Out of Nowhere

Also by Keith Botsford:

The Master Race
The Eighth-best-dressed Man in the World
Benvenuto
The March-Man

As I.I. Magdalen:

The Search for Anderson
Ana P.

Keith Botsford

OUT OF NOWHERE

The Toby Press, *London*

First published in 2000 by
The Toby Press *Ltd, London*
www.tobypress.com

Copyright © Keith Botsford 2000

'O Brother!' first appeared in *News from the Republic of Letters*;
'Along the River Plate' in *Stand*

ISBN 1-902881-24-9 (C)
ISBN 1-902881-25-7 (PB)

A CIP catalogue record for this title is available from the British Library

Designed by Fresh Produce, London

Typeset in Garamond by
Rowland Phototypesetting Ltd., Bury St Edmunds

Printed and bound in Great Britain by
St Edmundsbury Press Ltd., Bury St Edmunds

Contents

O Brother!

I

(1994)
Jim

The car was a maroon '86 Honda and it was parked off the highway facing due east on top of a hill on the state road between Belleville and Tonopah. It was as if the driver had parked there and gone to sleep waiting for the sun to rise, which it was just doing, trying to melt the rime on the windshield. The windows were all up and the doors were locked, and the man inside who wore sunglasses was about as still as you could get, well-dressed, about seventy, his hands on the wheel and looking straight ahead.

In the Rosedale Bulletin, State Trooper Walter McCombie Jr described the scene as: "Like one of those modern statues. A car in the middle of nowhere, a guy driving, a kind of memorial to the American Motorist." He had knocked on the window hard, pointed his flashlight at the driver, used his bullhorn. Nothing. The sun came up and he noted the dead man's shoes: "They were expensive and beautifully polished. Everything about him was neat."

Then he radio'd for identification, the medical examiner and some help from the four-man local police department. Two local cops came up from Sam Wells (Pop. 476), way down there at the bottom of the bluff; when they'd taken pictures and dusted the driver's side window for prints, McCombie broke the window and the ME who came with them said he thought the man died around midnight.

Which meant the driver had been wearing sunglasses all night. Not so odd out here, he said. "Some people sleep with them on." There was a quarter-tank of gas left, so it wasn't a case of running out of gas. The lights were off. The driver's wallet was missing.

An ambulance came up a half-hour later and took the body away. A tow-truck followed and did the same for the car.

By 7 a.m., the State Police had established that the car was registered to Anthony Mount of 1405 Buckeye Trail in Sam Wells. A local cop was sent there to notify Mrs Mount and McCombie met him there.

McCombie was struck by the emptiness of the place, the noise his patrol car door made slamming shut. A lone house-bound dog a hundred yards away barked. That was it. The house, one of a dozen two-bedroom ranch houses dropped on the desert at the edge of town, was empty, no one was home. The two men walked all round the house. The curtains weren't drawn, so they could look right inside. "Nothing to see," the local cop said. His name was Bill Humphrey and he was wizened and dry.

"And nothing to do," McCombie added. "Shoot! Why come out here to die? I mean, if you're not from here."

"Lots do," Humphrey said, lighting up.

McCombie then drove to Rosedale to rustle up a judge, because they needed an order to break into the man's home—a dead man's home is still his castle. That took until 10 a.m.

When he got his order and got back to Sam Wells, Bill Humphrey was talking to a frizzy-haired, leather-skinned lady who said she lived around there. She saw Mrs Mount maybe once a month at the beauty parlor, half-price on Tuesdays. She wanted to hang around, but McCombie said, "Let's get on with this."

They jimmied the front-door lock and got inside. All there was, was second-hand furniture, cheap rugs, and in the ice-box, half a dozen stale chocolate doughnuts that had been there two weeks or more. Just about nothing else. Except on one of those wooden trees at least a dozen hats, perhaps more, hats and caps, all colors.

"I guess he liked hats," Humphrey said.

The matrimonial bed was made; a lot of videos were shelved in alphabetical order. But no mail. Nothing in the box outside. No papers. No sign anybody had been living there for some time.

5

The next day's paper quoted the police as saying that at first they thought the Mounts might have been moving on to another place, but a brief check of the local realtors ("Desert Acreage!" "Retirement Homes!") established the house wasn't listed. Of course, that didn't mean the Mounts hadn't moved, or weren't about to, but if so, what was Mount doing up there on top of the hill facing towards Sam Wells, and not going home?

Some other neighbors said they saw Mrs Mount from time to time, but hadn't seen her recently. They couldn't remember if the Honda had been there or not. As far as they could remember, the Mounts had moved in two years back, and one woman thought they came from back East. Mount had the kind of accent they described as being "like you hear in war movies, sort of like Cary Grant". They made Tony and Eileen—except for the way he dressed and talked—like most people in Sam Wells. Most of the homeowners along Buckeye Trail had sold up somewhere else and moved to the desert so they could have a good, cheap life and last a little longer in the dry air before they passed away.

It wasn't that dead a place like it sounded, they said. Sam Wells had a nine-hole golf course, an American Legion Post, there were some drinking-holes along the highway, and there was a funeral parlor, the "Sunrise", a few miles west on the Rosedale road.

By the third day, the dead man's social security records turned up in Rosedale. They showed Mount had a small disability pension from the Second World War, in which he'd suffered a nervous breakdown. He had also been making regular visits to the Rosedale Veterans Administration Hospital.

His wife (his second wife) was called Eileen and she was a thrifty, sandy Newfoundlander. She had worked as a senior secretary at the Prudential and retired ten years earlier. A former Pru personnel director was traced who said she thought Eileen had a sister in California.

The probable cause of death was listed as heart failure and the time of death about an hour or two before sunrise. Though the dead man had a history of emphysema, there was no sign of a final struggle to breathe, no disordered clothing or starting eyes.

In time, they found us, his family: la Mamma (pronounce that Italian), kids he hadn't seen in some years, and myself, his brother, who loved him quite a lot, whatever anyone thought.

*   *   *

Mandy

Sure, Dad liked to drive. A big, black Mercedes best, back when. There are pictures of him at the wheel wherever he was. Being free to move, to move on, the luxury of that. Turn on the TV late at night, you see lots of Dads: in black and white. They put on calfskin driving gloves, wear a cap or a hat (in winter a foulard), climb into a superior car, and usually lose the girl to a brawny more down-to-earth type. When I heard how he was found, it sounded appropriate. It brought back lots of cars we'd been in as kids.

Grandma Mount—Nonna to us—was listed as next of kin, not us, not Uncle Jim. So from Sam Wells in Nevada they somehow located Grandma Mount at the Cardinal Spellman Home in New York, where a social worker said Mrs Mount was ninety-nine and could be of no help. She said she would try to notify the brother of the deceased.

It was Uncle Jim who called up to tell me Dad had died. The picture was pretty sketchy: "Just sitting in his car, as if he drove up there to see the sun come up and parked. But the car was pointed home to Sam Wells, and there were no signs, they say, that he turned around. He had to have been somewhere else." On the phone, Uncle Jim sounded as if he was trying to stay out of things; at the same time kind of amazed, as though it didn't make sense, but maybe with Dad it did.

I think I was ready enough for Dad dying from the time he remarried Eileen and went West. He'd been sort of dead for years. If anything, I was glad for Dad. Pain was what always worried him, and it sounded as if he'd gone without any. But I'll still miss him, for all the things he might have been to us and wasn't.

"You know where your brothers and sisters are," Uncle Jim asked. "You could help by calling them up and telling them. You need to ask what they want to do about your Dad." About the body, which the authorities were keeping in the county morgue. He said, "You have any idea where Eileen might be?"

"No, and I'm not likely to."

"OK," he said. "This isn't the time to bring up old quarrels."

Wasn't he the least little bit sorry? I asked him. "Sure I'm sorry, Mandy. But you've got to be glad for him. He didn't have much left to live for."

I said that if it was OK with him—knowing he hated the telephone, and none of us nephews and nieces ever got to see him much—I'd call him back when I'd told the others. He said that was all right with him.

I called my youngest and favorite brother, Adam, first in Korea, where he was teaching English to businessmen. Uncle Jim calls Adam "the almost normal one". Adam didn't have the money to come back for the funeral, but said he would try. He had no idea where Eileen was: "I never once had a letter from her."

Tessa was at a Bible Study school somewhere in Texas and I'd misplaced her address.

My older brother Danny has been living in Uruguay with his snobby wife and three kids for some years now. He said he didn't give a damn how Dad was buried or where. "He was one sick guy, Mandy," he said, "and I feel a whole lot better already." Danny was calling his father sick?

I called Uncle Jim back. As far as I could see, what everyone wanted was, we'd be happy with any arrangements he made. That made him peevish. "What do you think Dad was doing out there in the middle of the night, Uncle Jim?" I asked. "And where was he coming from or going to, if he hadn't been in the house for some time?"

He said sourly my guess was as good as his. Maybe he'd pulled over, not feeling well.

There was a history there: the two brothers bad-mouthing each other, as if they had nothing in common. Like his mother—powerful genes were at work there, making him short-legged, black-eyed, stocky, a relentless family man, a furious eater—Jim had the capacity to hurt. Dad didn't. He was always kind. And fun. We never knew the man both of them called "Father", who was apparently vague, dreamy, rich and obsessed with machinery of any kind. The most Dad would ever say, fondly, about his younger brother was, "Oh, you know Jim, he's a bit pretentious and full of himself."

The rare occasions we saw Uncle Jim, if we talked about Dad ("How's tall, fair and handsome?" he'd ask), it was Dad he built one of his cases against. Ladies and Gentlemen of the Jury, the defendant bled his Mamma white, he abandoned his kids (us), look at the flop he was! We figured this was his Italian-in-Chicago tough guy act, but deep down, because they were Dagos, they loved each other. And Jim had to be the way he was because that was what worked in Chicago, where dogs ate dogs.

The fly in the ointment was the *nonna*, Felicità, our very own Italian matriarch. Dad was the older brother by five years, and in her eyes, Dad could do no wrong. Yet she would hardly see us. Why couldn't Dad have done what Jim did? Marry "suitable" Catholic women, make her the family she wanted: since Jim's many kids were all happy and successful where we were a mess.

Uncle Jim sent me a ticket and we met in Reno airport, just the two of us. His beard showed grizzle, one leg shuffled; he didn't like burying his brother, like dying was another failure on his part. He was angry at Eileen, too, and Dad going back to a woman he'd walked out on after five or six years of unutterable boredom. "Why go back whimpering with your tail between your legs?" he asked as we drove south from Reno.

I said I agreed: it just seemed crazy someone so Scotch-Irish and organized would have walked out or shut up the house and left Dad alone. "I guess they had nothing else but each other; they needed each other's social security checks to live on. Nevada was, you know, their death deal." Only she had gone; she wasn't around to bury him. After what she'd done to me last year, that was OK with me; I never wanted to see either of them again.

And Dad I hadn't seen again: except in the pictures the Sam Wells cops showed us the next day. Great big glossies of Dad sitting in his car just as they said he had: as if he were still driving, the sunglasses on his narrow, hooked ("aristocratic", he called it) nose, his lips just parted. I guess he was still a good-looking man, vain right to the end, in a brown hound's-tooth jacket with a grey cardigan underneath. No tie. The shirt collar clean. The trooper was right. He looked painted or sculpted. We followed the cops in the big, white, rented Lincoln Town Car and visited the spot where he died. You could see for miles in every direction, and there wasn't anything to see: just a lot of ochre-colored earth, mesquite, rocks, and houses huddled together like trailer parks, stretching out into the distance. It wasn't just the landscape receding from us up there on the hill, it was my Dad, Mister Elusive.

I called Adam the night before the funeral, the way we always called each other for support. I said, "Whatever we think, the guy had style."

The next day there was first a "viewing" in the Sunrise Funeral Home where a young man explained how Dad would look and feel ("Two days' growth of beard and kind of remote. It's a bit strange at first. Some people don't like to touch the departed. Everyone will understand.")

A veteran, he lay on his gurney with the stars and stripes tucked up to his chin, otherwise grey and pretty peaceful, his eyebrows puckish and wispy; very cold to kiss, which I made myself do, and Uncle Jim did too.

Then we drove behind the hearse to the cemetery at the edge of town. It was a creepy place: you felt the sand shifting around under your feet and between the bones, and the grass they'd planted was all brown. The sun was weak, the air chilly. Uncle Jim and I threaded our way back among the fresher graves. Apart from a couple of teenagers who went in a car crash I guess, everyone in there was old even before they died. At seventy-one, Dad was just a kid.

Then a priest said a few words out of a manual that could have been about any "dear departed". Whatever we saw, through tears or dry-eyed (or simply embarrassed by the incongruity of this death), shifted as we stood there, blown-about in random fashion, was reclaimed, earth to earth.

"Great send-off," Uncle Jim said, buttoned up in his coat with a Western hat on his head which he had to hold with his hand when the wind blew. He turned to slip an envelope to the priest. I didn't know if he was being sarcastic. "They should have buried him in the car, like that woman in California. He always did like getting in it and going someplace."

"I guess this is someplace, huh? You must have loved him once," I said. "He's your only brother."

"Was my brother. When I was a kid, I adored him," he answered. "I used to worship the ground he walked on."

Uncle Jim looked away now and then, maybe he was crying, and when he threw his handful of dirt on the coffin after me, he said: "He was a lousy father but a sweet man. You should feel sorry for him."

I thought, two good-looking, sexy old men (Dad had the better teeth, but after spending twenty-eight grand on them he should have) with the *nonna's* charm. She could turn on the charm all right: like all real bitches. When she claimed to be a helpless woman, not to have been so educated in Philadelphia when she was a little girl, "Scusa but I still make mistakes in English". We kids didn't get any of that charm. On us she stomped with the cane that held up her disintegrating hip. Jim probably hadn't got that much either. The charm went into the ground with Dad.

When we reached the car, the Sunrise Funeral people were standing about their hearse. They wore string ties. Uncle Jim looked briefly through their itemized expenses. I said, "What does 'perpetual' care mean?"

"Forever."

Discreetly, the oldest of the morticians asked Uncle Jim if he wanted the plot next door for the widow. Or for himself. Uncle Jim damn near snapped their heads off. I saw his point. When Dad married Eileen, or married her again, that wasn't undying love; it was a last gasp, a marriage of convenience. As for himself, as he told me, it was Tykes v. the State of Illinois next week. Relenting, he said, "I can't afford to croak just now. But thanks for the thought."

When the service was over we drove back to Reno and the airport. I guess for both of us things about Dad had started running backwards in our heads: I'd remembered one thing, Jim would remember another. And when you got past the recent things, the quarrels over their mother, then it looked better.

*   *   *

Jim

I know you, Tony, I said over his grave, not knowing I'd be back there or thereabouts often in the next few months. You weren't going anywhere, you were running from something. Like nearly fifty years ago when you limped up to the Jersey shore with the mast chopped off the yacht you were bringing north from Florida, the sheets smoldering. You were so legendary to me then, with your stories of riding elephants into Princeton's eating-clubs and collecting Roosevelt dimes you could dump into the local ponds in protest—I didn't even think twice before seeking to save your bacon. My hero.

My first thought when I was in Sam Wells was, what kind of shit have you been in? And what sort of a way out is dying?

I have a practiced eye: I offer salvage in shipwreck and the general rack and ruin of marriage, partnerships and crime, the commonplaces of the day. From the start, hearing the cops talk, knowing how cops talk and think, what happened to Tony told me there'd been a crisis. Whatever it was, why didn't he get himself a lawyer? Or call me? Instead of which he was dead and there wasn't so much as a peep from Eileen, so how would I ever find out what really happened? Whatever was wrong, she'd walked out. I doubt without a reason, for the woman completely lacked imagination: just as Tony had too much.

Or maybe the something wrong was something that had gone wrong with her: one of those afflictions of the pre-dead for which one goes to ground. Something sudden?

And how about Mandy? She's been shopping around for a father, for someone, since she was about three or four—the first time her mother went crazy. In that orphanage of horrors where Mama had put the two girls: in hand-me-downs, pinafores, butchered hair—because Tony, her Tonio, couldn't possibly cope, could he? He was in Peru making fertilizer out of fish-meal, earning money; how could he look after four little girls and boys? We all had to do our bit and pray God. Because their mother had always been crazy—like her mother.

The nuns had been posted at the four corners of the asphalt playground when I brought Adam to see them, their rosaries swinging like knouts. Adam, the youngest, was just two when he came to live with us. He burst out crying in terror when he saw his sisters and clung to my hand. Let's hope he doesn't remember. And I wish I didn't. But the dead Tony, a sort of parable who'd gone before me in life, clung to me all the way to O'Hare.

Then we were sitting decorously, my wife Francine and I, in a half-acre of Chicago's best soft grey furnishings. Yes, we've moved up in the world—Mamma saw to that. Yet below us, the Lake was darkening inimically, like a desert but less purple, more black. And you never quite forget the early insults or the way the water shifts on the lake as your life can. Some of Tony's problems came from his feeling everything would always be the way it had been.

We were waiting for our dinner guests to arrive. Francine looked immaculate and the Kid (for me, the very last one) was watching basketball with a college-certified minder supposed to keep up his French for Francine's sake.

When I had finished telling her about the funeral, she observed: "Brother Tony was not the sort who goes off on a trip without a wallet, driving license, credit cards."

"If he had any left."

"Of course he did. Everyone always believed in him. And if there's one thing you would have said about him it was how orderly he was. Well-shaven, clean, neat: in those respects, the perfect gentleman."

Those stamp albums, his LPs, (the videos, Mamma's

investments!), all in alphabetical order! Look at his hand-writing! He kept accounts the way Moses chiselled the Tab-lets. Forgive the use of the word "chiselled". They weren't crooked, they were just imaginary. How else do you go through a halfquarter-mill in a few years? "Maybe somebody stole his wallet," I offered.

"You said the car doors were locked from the inside," she answered with French logic. Then she put the picture I brought back from Nevada face down on the table. "You shouldn't keep that around," she said. "Maybe you're sur-prised he died. He doesn't look surprised. If anything, he looks expectant."

I turned the photograph face up again and studied my dead brother. Even dead he had a good weird face: olive skin, luscious Italianate mouth, eyes set asymmetrically and far apart. I said, "It's not everyone gets to see his brother parked and dead."

She looked at me sharply. "Jim," she said. "This is me, your wife. Don't be someone you're not. Tony is just the beginning. Then comes your mother. It's going to take you a long time to dig out from under that history. It deserves better than smart talk. His kids and your kids deserve better."

One of the few irritating things in what looks to me like a flawless and final marriage is that Francine is nearly always right. Tall, elegant, senses sharp—ear, mouth, eye, nose—smart, right; her emotions deep but submitted to a daily grilling; her manner lofty, but spiced with a grin of a *jolie laide*. She was right again: the time to lay ghosts is when they're still fresh in the mind.

17

I admitted that since hearing from the home that Tony was dead, I'd been talking to Tony. It was a remembering thing. Getting Mandy and myself and others to remember what was Tony really like—who was this guy?—started with a lot of questions I couldn't answer. Tony's character was dead and gone, it wasn't going to change any more, end of story, picture snapped, nothing for Tony to add or take away. But he himself wasn't concluded. As I told Francine, "You know Chicago judges can be bribed, but you don't know for sure—until you get shafted—just how much or how badly: not until they've concluded."

"So I've been telling you. Some of your kids wrote while you were away. They don't seem to have been taken in by all your anger over Tony. Nor am I. I've been around you ten years now. They've been around the pair of you for twenty, thirty years, which is a lot more than I'd be willing to take on if I were in their shoes. It was more complicated than you make out, and they know it. Relax. You have a right to be shaken. He was the last one remembered you as a child. He was your older brother. He had rights on you."

She handed me two or three letters. Their condolences made me feel bad. "I thought he was really nice," one of my daughters wrote from Prague. "He was always nice to me."

"They loved him, I loved him," I said to Francine. "He was a goddam lovable man. The guys at the Shannon Bar round the corner from la Mamma's necropolis loved him; his stockbroker loved him; priests loved him—he repented regularly. What can I say?"

Later, we sat at dinner. Just old friends, including my partner, Frank. They'd all called up to say maybe I didn't feel like a dinner: in the circumstances. I said, rubbish. I wasn't shocked; I was just puzzled.

Over dinner, I told them the story of Tony's death; I said I still felt misgivings. We discussed poor old Tony as we discussed cases out of court. There was a party said it was obviously an accident: he'd taken the wrong medicine or done something he'd been told not to do. Another party said the way I'd talked about him—"Wasn't he something of a con man?"—this had to be an insurance scam. They asked about an autopsy. I said, not that I knew of, and there hadn't been any insurance.

They were having a good time. Tony's death had taken on fantastic overtones. It was the kind of story my friends really liked. You could swap grief for a joke among people who didn't have to be tactful with each other, and it had all happened out West where you expected weird things to happen.

"Doctor Kevorkian or someone like that," Frank said. "Farewell to your arms. Just do it. Go."

I said, "Are you trying to tell me seriously he committed suicide? For Christ's sake, he didn't have to up the schedule. He went out there to die anyway. He had only 29 per cent of his lungs. He was shot in all sorts of ways."

Why did I short-circuit the suicide idea? As I told Francine when everyone had gone home, because Tony looked damned cheerful, and he only had that look on his face when he had some scheme going. For some crazy reason

I smelled woman. Maybe it was just Old Reliable Eileen not being there. Maybe it was habit. And maybe it was old smarts about Brother Tony. I mean, there usually was one, a woman, wasn't there?

That all had to wait. When I finished up Tykes (I lost, as though Tony were looking over my shoulder), I went to New York.

These visits to my mother in the home were never pleasant. I hated signing in downstairs like a delivery boy. Who was going to steal one of these people? I hated the whole preview of death, the Coming Attraction. I hated walking past the chapel with its perpetual candle and its lying stations of the cross: why not put honest pictures up on the walls to tell the clients what life's really like between arrival and departure? The weekly dances, the craft nights, bingo, sing-alongs. I hated the big freight elevators whose doors were specially timed for the lunch-and-dinner wheelchair derby and the slow, slow trip up, stopping at every floor to the twelfth. It took too much time. All that time to think about the unloveliness of the human condition.

There was a real question this time, too. Do you tell a ninety-nine-year-old woman her son is dead? Not just her son. A son would be one thing, and bad enough, but Tony was also the lifelong object of all her desires. Dead? And she was alive?

I was never sure she wasn't just pretending she didn't understand. Why bother to tell her, if it's bound to hurt.

She was up on her high bed, half in and half out of this world. She looked like some small and very old angel adrift. She was in a white gown; her eyes had had the dark currant color washed out of them; her skin was so wasted you could give an anatomy lesson, joint by joint. This was a human being who'd gone back to the diapers and feeding habits of infancy, and along the way passed backwards through all the stages of her life: through my father who had betrayed her twice, once by shedding her and then by killing himself; through the beautiful young woman she'd been before she grew fat, with a wave to the Italian nightingale who'd sung Mimi at the Civic Opera (and met Father, a music-lover who sent her the flowers she had viewed with such suspicion); then back among her turn-of-the-century family—hooded-eyed grocers and restaurateurs, vast, sombre, careful men in dark hats and her older sisters who had turned out remarkably childless but had lived to a great age.

This woman had been around a hundred years as a human being and she frightened me. If I didn't come for a month or two, she knew it and cried somewhere inside; malevolent as a child, she was saying, "It's going to happen to you, you'll see, you'll see!"

I sat down and held her hand. Some days after an hour or so the wiring might connect, a little spark of electricity leapt across the furrowed ridges of her brain. By now this rarely produced recognition. I couldn't just treat her like a two-year-old. I remembered everything she was, which was still inside her: Tony and me as much tots as she was now, what she thought when Father left her and worse, later, when he killed himself and we, Tony and I, were taken off the first and only time to see where she came from, Agrigento, when she was nine. A holiday on which the young Jim had pointed out another of her follies, to have called me James when I was, so her cousins left behind said, so like her, and my brother Tony, Tonio, when he was, or wanted to be, so purely Anglo and the cousins thought they were being treated by him as if they pushed barrows.

Usually I tried to think of things she might like to hear; today I had to tell her things she didn't want to hear. The technique was to hold her hand and feed her the word "Mamma" and my name: "This is Jim, Mamma. Do you know who I am? Mamma, this is Jim." If that didn't work, I could try my few words of Italian and she might smile wistfully.

This was when she was most dangerous. She seemed to be asleep—from the effort of thinking where am I? Who's this?—and suddenly it hit her and her hand fairly jumped out of yours, a recoil like a shot.

I said, "Tony's dead, Mamma, he's dead."

She looked at me imperiously. "You shouldn't talk to your brother that way, saying things like that," she said, angry and spiteful. "He's older than you and he's had a more difficult life. You both have to learn how to get along."

II

(1993)
Mandy

Dad had disappeared from one day to the next.
Not a word to me. Not a word to anyone. I called him up
as I usually did once a week or so and the telephone had
been disconnected; when I went by, the super said Dad had
moved out.

Uncle Jim says he got the news via a letter from the
Manufacturer's Hanover bank, Nonna's trustees. Or rather
two letters. The covering letter from the bank said Dad had
decided to move out West for his health. The other letter
was from his brother. "I don't have your dad's letter," Uncle
Jim told me. "Lawyer though I am, rage got the better of
me that day, and I tore it up."

I don't believe that. I think Uncle Jim kept it, but
for his eyes only, because it had really got under his skin.

If he didn't keep it, he had it memorized, because whenever it came in handy, he could quote large chunks. So that unless the letter was very long, I've heard most of it by now.

The gist came first. Dad had decided to save his own life, or what was left of it. And Jim should see if he could do any better than he had: with what remained of his mother's life, his, and life in general. Dad's "I hereby resign", came out immediately and was repeated often. Then came, "I'm going back to Eileen, and you can do us a favor. Neither she nor I ever want to hear from any member of this family ever again." Funny that: they're the very words Mom used in the clinic when the three Mounts went up to visit her.

The balance came in sardonic sides. "According to your father I'm conceited, I didn't even try to understand his situation." There was more and worse. There was ire; there was hatred. There were grievances that went back to childhood, and betrayals; there was his *character*, his *nature*; there were details that hurt, lists of what people (wives, mainly) really thought of him.

"He left nothing out. He was sick. He said about his beloved Mamma that he didn't care if the old bitch died. As long as he didn't have to watch it happening. I quote, 'I've had it. Up to here. I've carried the can all these years. It's yours to carry now.' I said to myself, that's that. He's done a bunk."

It was his wife Francine who said back then, "Listen, Mandy, you want to keep it cool with your uncle. He's mad as hell. But I don't see how he can blame your father. Jim didn't actually volunteer for the job of looking after his mother. He left that to Tony. You reap what you sow."

Then there was the money. "She's not of sound mind!" ("She" was the *nonna*.) Francine said, "Jim worries about what your dad's going to live on now. He's already sore at what your father took from her before he left. But don't worry about that. What your dad spent was money for services rendered. In his saner moments, when he's not enraged by your father, Jim knows that. I wouldn't have lived all those years cooped up in that tiny apartment with her for a million dollars a year. And yet God knows I was trained to *serve!*"

*   *   *

Jim

Mandy has a weird, overheated effect on me. I could never put my finger on it until I took the Kid to the Museum of Science and Industry and we heard through earphones what some kind of African cricket goes through to attract his mate. The cricket sounds desirous, but irritated, frustrated; with Mandy, I hear the rub of her panty-hose along the wire as if she held the receiver between her legs and her voice emerged from between her copious thighs.

I remember, maybe six months after Tony did his bunk and I was beginning to get him out of my mind—like a client whose unpaid billings I've written off my taxes—I was in Milwaukee on business, and Mandy called. She must have got the number from my office.

"Listen, Uncle Jim," she said huskily, "I've got something really great for you. You got a pencil and a piece of paper?" When she gave me my brother's address in Nevada her voice shifted: from the ingenuous child who wants to please to the near-forty-year-old who has to make up with enthusiasm for all her failures—all at once and right now! "Hey! I actually *saw* him. What do you think of that? You should be out there when night's falling. Very purple."

This is Mandy's old come-on to her Uncle Jim, tried once a year: routinely before Thanksgiving or Christmas, at one of those times when families *ought* to be together. ("Can I come up this Christmas, Uncle Jim?")

I said: "What the hell did you go out there for? Tony and I may not have talked since he took off, but I've got his number. I got it off the bank: in case something happened to your *nonna*."

"Come on," she said. "You can't tell me you're not curious. You want to hear what the house is like? It's real small. There's just one bedroom, so I had to sleep on the sofa in the living room, and they go to bed at nine."

This was my niece. Why do Tony's kids make me feel guilty? Whose fault is it they had such a rotten life?

"So, how'd it go out there?" I asked.

"Fine. Until we took this trip to the Grand Canyon. He hit me, Uncle Jim."

"Hit you, did he? What were you up to?"

The last few years, those rages of his had got worse.

I didn't like getting too close to him. His anger was like a drive-shaft: it made his wheels go round. It was obvious he could kill: the way someone with hardly a lung left will kill for one more gasp. For all I knew, maybe he had killed, on his travels: in some back-alley in Pakistan or Peru. He got into altercations on the public by-ways: on Lexington Avenue or Park (he didn't stray far from Mamma's apartment). Someone jostled him, someone bought the banana he'd picked out on the fruit-stall: usually a Kike or a Nigger. His hands shook; the anonymous, flat, checkered cap on his head simply emphasized the choler on his face. There was in him this aggregation of discontents, this viper's knot of fury. He had lungs like tripe and a heart with dodgy valves but he could rip a phonebook in two, just as Mamma couldn't read but could still spot a fly at twenty-five feet. Their apparent weaknesses were a con; their charm was their feint. Both of them were full of the magma of sick love; they needed their vent-holes.

When I was younger he could come at me with his eyes white and his lips drawn back like a Labrador's. I was present when he knocked his oldest son Danny across the room once. You want some nice odium, look at those two! Of course Danny is a nutter; he inherited genetic ire two ways, from Tony *and* from his own crazy mother.

In our New York days, Tony would go to a bar to repress (sometimes, to hone) the anger. His hand would hold the tumbler (ice and straight scotch) as if it would gladly crush it. This kind of crazy heat is just under the surface all over America. The prisons and courts smoulder, the public toilets, the clubs, the Marines, ordinary life, are in slow burn; the heat's even whiter, it's meltdown in the *Family*.

People don't know this. They read self-help books, see shrinks, play games, wear crystal pendants, sue; and all you need is love, with which they're all filled. With that much denial around, how do you get through to them with the truth?

Anyway, Tony's kids have this charming habit of passing round whatever I say, chewing on it, storing it up. Mandy was perfectly capable of using her office phone to call Danny in Uruguay—"You know what Uncle Jim says about you?"—so I played it cool and diverted her from what she really wanted to tell me, that my brother had whacked her in a rage, but I would never do such a thing, which was why she was willing, no eager, to transfer her affections to me.

"Hey listen, honey, these are the hidden resources of parents. What else have we got if we can't smack our kids? If he whacked you, he must be in good health."

"It's sick."

"*He's* sick, poor bastard. Tell me what happened at the Grand Canyon."

She paused. This was when Francine would usually poke her head around my study door in Chicago and say it was time I got some sleep or at least let her get some. But this was Milwaukee and a year ago. I couldn't hang up on my niece. She was determined that we were in this enterprise *together*. And no one else was interested.

What happened was that Tony wanted to go out for a drive and a picnic. In the Honda. No doubt a series of picnics resided in his memory of childhood—picnics in the fair Vermont countryside, in the Appalachians, on beaches north of Jacksonville, Florida. And what lodged in his memory was imagery applicable, like a transfer, to others. Picnics were memorable, by definition.

Childhood, Francine says, is a golden rope: you drag it after you all through life, like the Minotaur's thread, so that you can always find your way back. "Of course, like an umbilical cord," she adds, "it can also strangle you."

*   *   *

Mandy

The way it started was like this, I went to see the *nonna* in the home. She didn't know who I was, but there were some postcards the nurses had stuck in the frame of her mirror: a big cactus, a cowboy, buttes. I picked one out, figuring it must have been from Dad, turned it over, and there was the postmark, Sam Wells, Nevada.

At first, when I got his number from the phone company, I was just going to call him. Then I thought it would be fun if I went out and saw him, how surprised and all pleased he would be.

Uncle Jim won't believe it if I say we started out having a good time. Dad and me. Maybe not right away, though I could see Dad was pleased inside—we had a thing going, him and me: just Eileen made me take the rental

car back to Avis in Rosedale—"No place to go out here,"
she said. "Don't waste your money. We'll drive you back
to the airport." I took the car back; Dad followed behind
in the Honda. We lunched in Rosedale and had a few
drinks, which Eileen didn't allow him. We had one or two
more in a bar outside a place called Hawthorn where he
introduced me proudly as his "new girl friend".

Once he got talking, he said for some reason we kids
remember only the bad things. "How about the good
times?" A polo game in Africa he had filmed and showed
us as kids, the fantastic apartment in Paris when he and
Eileen were first married. He'd draw these good things out
of some long list in his head, they made him feel good;
only he never mentioned any one else in those places, he
was always alone. They were his places.

As I told Uncle Jim when I called him to tell him
where Dad was, I couldn't remember *his*, Dad's, good times,
and Jim said, "There must have been some."

Even if we did get back late and Eileen was sore, it
went all right until he got sentimental over dinner. It was
some sort of Irish stew. Eileen was tight-lipped. But when
Dad helped himself to a scotch, Eileen did too because I
was there, so I had one too. I could feel him getting emo-
tional; he'd wipe his eyes when he thought Eileen wasn't
looking, his lips trembled; he just looked very frail.

Suddenly he said we ought to see the Grand Canyon.
Eileen must come along. He looked longingly at my cigarette (I almost never smoke, but I wanted to defy Eileen)
and said, "We'll all go." We were all the family he had left.

It was also like the Grand Canyon wouldn't be there any longer if we didn't get to see it.

Eileen said, "When?" and asked how long I intended to stay.

For several days after that Dad just drove around. First because he wanted to show me how he'd changed and felt better out there; then because more and more good things came to mind; but mainly because in the house we didn't talk much and Eileen hardly said a thing. Dad would ask her if she needed the car; if she didn't, we went off in it and she looked relieved. She stayed home, mainly cleaning and painstakingly reading home decoration magazines.

Dad said I should ask him questions about the past: or everything would be lost in someone else's telling. For instance, neither Jim nor the *nonna* could be trusted on that score: "They were always against whatever I did. They didn't want me to marry your mother."

These conversations—no beginning, no end—slid around in my head. It seemed to me he'd either been *reading* about those happy times, or he'd seen them in some *movie*. He *wanted* life happy. We kids had picked that up from him. Mom's new boyfriend was fine; Eileen was a good sport; next week, next month, all our dreams would come true.

We'd stop in some bar in Rosedale for a beer, Dad saying, like he really cared, I ought not to smoke, and me saying he shouldn't drink, him putting a finger to his lips and saying "Sssh!". Making funny jokes about my sex life. The way people *liked* him wherever we stopped, looking at

him the way we kids often did, like some fabulous character
from a book or a movie, telling stories, laughing as though
he didn't believe them himself.

Then we went to the Grand Canyon. It was a long
drive. Dad drove and I sat in back, staring at Eileen's stiff
curls and the collar of her windbreaker.

We got there finally and parked in a picnic area on
the rim of the canyon. Dad got out of the car, stretched
and wanted to go and look at the canyon; Eileen—she
looked like a woman who's lost a lot of weight deliberately,
but it just hardened the edges in her face—wanted us to
eat first. She was hungry.

Dad gave up on seeing the Canyon right then, and I
reckoned I was going to lose out in any fight like that, small
or big. Dad had *asked* to come back. This corner of Nevada
had been her choice. Eileen had the power and she showed
it by her manner, the impatient way she handed me all
the things to carry to the picnic table: cooler, paper cups,
sandwiches in waxed paper.

When Dad sat down, he was breathless. Eileen asked
if he'd taken his pills. He said he'd forgotten them.

Eileen turned on me. "Your father shouldn't be here.
Can't you see he's a sick man? All this carrying on is for
you. You let him drink. You drink. For a year he hasn't had
a drink in the house. What are you doing out here anyway?
What do you *want*? No one asked you to come." And like
a glacier she wouldn't stop. She was an impersonal force
without the slightest feeling. "Your father told you he didn't
want to see any of you again. How dare you force yourself

on him? You kids are all selfish, you never think of your father except when you want something from him."

Uncle Jim said, "Did you at least stop there? You took it from her?"

Of course I didn't. I was surprised and hurt. I looked over to Dad for support. He was somewhere miles away, turned around and away on the picnic bench while Eileen bent over a paper plate heaped with chicken salad. I'm sure he had just taken a quick swig from the flask he kept in his pocket.

"What did you *say?*" Uncle Jim insisted.

"I don't remember. I just burst out. I must have said something like, he was our father whether he wanted us or not. And who was she, and . . ."

"You said she was just a secretary, she was jealous because she hadn't had any kids, you said now she was too old to have any."

"Something like that."

But I pulled myself together. Dad was looking at me from across the table that way he has when he's boxed in, when he's ready to get up and go, go as far away as possible. I said I was forty and a grown-up, and I didn't want to be talked to like that by Eileen.

Dad stood up, he went all white and said, "Don't you dare talk to Eileen like that," and then he leaned across the picnic table and whacked me. Eileen packed up the lunch, he got in the car. He was in such a hurry, I had to jump in the back seat. They would have gone without me.

We drove in silence—I mean absolute silence—back

to Sam Wells, and then another hour to the airport once I'd picked up my things from the house. I begged Dad not to bring Eileen along to the airport. She got in the driver's seat to make sure, gunning the engine. "God knows what wickedness you'd get up to if I wasn't there," she said. Dad didn't say a word. He got in alongside her and I rode in the back again.

When we got to the airport, Eileen got out first. She reached in through the back door, grabbed my bag from next to me on the seat and threw it onto the curb. I retaliated by reaching between the front seats and grabbing Eileen's purse, got out, picked up my own bag, and ran into the terminal. Eileen didn't even look back.

The last thing I saw was Dad looking straight ahead through his sunglasses so you couldn't see what he was looking at, and Eileen slamming the door and bang! driving off. They weren't even going to try to get the purse back. Not if it meant talking to me. I got ninety bucks.

"Dad's an escape artist," I said to Uncle Jim.

"You bet." And he added, "That's why he wears those sunglasses: even at night out on the empty highway."

*   *   *

Jim

When this call of Mandy's came back to me—it required some work—I lay there in bed alongside Francine and her easy breathing, and thought about Tony's empty house out in Sam Wells. I saw the cops walk in through the jimmied door and look around, go into the bedroom, the bathroom, the kitchen, the lounge; they emptied drawers, poked around in the kitchen and closets; and found nothing as someone might walking round here if Francine and I vanished and the Kid wasn't a kid but someone like Mandy. The house spooked them. They didn't just walk around as they would have at home; they didn't have any idea at all what they might find. A house contains a lot of the persons who live in it, and yet, when it's abandoned there's nothing much left of who lived there.

I'd talked to those cops. They were big, beefy, healthy types; they were used to the hard things of life. Like me, they knew damn well Tony and Eileen hadn't just left: something had happened. I talked several times to Bill Humphrey. He agreed something was wrong, but what did the police have to work on?

I've been back twice already on my own, interviewing people, checking leads. It always comes to the same thing. They haven't really gone. They haven't put their house up for sale or rent; cancelled a single appointment; closed their bank account; notified the Post Office; left a forwarding address for the all-important social security checks.

It was all wrong. Brothers die. One kisses them goodbye, one forgives. I should have been in Sam Wells going through his shirts, diaries, Cartier wallets with gold pencils inside; I should have embraced Eileen, and consoled her; together we would have sorted out Tony's stuff: what she wanted, a keepsake for me, what the kids should get. When the funeral was over we would have sat on naugahyde sofas in that drab little living room and I would have advised Eileen on her VA benefits, and asked about his will.

Instead I had my brother's cold body, a photograph and an empty house: with six chocolate doughnuts hard as rocks in the ice-box and a collection of hats on a tree. And Tony still sat on the crest of the hill and looked down on Sam Wells and his house. He'd sit there eternally, I thought, beaming at some private joke. He wasn't coming back. He was having one of his goddam fantasies. *That's* why he looked so peaceful! It wasn't real.

III

(1990)
Jim

I am flying out to Reno again. Each trip and every day
now, I try to catch some fugitive traces of my brother's
past. Among these fragments, his kids, his daughter Mandy,
rarely seen, but also never really absent. These kids had
weight. Hard to tell if they screwed up or were screwed up.
I'm told that when Adam took his bride to meet his dad,
Tony slammed the front door in Adam's face and said:
"Take that fucking Korean of yours and get out of my life."
Which, to Adam's credit, he did.

The more often Tony was drunk, the harsher and
more irrationally abusive he was, the more those two,
Mandy and Adam, craved him. Adam wrote his Dad long,
confessional letters Tony never read—he told me once they
made him physically sick.

Not sick exactly. Their very existence fatigued him; the weight was guilt: when we'd like to do good and just never get round to it.

Mandy fell into a different category. Here was this hefty, generous girl with enormous vague eyes and (Mamma's granddaughter) dark olive skin, and she didn't bitch; she was just hungry for all the things in life she hadn't had, in her case, especially someone steady in her bed. Marriage, kids. Wasn't everyone doing it? Her crazy mom had just done it with a fitness freak; I'd done it for the third time; Adam had done it; after about five kids with him, her big sister Tessa had taken up life with her everlasting Jesus in the shape of a Nigerian preacher. With the *nonna* gone into her home, Eileen long divorced, her dad might do it too. I know for a fact he went a'wooing. Why not Mandy? Well, I can't answer that: maybe just a tad *too* generous?

About then, when I saw her in New York, she had a lank-haired Hungarian pop musician in tow. Whatever else he was, Arpad wasn't Mister Right. A child of seven would have figured out why he was there: he needed a place to stay in the city and Mandy was a well-made bed. But this wasn't enough for Arpad. This ex-Mongol with a hatchet face had figured out America. He imagined life had pissed on him, he pissed on Mandy. Barely glancing my way, he sat coolly on her sofa, snuffling up from his dirty hand something paid for by her job in some film production company.

It was painfully obvious Arpad would walk out and

take everything she owned, which is what happened. After
five minutes of Arpad, I said, "Come on, kid, let's get out
of here."

Later, in a bar where they seemed to know her pretty
well, we talked about her dad and her. In her eyes, it was
a question of entitlement. A girl had a right to a mom and
dad, and somehow if you worked for it hard enough, and
you believed in "I'm OK, you're OK", you either should
have or could acquire both or either. This dad, unlike her
real one, should be cuddly and love her and give her away
at the altar in a grey suit and top hat.

This wasn't what she had. I was supposed to fill the
want. "You could help me, Uncle Jim. We're all a little
crazy in my family."

I could help her, but what would that entail? I had
kids of my own, lots of them. Everyone wants a piece of
my soul. Then as now, I adorned myself with what Francine
calls "the Higher Selfishness". That is, all the good reasons
I have for self-preservation in a sea of pleas.

For instance, this morning, having to get out to O'Hare,
I go outside to dig out the car from under a heavy, wet snow-
fall. The meter maid, a bulky black woman in heavy goose-
down, stands there writing a ticket as I arrive. She doesn't
apologize. No, she tells me what it's like to put in eight hours
of ticketing in leaky boots. She too wants my sympathy. We
agree Chicago slush is hell; perhaps we should sue the city;
it's too bad, but I'm going to get the parking ticket anyway,
snow or no snow. The Higher Selfishness says, don't even
think of her as human. May her boots leak.

This, Mandy, I wanted to say, is why you're being deprived. Your dad's mind doesn't function primarily in the here and now. Tony's a prospector, a projector. He's always got some unlikely scheme going. For a year or two, back then, he had been spending the few hours he was awake doing demo tapes. Music moved, transported, him; he had a deep, sexy voice with a carefully cultivated accent; why not one more creepy classical disk jockey? With music he could swap one world for another. There was a small apartment off Lexington, there was the 1812 Overture with all the cannon. Where would anyone rather be, if he had the means?

Then at thirty-something don't you think it's time you gnawed through the umbilical cord? Don't you find something sick in your father still shuffling about in the same twelve-by-sixteen room he occupied when he was fourteen? Twice your age and still getting up in the late morning to find his breakfast cereal and cup of tea waiting for him?

Can't you see that everyone around Tony has been marginalized? It's been going on for years. As Mamma's capital diminished and the demo-tapes were sent round America with an impressive and probably false c.v., all the *things* that could connect him to us also disappeared. Isn't that Mamma's silver mirror on your mantelpiece? No doubt the Nigerian Church of God has Mamma's linen. Down in Uruguay, they dine off Mamma's silver.

The big red Persian carpet that had always been in her living room was also gone, and when I saw Tony the next day, I said, "Look, you're selling stuff that doesn't belong to you, and I don't mind, but I'd like to have something to remember what this place was like."

"Mamma's medication costs a bomb," he answered. "I had to give the home some money."

"Let's see the check."

He laughed; he always did when he was caught out.

When it became a matter of just clinging to the wreckage, surviving in the open sea, more and more was cast off. By subsequent visits the tapes and records had been sold off at a vast loss; music had joined other rejected incarnations.

It doesn't take genius to figure out why he got rid of Mamma's stuff: she had to vanish. All those years when we were kids we sat there at the same dining room table being told to eat up our liver and drink up our milk; leaving the place as it had been would have meant being locked into the past when what he wanted was a new life. He could take his revenge on the old one by chucking everything out.

The carpet showed malice and intent. Tony wanted to make sure nothing was left. Next thing he'd be putting the bite on me to come to the rescue: say a few hundred bucks a month. And that happened too.

When Mamma's apartment was as empty as the house in Sam Wells would be, he went out there and started emptying out some more.

Sure, as Francine pointed out at the time, there was a little bit of revenge. But it wasn't all against me. There were indeed old scores to settle. Fine. But why lie about it? I said to her, "You remember when Tony called to say he'd been followed up to the apartment by a black who tied him up and robbed him? I asked him if that was how the silver went missing? Actually, I was worried, a man his age living alone. So I asked him, did he report it to the police? He said sure, but this was New York and they don't care. Then I had my secretary call all the local precincts. There was no report of a robbery. What gets me is, he didn't need to lie."

But even now I can remember where everything was in that apartment. Increasingly, as I think about him, I bring back what went on there, the stuff I'm writing up.

The reason I'm going back to Nevada again is, my partner Frank was at law school with Harry Blofeld who now practices in Reno. When Blofeld rang up for something or other, Frank mentioned Tony's death. Blofeld said he knew someone in Esmeralda County who could help out with the estate, and maybe other things, if there were other things to look into.

Now Blofeld meets me at Reno airport and we drive down to Rosedale together. The next day we appear in court to testify that Eileen Mount can't be located. Nor so far can a will, or any insurance policies. There is something troubling about this, I tell His Honor: "Both my brother and his wife were very systematical, orderly people." And I am not satisfied with the account of his death. I add, "My mother is ninety-nine. I'm only brother to the deceased, Anthony Mount, and on behalf of his four children I need letters of administration to settle the estate."

The judge wears a dark brown suit, he has natty, tiny teeth. He says yes, only no money can be disbursed from the estate for a year and a day; by then he hopes we'll have found his wife, "and everything else you need. Any idea where Mrs Mount's gone?" he asks civilly, one colleague to another. I say, none. "But if my brother has any money, Judge, it's sure not his."

"I see," he says back. "You folks need a good PI? Sounds like it. Unless you want to do all that digging yourself."

That's how I come to hire Harland Delattre, who is recommended by the judge, a good man, a retired forensic cop. I call him up from the hotel and we agree to meet the next day. Curiosity about Tony's end. Nagging doubts.

Meanwhile, the simple things I can do and have been doing by myself. There is no mortgage on the Buckeye Trail house; the title is in both their names, but Eileen seems to have been the one who made the actual purchase. Taxes are minimal and the house is valued at $80,000, though the market, currently, is slow. The Citizen's Bank in Rosedale which has title to the Honda for another six months at $227.50 per month says their joint account was closed by Mrs Mount three weeks before Tony died. The average monthly balance was something like $1,800. "Sorry about his passing away," the manager says.

The government checks for both of them are still coming in three months after he's dead and she's gone. I write Social Security to stop Tony's checks and tell them that Eileen's current whereabouts are unknown. At the police pound I get the Honda released and towed to Buckeye Trail. I ask the local cops if they've done any investigating on the car and they say no. Except for the broken window and what they'd had to do to get Tony's body out of the car, it was pretty much like they'd found it. When I'm finished with all that, I go out to the cemetery and stand a while by his grave. As Mandy said, the time just before night is very purple.

IV

(1987)
Jim

It was a tough night. I don't like being away from Francine and the Kid. I'm not that fond of digging around in the past. But the question is there, just when did Tony start freaking out? Back seven years ago, before Mamma went in, he and I still talked to one another. I knew that looking after Mamma depressed him, but we had made a sort of joke about it. "How's the odd couple?" I would ask.

I don't suppose you can rule out suicide. Reasons a-plenty. First there's Father; then the fix he was in as custodian of Mamma's gloomy Italo-American humors; his lousy health. There was a lot of solid American defeat built up there: he'd flunked his marriages; he seldom worked; the early vigor, and the bright hopes had gone. True to Italy, he'd left his Mamma's apartment now and then, a few years here, a few years there, but never forever. And it was all sandalwood-smelling, maternal bosom now. Except for Mandy and Adam, though that may have been a comfort, his kids weren't around; the ex-wives (I'd handled both divorces for him) were bitter, if resigned. And more immediately, I remember creditors baying at him over the telephone: his dentist, hi-fi companies, high-level *traiteurs* from whom he ordered up the meals he pretended to cook.

If you'd brought Mamma's huge family together, if any of them had lasted long enough, they would have said Tony had no place to go. That pocket-handkerchief, vaguely Moorish (it had unambitious arches) one-bedroom Manhattan apartment was still there. It was home.

He made stabs at getting out, but he never got used to accounting or to being accountable. Recently there'd been a livery service job; it lasted four months. Then he took an air hostess home with him and they fired him. He said, "How did that hurt business? Bloody Jews!" Then his polished manners got him a job with the "arrangements" section of the Carlyle, running two debutante balls: until the accounts didn't tally. He was meticulous, but he had expenses. Could he help it if the liquor store he bought from gave him a modest cut? It was good for business all around.

Ultimately there was Mamma. There's probably a name for their cohabitation today: some syndrome with suitable initials. Francine, coldly logical, said: "They deserve each other." Others thought one or the other, Tony or Mamma, was a hero or heroine. I saw it was the Ultimate Bonding: 'til death do them part.

Mamma owned him; he spent her money. But he *paid* for that little fact in all sorts of ways. Life in her cramped apartment was no joy; drinking didn't improve it.

One time I was there—when Mamma was still shuffling around the apartment bringing him the cups of tea which he converted into whiskey-and-water (with her bad eyes they looked the same)—I found her, dressed in stern, self-depriving black, in the narrow front hall with three heavy suits hanging on her brittle arm. Ninety-something, she was going to take them down to the cleaners, because with his dicky heart Tony couldn't handle weight. Bottles that had long lurked there, hidden in his closet, clinked in their pockets. The bottles she heard. "Just ginger ale," he told her. "I get thirsty."

He could have said he walked on water and she would have believed him. I was angry. I went back into his room (that had been our room as kids) and in less than a minute I found a flat pint behind the Slonimsky dictionary I'd given him. "You hide ginger ale now?" I asked. I said I didn't mind his drinking; in his shoes I'd have taken to drink long ago. But did he have to lie?

He said, "You don't know the half of it. *You* don't have to watch her falling apart." But I did: every time I came to one of our awful reunions. Preserved as it was forty-five years back, the table in the dinette was Louis XV, the chairs were of tulip wood, a bakelite radio I gave her in 1942 played WQXR. Her smile, no longer girlish, had survived too; she beamed with grim, familial satisfaction at her two boys as though they were still the adolescents of yesteryear: when in fact we as a family were *condemned.*

When she stepped aside into the kitchen with our dishes, Tony whispered how the day before she'd dropped a sugar bowl, and a week ago she'd panicked because she couldn't get out of the bathtub and couldn't let him in to help because she'd locked the door (against instructions) and because she was naked. "*You* didn't have to listen to her crying for a half-hour."

Fair enough. He earned his keep. By any means-test I know he qualified. He needed food, lodging, pocket-money and mother-love. The only trouble was, he could never have enough of the above. Or hang on to any of it. Just, please, let's not kid ourselves as to what this meant. It meant that in no time there would be *nothing at all.*

That was the last time I saw us as a Family. Her dissolution, already visible—hair in wisps retreating from the skull, gums from the teeth, skin from arm and hand—got to him. Living with her remainders, boxes of clothes in the closets, a smell of moth-balls, drove him round the corner to a selection of bars where he perched nightly, cap on head, right leg jiggling on his bar stool, until closing-time. That was the end-of-each-day routine. If it got bad earlier in the day, his chief distraction was Doctor Silverman down the street—there was always a gum to resect or a root canal to worry.

Sure, he needed to get out. Well, dying sure got him out of things.

I write this stuff up (I promised Mandy, and it's for the record anyway) in the same room of the same motel I stay at in Rosedale. I've always loved the anonymity of motels; they are places that let you think.

Harland remains as laconic as the landscape. His hair is no more than a slight, light-brown haze on his suntanned scalp; by nature he is as suspicious as a stray cat. Today we were out in Tony's garage on Buckeye Trail, standing by the Honda with its broken window. Harland rubs his long, pointed chin and wants to talk detritus: what he's handled with tweezers and put into little plastic bags, what he's found under the front seat, where the back seat folds down, under the rubber mat, driver's side, on which Tony's polished shoes once stood up at attention, and under the fake carpet in the trunk where the spare is, in glove compartments and those slits in the doors where you stash maps. He has become that comforting modern figure, the Expert, the man to whom you hand over your life, your law, your taxes, your soul. "Cars have stories to tell," he says. He talks about buttons, bits of paper, human hair, thread, candy wrappers, cash-register print-outs, cigarettes—"I thought your brother was too sick to smoke? Her, was it? The wife?"

Since the cigarette butts bother him, I tell him Eileen didn't smoke either: "She was much too clean. My brother probably sneaked a few smokes, but he smoked little thin cigars."

"Why do you say she 'was' too clean?"

"It's just a way of talking. I don't imagine the two of them dying at the same time. Frankly, I can't imagine her disappearing, either. And now you show me all this stuff, I'm surprised. Tony always kept his cars clean. His daughter visited a year ago. She smokes. Sometimes."

"These are recent butts."

We move through the rest of the house, where I've been sorting out a pitiable mound of keepsakes for Tony's kids. "It's not just that something's missing, I mean, some particular thing," I say. "It's the sheer, awful emptiness of everything here. It's like everything is missing."

"Except those hats, anything older than the month he dies," nods Harland. "There's even less of her. Looks like she took all her clothes, for instance. Usually you find a pair of old shoes or something. She's a blonde, his daughter?" I nod. "That accounts for these hairs here. She must have sat up front. If this is her hair."

"They went to the Grand Canyon two summers ago. I thought she said she was in back."

"Uh-huh. So she smokes? Recently."

I hold a few strands of hair in my hands, sort of reddish. I don't remember any red in Mandy's hair. It's more golden.

To Harland evidence counts, feeling doesn't. He only likes writers who give facts. The sun is the sun; it's not like anything else. Same with death. But what am I supposed to make of this detritus? Is this little pile what Tony was? Already he gets less real by the day, and I have to remind myself to think about him.

At night I listen to the wind blow, uninterrupted, across the desert. The season is changing. I can't sleep properly.

At some point in life there are always choices. During

that visit to New York I called Francine. "They can't go on like this," I said. "Two terrified people in 350 square feet who love and hate each other to death. If we get Tony out and provide some help, she can survive. Or she can come to Chicago."

"Over my dead body," she said. To mother *or* brother. Francine wasn't being uncharitable. Only she was married to me: not to the two of them.

I can't escape the fact I knew all along what was going to happen to the odd couple. Adoring mother, adored Mother, that's a complex knot. To undo it, Tony was going to pack her off. And wherever he packed her off to, she'd die. Of deprivation, of pride. Not die in the body—the women in her family last forever—but die in the mind. And she'd take him down with her. For company.

The next morning, that visit, was a Sunday. When I arrived, Tony was going round the apartment with his scooper-dooper. When Mamma wasn't looking, he picked up the little hard turds she dropped. Before we headed off to church he said, "Mamma, remember to go before mass." It wasn't something she could acknowledge, so she pretended not to hear, but glared at him anyway.

Unfortunately, Tony's wavering nature also included kindness and generosity. Superb, dramatic, perfectly genuine ripples of feeling flowed from him, tears welled: of pity for her and of course for himself. Stored up in him was the golden child he'd been. His memory was longer and better than mine. He knew his Mamma at her apogee! Fell in love with the best of her! Attended her sittings, her fittings! The reduced circumstances fell on young Master James, who sat with her weeps as her marriage collapsed: with the suddenness of a landslide. Because of those memories, that memory, life in the Here and Now was, for Tony, awful. It is always more awful for those with rich streaks of sentiment, who capsize at high mass from the incense and the music or the terrible wistfulness of autumn leaves being burned. Oh yes, it should all have been different. What had gone wrong?

The collective sense of humiliation in that tiny apartment was huge. Here's an instance that popped into my mind from that same weekend. On the way to mass, she took his arm the six blocks to Saint Ignatius. She wore a fur coat that had belonged to one of her sisters and her face was wrapped to its Mediterranean nose and weakening eyes in a plaid, wool scarf. She couldn't stand his pace (it was so slow), nor he hers (it was so fast, uneven and fretful). Tony said, "I can't breathe when it's this cold"; she raced ahead hobbling on her bad leg, saying, "Anyone would think you were an old man, the way you walk." She would never have dreamt he could feel humiliated.

Mamma still had her deadly marbles, and with them, the power to insult. After mass, she put him in a cab and slipped him five bucks. It may have been because he really was better off in a cab, but again she noticed nothing about how he felt.

She took my arm on the way back. "You tell me what I should do, James. He has no sort of life with me. If I go into this nursing home, he may pull himself together."

"He may, but living together is what keeps the two of you going. You look after him, he looks after you. If he really wanted to get out he could have done that years ago. When he still had a job of sorts."

She looked at me with pain. "Oh, he could never have done that," she said. "He would never leave me. He always loved me more than you did. And he's never been well. Not since the war."

"Look what all that love got him."

"So you think I should stay?"

"I think you'll die worse if you go."

Talk of choices. There are parts of people truth never reaches. A month later she was In. Tony called me to say he "couldn't do anything else". The Spellman Home had a vacancy and he had to say yes or no right away. Right. Tony was trapped. He couldn't very well say, "My mother's a threat to my health, I'll wind up *killing* her if she stays another day. Take, oh take her away." Tony had to represent her Going In as an Opportunity—those you have to grab right away.

Either she was disappeared, or she sacrificed herself on the altar of motherhood; or what happened to her no longer mattered. One night she signed everything over to him, like a nun marrying Christ. The next morning in she went. Why did she have to go in naked as a babe? Because that was Tony's wheeze: he'd got her into the home as an indigent, and to do that, he had to take over her money. That was the sudden Vacancy: a charity room. "Everybody does it," Tony said. "Everyone cheats. Otherwise, when she dies, the home gets the whole lot." At the beginning the apartment looked cozy, all her things in place: keeping alive the fantasy, which Tony *needed,* that Mamma was still there. Or, as he said, that she could come back any time she wanted. Imperceptibly, it became his apartment. New Scandinavian furniture arrived; twenty blocks away, Mamma faded. "They have every sort of service there," Tony now said. "Weekly dances, mass downstairs, company, TV, medical supervision."

I said, "Would you go in? Would you *choose* that?"

The first time I saw her *inside,* I thought about how fast she'd gone from walking to church to sitting in an armchair all day: not really watching TV, just changing patterns of light. It was a big fall. It was why she said to the occasional visitor, or me, "That was a wicked thing to do to me!"

"Why did you do it?"

She complained bravely. "No, I'm not angry with him. It was impossible for him." But in the middle of the night, I heard, she got angry with her nurses so they dosed her. She retaliated by refusing to read; then, by degrees, refusing to recognize her visitors; or falling asleep while they were talking.

When I proposed the trust, Tony hated the idea. Mamma could still, just, be reached with reason. I told her that if Tony continued to have unlimited access to her money, there'd be nothing left. So she signed. And went to sleep.

V

(1985)
Jim

I t was at about the time Tony and Eileen were breaking
up and after his heart attack, he went for a brief walk in
the winter woods behind their rented house. He talked
about the pain, but also about the wonderful democracy of
his survival. He couldn't get over it that when his heart
stopped his roommate—"You know, just anyone, no one
at all!"—rang the bell, and rang and rang until a nurse
finally showed up. By then Tony had been technically dead.

I asked him what it felt like.

"It had this 'at last' feeling about it," he said. "It
wasn't like sleep. It was like a comfortable buzz, a place
you could go to and no one could get at you."

Then of course they pounded and beat his chest and
stuck masks on his face and that moment was gone.

Mamma had undergone her bypass operation the year before.

The two of them lived really parallel lives, and even now I can't get over his being dead and her still alive. She couldn't either if she were in any shape to know. But it hits me each time I go to New York to see her. Still trying to get the message of his death through to her, I say "Tony, Tony" to her and sometimes she smiles a grim, fleeting smile. There is someone called Tony who wanders about in her mind, but she doesn't really care to talk about him.

VI

(1982)
Jim

Twelve years ago, Francine was still a new wife, and sassy. She went around Chicago calling herself the "current wife", and we were only rationally, diffidently and exploratorily connected. "A year away from your law's what you need," she said; so we went to Tuscany together in June, and I fell for an old mill-house that was stony, cool and green—in summer. "We just weren't thinking," she says now.

When we got a letter in Mamma's emphatic Catholic hand saying they were coming down it was winter. In winter the place was a misery. The house was at the bottom of a deep valley; it was wet and cold; the sun came over the hills two hours a day; when it rained the river crept under the doors and when it receded the rats raced almost soundlessly down the stone stairs.

It had been planned meticulously (by Tony) as a last, expensive, perfect trip, a Grand Tour prepared as an actor might prepare a big part; so that I assume, this being a sort of ultimate fantasy, this is how he saw an ideal life. Tony could sightsee Scottish mists, wartime English chums with country houses; in Sicily Mamma, still hale, could devour ices, her beloved coffee and cousins known by correspondence. Francine and I lay across their path.

But the trip through the Alps, with Tony driving, hadn't been a success. They hit an early storm as they started up the Saint Bernard and had to stop half way in a cheap, crowded, unheated hotel. As I understood from Mamma's telling, Tony had got drunk, made passes at a waitress and been tossed out into what was now a blizzard. The door locked behind him. She stayed inside shivering in her lace-up boots and thin black dress by an electric fire with a single bar. The result was that when Tony reappeared the next morning they had to repack, abandon their rented Daimler and pay exorbitantly for a taxi with chains to take them back down.

They took a train the next day to Milan. In Milan, Tony fell ill.

They turned up at the mill in an ambulance on a foul, rainy day, Tony stretched out in the back with pneumonia, an oxygen mask strapped to his face, Mamma up front, looking grim, exhausted and anxious—the expressions on her face were always sharper than on his, the wounds more obvious and habitually revisited, life and loss more harshly real. "Something always happens. I can't go on like this," she said. "He's not his real self when he drinks, and now he's got pneumonia."

We led her into the mill and gave her coffee by the fire while Francine called all our friends to find a clinic. When at last we found one that would take his US insurance, about an hour away, I went out into the rain and told Tony what was happening. Mamma could stay with us; we'd see to it that he was OK. He didn't seem in the least bothered by his condition. "Do you want me to come with you?" I asked.

I see him now waving at me cheerfully from his stretcher in the back and saying, "Your turn with Mamma."

It turned out our house was really a detour. She hardly knew Francine, she'd been attached to both my previous wives, she thought our house was likely to be bohemian and uncomfortable; she'd come to ask me if I thought she should go on living.

Even as she grumbled about the damp and the chips on our coffee cups, she outlined her agenda. Before leaving, she'd had a check-up. She was coming up for ninety. Should she have an operation? The doctor had told her a heart-valve wasn't working; it could be fixed, but at that age you never knew; but if she didn't have the operation, he was unwilling to say how long she would last—and what would happen to Tony if she died? Like all of us, she saw death as something terminal, not as a dreadful lingering.

Francine told me to stay out of it. "It's *her* heart," she said. No matter. My mother asks me a life-and-death question, I'm not going to duck it. I told her ultimately it

59

was a matter of how you lived after they fixed your plumbing, and how much you wanted to live in general. If your life is good, you've got things you want to do, you're not alone, fine. Otherwise, no. The way I see it, and what the cardiac boys won't tell you, is that you go on rotting all round the damned little machine; it ticks away endlessly, but the rest of you is finished and knows it. Another ten years in that stifling apartment in New York with Tony? Forget it. It was dumb to outlive oneself.

Between these discussions of ultimates, I visited Tony. Of course, they loved him at the clinic. He was a Big Spender on the "extras"; he regaled the night staff with the sounds of mock-battles or of a short-wave broadcast from darkest Africa. He looked better than he'd looked in years: as he put it, "at last really on holiday, thinking of no one but myself." He'd fixed it, he said, so he got whiskey mixed with his oxygen—I hope that was just one of his jokes.

He seemed startled by what I'd told Mamma. He may have thought her immortal like a fury: "I don't know how you can justify telling her she ought to die."

"I didn't. I just tell her she's going to." I looked him over appraisingly, aware her Number One argument was, "Someone's got to look after Tony." Because I wouldn't.

How durable was he? The jury was out, but with his dreary marriage to Eileen behind him and still some spring in his step, projects afoot, I thought he'd outlast her. Besides, they needed each other. "You two have a contract," I said to Mamma. "There's no contract without consideration."

"I'm considerate."

"Not that kind," I explained. "Consideration is what you pay, without which a contract is valueless. You've both been paying for years."

"You're always so sure you're right. You always think you're smarter than anyone else," she smiled furtively, as though she'd scored a point.

She stayed with us a month while Tony recovered and she hated every minute of it, I think. The mill was bitterly cold, she wasn't sure what she thought of Francine. ("She seems completely detached. Does she love you?") The only time she was happy was when we took her to the clinic and she could sit on a hard chair by Tony's bed and hold his hand.

We brought him a *Wall Street Journal.* He beamed. The market kept rising. Only fools lost money. "It's all quite safe," he said.

I asked the clinic doctor how Tony was: Come on, the straight answer. He shrugged. "If I could keep him here, he'd live forever," he said. We looked at one another and established mutual understanding. He'd fake his report and keep Tony another two weeks in bliss. After which . . . well, the insurance.

I think *la Mamma* understood, too. "It's good for him without me for a while," she said and got on the train down to Agrigento. From which she returned amazed by the hours of bare, brown hills, the houses with blank windows that gave on the tracks, with how people managed to live down there: "All the women in black," she repeated in the guttural accent of her youth, "the husbands all gone, often the children. It's a fate to live so long. A fate."

And it's still going on.

I finish writing this just as Harland arrives. We make an odd couple ourselves and I am growing accustomed to him. He's at home most in road-houses with country music and beer that's practically frozen. When we sit down, he takes the seat from which he can watch the TV. Short, plump women in cowboy outfits walk by and his face relaxes sheepishly.

At two hundred dollars a day, he ruminates—slowly, like a man with time to waste reading every line in a local paper. He'd be good on the witness stand. He sees things simply and what we do back East in Chicago is pretty exotic to him; characters like Tony cross his ken only late nights on TV movies. He's glued to the Tony screen.

Our usual steaks arrive and Harland says, "Way your brother lived doesn't smell of money, but he looks like someone with money, everything he's wearing is expensive. That's what you're sore about, that he ate it up?" The Bulls are on the TV. The Kid's probably watching.

"Just the waste. We were taught to finish everything on our plates."

There are times now I think he's questioning my evidence. He chews with deliberation, the way prosecutors intimidate witnesses. He says, "Tell me about Eileen. Why'd they split up in the first place?"

"Money, I think. He lost the Paris job, she went back to work, and he didn't try very hard to get another job. His résumé was a short one."

"You saw her after they split?"

Sure, a few times. She came by to see Mamma. She looked to have lost weight; she was almost good-looking, in an upswept-hair-and-Hermes-scarf way. "I couldn't make her out. Then or now. She never complained about Tony; on the other hand she never said anything was right either. She was as self-sufficient as a refrigerator. A refrigerator doesn't care what you put in or take out. Its job is just to keep going."

"How'd your brother feel about her?"

"After the divorce? I'd say Tony was grateful to her; I had no idea why."

"You told me he was impotent? You sure about that?"

"That's what he told me a few years back. Why?"

"Because there's semen on the back seats. And the front. I got the report back yesterday."

"Jesus! I should have known! You learn that in court: the way people lie and hide, nothing's harder than knowing what someone else's life is like. Priests get blow-jobs in the sacristy, judges are on the take, your local ideal all-American couple explodes. You realize all we've got to go on about how Tony and Eileen lived out here is the one snapshot of home life provided by Mandy, a girl who is herself deeply bereaved?"

Given that little bit about what Harland calls "evidence", it hits me now how when Mandy was advancing this grievance against her dad—that he'd whacked her— what she *really* wanted to say to me wasn't just that he'd

63

hit her. No! She had another familiar agenda. What she wanted to remind me was, "Uncle Jim, you *know* he incested me."

"Just once," I explain to Harland. "He was drunk, it wasn't ordinary lust, and to hear tell, she didn't fight it. The incest thing is big with her; it gives her worth; it's part of the rich tapestry of family life."

But it was no fantasy. Tony told me about it himself: in tears, with the sentimentality of the true alcoholic: "I couldn't help myself, I don't know what came over me." Well, he wasn't the first man to get laid on a hot night by a fucked-up kid. (And yes, Francine my conscience, that's what I think really happened. It sounded more like frottage than the real thing.) "You want to hear about it?"

Harland pushes aside his salad which anyway he never eats; he nods imperceptibly. Sure he's interested in queer people like us. "The Mamma walked in on them. She'd probably forgotten Mandy was there. My brother was lying on the bed with his pants around his ankles. When he heard the handle turn he pulled the blanket up around him and pretended to be asleep. But there was Mandy sitting on the edge of the bed wearing nothing but a bra.

"No way either of them knows if Mamma saw anything. I don't think she did, but how do you know with her? Every night she brought Tony cocoa. I have to guess Tony was so drunk he forgot.

"So Mamma walks in and says, 'What are you doing there in the dark?' The girl can't say 'nothing' because it's pretty obvious what they've been up to. She thinks quickly and says she's just trying on a new skirt. She says, 'Don't turn the light on, he's sleeping.'"

"She must have seen *something*," Harland says.

"She saw what she wanted to see. You know what Mandy says every time she tells me this story? She says, 'He's the most lonely man in the world. He loves me because I kept him company.'" This is pretty much as Mandy tells it: cutting out the drama and the build-up, Tony's entreaties, the hot night, the air conditioner on full, the single bed, her excitement.

And as Francine reminds me, quoting some French writer she's partial to, ultimately whoever Tony balled, it was a reminder of his Mamma. She was Snug Harbor.

VII

(1973)
Jim

Once—I think it was in '73, the year Tony grew a beard like King George V, moved briefly to San Francisco, sold his stamp collection, and wrote off his children—he and I sat down and wrote down on a yellow legal pad what we could remember about Father. Not much: being five years older he had eleven things on his list, I had seven, and we had few in common. Mainly cars.

So many of our conversations I remember as a gazetteer of the imagination: as old soldiers walk the battlefields of their youths, and the graveyards. We would sit under a picture of Father taken up in the moon-mountains of Nevada where he killed himself in the snow, skiing smoothly down by the immense light of the night sky, climbing back up to his second wife's lodge, setting forth again, up once more until his heart, as he knew it would, gave out. The picture's enough to shut anyone up. Father's wearing a cowboy hat which looks all wrong on him, and he's looking into the distance, seeing nothing worth doing out there. We agreed on one thing: he made us both feel that, like his second wife and Mamma, we had let him down.

It was one of our periods of getting along, and I asked him what he thought our kids might remember about us. "Mine never ask a damn thing," he said. I told him nor did mine. Everything changes however when you're dead: either you fall off the edge and no one gives a damn or suddenly everyone's curious about who you were.

Mandy's out with us for Thanksgiving Day: with the Kid, a smattering of my other kids who haven't got families of their own and in-laws, and a remote cousin of Francine's stranded in Evanston. Of all of these, it's Mandy who's giving off heat. She wants it all: her dad, a "solid-truth" sandwich ("Give me the facts even if it hurts"): like raiding the ice-box at midnight. The rest, curious about their cousin, are cool; only why does Mandy seem to fill the room?

Rather than giving Mandy the floor at table, I take her into my study beforehand. "'73 was one of his better years." I tell her. "Your dad was pulling himself together. You and Adam were out in LA with your father and Eileen, I think. You would have been something like eighteen and fifteen. You remember?

"I'll say this for Eileen, she was straight with you: she did what she had to do. She opened up the cans of beef stew, put the OJ on the table, made the beds and put your dirty clothes in the washing machine."

"She didn't like us."

"That's a part of the job? She was your father's wife, not your mother." I see them back then. Good-looking kids, but very long and narrow-faced: nervy, overbred horses with flaring nostrils, like Di their mother. "One day your dad called me up and asked, could I make sure you made your connection at O'Hare. He was sending you back to your mother in Baltimore. You remember what went wrong out there?" Was it Eileen said, it's them or me? Could he not afford to keep them?

"He said I stole money from Eileen. I never."

The only thing Tony said to me was, "They're not my children, God knows where they come from."

I met them off the San Francisco plane: two teenagers with a kinky brother-and-sister act. They were like newspaper pictures of starving children. You feel sorry, but do you want one in your home?

And that was one of the good times. "Anyway, for six months Tony didn't drink and then he shows up here asking me for a job. Which I got him. He sold textbooks a client of mine published. Sensational he was! He'd sold fish from Peru, old oil drums in Nigeria, God knows what in Pakistan. He was the Supreme Salesman. The secret? He was selling himself, his many selves. But you know how it was with your dad. Something always went wrong. Probably he didn't really believe in oil, fish and big business.

"This time round, he *believed*. Textbooks were good,

education was good, my client's textbooks were the best. In his own mind, hitting the road between college towns in his company Mercedes, he was a professor himself; he sat on those big leather seats and lectured imaginary kids on what was in the books.

"However, one day the client called up. 'Your brother said he didn't feel safe with commissions,' he said, 'so I put him on salary. Less money, more security. A conglomerate is looking us over, Jim; they've checked the books. Tony is costing us a bomb—his sales are terrific, his expenses don't check out. My partners say he lost us the deal.' He apologized to me for having to fire him. 'Hey look,' he said, 'it's no reflection on you, he's a terrific guy, he just wasn't made to live with accountants.'"

"I was really sad. He had genius and he was so happy. But back he went to Mamma. She made him shave his beard off. She said it made him look old."

"You want to hear about a terrible Thanksgiving?" she says.

69

VIII

(1966)
Mandy

Well Adam, would you believe it, I was invited to Chicago for Thanksgiving! Your sister told Uncle Jim—he looks more and more like *la nonna* with a grizzly beard and these thick, hairy arms—I'll remind you of *our* Thanksgiving, *that* Thanksgiving! Uncle Jim was there! He just doesn't want to remember. I started to tell him about it: you know, remind him just how much we've got to be thankful about! He takes me off to his study so I don't upset the house and his wife and kids. You must remember. Mom was still sick, she'd taken up with Ray who used to belt us and wore red flannel shirts and boots and spent his time doing bench presses. We were in that uncomfortable house in Jersey. No one said anything to us, but it was obvious money was short. Eileen was off working all day and of all times Dad had picked that one to bring us all together again and play happy families!

It was Tessa kept us together. She and Eileen argued all the time. Tessa had left college and become a slave to Jesus; she played her guitar and sang cheerful hymns, went round the white colonial houses in our New Jersey 'burbs proclaiming Love. She was going to save Dad and Eileen by praying for them. She'd come up with Boma (his real name was Olatunwe) by bus from some mission, only Dad made Boma stay in a motel because he was black, wouldn't have him in the house, tried to lock Tessa in.

It's amazing how much you can remember if you try. Boma was short, his hair was straight like it had been ironed, he smelled of butter in summer. And just about that time Dad had found out he had a wife and God knows how many children back in Nigeria.

On the Great Day we sat down at table, Tessa's eyes rolled, she looked up as if Jesus were in the light fixture, and started "talking in tongues". I think Eileen was Protestant, Presbyterian maybe. Most Scottish people are. Dad asked Tessa to say grace. Nobody could stop her once she started, and after about five minutes, with the turkey getting cold and Dad poised with his carving knife, Eileen gave her a short sharp one across the face and told her to shut up. Wasn't Eileen the oldest in her family? I reckon she had practice.

Anyway, as you might expect, Danny broke into tears and called Eileen an "old cow". I can see him now, half angel half devil. He walked quietly out to the kitchen, picked up a serving plate as if he was going to help out, and carefully turned all the sprouts and sweet potatoes out on the floor. Then he came back and grinned defiantly at Eileen with that green-and-yellow mess behind him. Dad just sat there. His eyes were glassy. Tessa looked sweetly round the table and said, "Why can't we all love one another?"

I reminded Jim he walked out; he wasn't going to get involved. So he didn't see the way Eileen looked when it got through to her what Daniel had done. She grabbed him by the ear and hauled him off to the kitchen: him yelling, her voice like ice. We watched as she started pushing his face into the sweet potatoes-and-marshmallow, her hand white on his neck, her big butt facing us.

Daniel bit her on the back of her knee. Dad's eyes grew white, his hand shook, and his leg started going up and down underneath the table like one of those jack-hammers they fix streets with. Then he got up, ran into the kitchen— he could be quick back then—and whacked Daniel so hard he flew right across the kitchen floor and into the counter under the sink. You could feel the hate in him all the way out in the dining room. Tessa was praying, you were blubbering, and I sat there watching out for myself.

Dad started across the kitchen floor to hit Danny again, Danny was bleeding, and then, just as he was bending over and raising his arm, he suddenly couldn't move. He just stood there looking surprised down at his legs and wondering why they wouldn't move. It must have been some kind of early stroke or something.

Next thing I knew there was a cold draft in the room and Eileen was heading out the front door in a transparent plastic coat. Uncle Jim came back just as Dad went down on all fours and Tessa went over to help him up—all that while Daniel was having one of his fits.

Somehow Tessa got Dad back to the dining room and Dad slumped down in his chair. Daniel was screaming, Tessa was trying to comfort Dad, Dad just sat there crying too, he didn't give up crying for some time, but by then the rest of us were out in the kitchen doing the dishes and chucking cold turkey in the garbage pail. No one wanted to eat. You shut up quickly and washed up after us. You were always the only one of us never asked questions. I helped put Dad to bed. Uncle Jim called the doctor.

I told Uncle Jim you can't expect things to be the same after something like that.

*   *   *

Jim

Two days go by and Harland's in my motel room. Harland says an autopsy *had* been made. "Your brother was a mess. It's a wonder he kept going. He had about twenty per cent of both lungs, his heart was shot, his liver was gone; he would have died soon anyway." Then he says, "He was miles over the limit. The only thing in his stomach was bile; and a cocktail of pills. You name it, he took them. I go for the obvious. I reckon he went back on the sauce and Eileen left him. I see her as one of those self-righteous broads you get back East. She wouldn't have approved of him and his daughter having it off. You still interested in finding Eileen? Find me her maiden name, I might run a trace through the force here."

"MacSomething, that's all I remember. I can't even remember where they got married. Someplace hot."

"He like kids? Young girls? Besides his Mandy? They're a young woman's hairs." He says, "Suppose I follow his route backwards; he must have stopped at somewhere to buy the stuff. Chances are he had a place he went regularly, even if he bought his drink in a brown paper bag and chucked it out the window someplace."

Girls? There always was one, I tell him. "I thought that up all by myself."

"Evidence," he reminds me.

"You ought to talk to Mandy. Give her a chance. I send her what I write up: like a serial you see backwards from episode thirteen."

"You talk to her?"

"Lots. I just don't want to be adopted. Last time she called she was talking about Tony's funeral, how quick he was gone, didn't I find it weird? Compared to the death, the funeral was straight up and down, priest and flag and God Bless America. Now he's dead, she's taken to her Dad dead like a convert taking first communion; she's been eating him ever since."

"What sort of chance I should give your niece?"

"Good lawyers make scumbags sympathetic. Tony's an easy case. I'd like his daughter to like him. By the standards of the day, she's a good kid. Only she's got this pursuit of happiness business deep within."

"I agree with you there. Worst thing they put in the Constitution."

"Mandy wants to know if he was happy with Eileen."

"Was he?"

"The answer is, on balance, yes." As he'd been happy with selected nannies from his childhood, ladies generally big-bosomed and always half cross, wholly indulgent, perhaps amorous and reckless, often French, but always disciplinary when Mamma was around. Father's idea, and Mamma's to get rid of them, often enough *in flagrante*. "Eileen took French lessons for his sake—so she could keep up. But without much result."

We head out of the motel in his pick-up and I make Harland stop where these supposed Nevada girls of his are hanging out. I imagine them in short shorts frayed at the bottoms, tight all round. I'm in the mood for a few drinks myself. He starts out disapproving, sticking to his icy beer. But on the second or third stop, with a restaurant thrown in, he takes to bourbon. When we've had a few which, being used to them, he handles better than I, the girls begin to look ferociously young and the men looking at them are mostly my age or at most Harland's. Even in the fierce air conditioning of the Dollar Bill or the Last Nugget or wherever, they knot their shirts above their midriffs to push up their athletic breasts.

Harland watches me impassively, sipping. "I do hereby note, Mr Mount, you're not past it yourself."

No, I'm not. I see young girls with their pump-action guys, I think of what they're missing. "I've got this weakness for the girls out here: round twenty-five to thirty. Have to tell you that. They all look like they've been abandoned, like a tree that wants watering. Shows in their eyes. You notice? They stare far away like something good's going to show up." I also like their dry, freckled skins, the way they fall in with you, being slightly crazy, and will do just about any damn fool thing you can think up. "Know who my favorite actress is? Cissy Spaceship, my wife calls her, Spacek or whatever her name is. My first girl was from Oklahoma, she was something. I never wanted to stay East.

"I reckon you should never have asked how my brother and Eileen split. That's no problem. Ask rather why they ever got together. I'll tell you the God honest truth, I never really liked her. She liked cut glass, her bathroom was ultra-sanitary, she kept stuffed animals on both sides of their bed—this was in Paris when they started out—she was rigidly engineered, you know: tartan skirt, large and motherly on top, pearls, smooth neck, down on cheeks and upper lip, up on top the big hair of the times. I never looked at her that I didn't think what a wonderful ambition it was for her to be married at all.

"It's all too easy to fool Mandy, but the truth is the only woman her dad ever loved was Mamma, and he married Eileen only to get away from her."

"Yeah, but what I don't understand is why he loved his mother so much. They don't sound much alike. Your brother now, he sounds like fancy folk, like he's better than other people. The way you talk about her, I think of you."

"Great beauties both of them. Beautiful people spot each other: same way homosexuals know whose knee to lay a hand on. Nothing much left of *la Mamma* now, but once . . . How else did she get out of Philadelphia?"

But I'm pursuing a thought that's been bothering me some weeks. It wasn't just Tony and Eileen, but there was also Tony and Di, the mad mom of his kids. "It has to do with semen," I tell Harland. "Mamma spotted that from the start. When Di—that was his first wife—flew off to the equivalent of Timbuktoo to get him to marry her, where she got him was between the legs. Sex."

From what I've heard, when they went back, married, the stuff flowed, endless and majestic, like the Congo, carrying all those nutrients into her fertile, crazy womb. "I had this intuition about a woman right away when I came here with Mandy for the funeral and saw the house empty and Eileen gone. But back in Chicago, when I said how he died, people said he killed himself . . ."

"One way or another, maybe he did."

"It was the look on his face. Positively beatific. I shouldn't have fallen for it. Had to be a girl."

On that, we move on to another place. Somewhere younger still, more jammed, noisier. Here the girls are wearing gingham shirts and the boys sport cowboy boots elaborately tooled. The girls look constantly fresher—except for those who perch on stools at the bar alongside us.

"A son of mine worked bulls one summer out in

Minnesota," I tell him. "He used to collect the stuff, the semen. You work the prostate and hold a plastic bag underneath the bull's dick, a forearm long. Enough to blow your mind. Tony did to me what the bull did to my son. For instance, it would happen when we were young we might share a girl. You could say I have collected testimonials about this prowess of his: not to speak of the time he and Di visited us somewhere—I forget where—and Lou, my first wife—not the Oklahoma girl—had to wash out the sheets. Still *wet*, His and Her liquids. Lou was worried about the mattress being stained."

"We ought to get off this shit," Harland says. "There are times you worry me, Mr Mount." (I keep telling him to call me Jim. He won't, because that would make us equals.)

I pay no attention. "A deeply sensual man, I guess," I say to Harland: "His first wife's doctors—when she had to go Inside in Wesport, Connecticut—said he had literally fucked her mad. He *exhausted* her. Who knows what he imagined when he made love, what he really saw in *them?* I know Di was always languid: a tall girl, lolling on chairs, sofas and the sides of beds like a dog's tongue hanging out.

"I can't get over your semen samples. I suppose you're sure they're his, not a previous owner. Back seat, front seat. I thought that was all past. That's what he said."

"I've known people to go off the tracks both early and late," he answered. "But most folks are consistent. With your brother it could be either way. Maybe he lied to you."

On our last stop that night, one of those purple nights

Mandy goes on about, we're in a place called Hawthorn where there's an Army ammunition dump and not much else. The girls here sag on their flat shoes; the boys watch TV and the only time they move is when they reach back into their jeans to check out how much cash they've got left.

Harland says before the last stretch to Rosedale and hitting the sack he ought to tell me he thinks he's found a girl called Rose who remembers Tony.

"Jesus! Now you tell me! How'd you manage that?"

"Just asking round," he says. "'Seen an old guy, you know, continental type?' Show them the photo."

"She remembered him?"

"I'm a cop of sorts, remember? I didn't say she remembered anything. All I said was, she recognized the picture, your brother. I could tell. Then a minute later she said she wasn't sure."

"You think he was with this Rose that night? If he was, she can't just have got out of the car up there on top of the hill and walked home."

"Could be. Could of panicked, if she was the one that night, which I doubt, could of hitchhiked home. Someone, I'm pretty sure of that. What I'm trying to tell you, Mr Mount, is they remember your brother. Turns out he was a Friday-night regular. Did magic tricks. With cards. Sat at the bar and played poker dice."

"Where's that?"

"Right here."

I look around as though I'm going to see Tony at the

far end of the bar, with sunglasses, a cap on his head, a smile of his lips. "Here? So what happens now?"

"I go find her. She ain't here tonight."

Rose, honey, I sure hope you did give him one good time.

IX

(1956)
Jim

I have bad dreams that night. I dream about girls with pointed, 1950s breasts, and when I first open my eyes Tony's ex-wife Di is sitting impassively at the foot of my motel king-sized bed. She is blond but with thin, dispirited hair. Her lipstick is smeared and her dressing-gown, idly parted, reveals powerful, soft and dimpled thighs. I drift back into sleep with the memory of her in a vast and heavily mortgaged house in western Massachusetts, and of a sour smell of kiddies, the dire and squalling result of all that seed. In the distance behind steaming romper suits on a line, plastic mugs and cereal bowls, a press clatters Tony's greeting-card business into bankruptcy.

In some decor like that, in the kitchen of that house and in the freezing, early hours of a winter morning, Di sought repeatedly to stab herself with a heavy meat cleaver, and instead of being dead wound up with a sprained wrist, bad bruises and a nasty bunch of deep slices which bled a lot. That was how, in the blood, Tessa found her: come down in her nightshirt with Adam's empty, formula-clotted bottle. A mother already, Tessa had staunched her mother's wounds with kitchen towels and already washed the cleaver before going up to tell her dad something was wrong.

Ironically, Tony was going through one of his many transformations. In this one he'd gone on a retreat with Mamma; seen the Light; and remained cold sober if distant during the ensuing weeks in which Mamma dispersed their kids—Adam to me, the two girls to the orphanage in New Rochelle and Daniel to Di's sister in Baltimore—while Di was packed off to a sanitarium in Westport, Connecticut.

How could Di have done a thing like that? Mamma asked. She knew the answer: "It's God's punishment." But why punish the kids? Lou and I asked. Never mind, black eyes flashing, Mamma marshalled her forces—especially the nuns of New Rochelle who had God on their side—as for a natural disaster: Tony had to be saved from himself, Di to be sequestered (otherwise there would necessarily be more *bambini* with which Di clearly could not cope), the four children spared.

Maybe two months later, Tony drove Mamma and me out to the clinic for a visit. In Mamma's high, pre-war Pontiac—used about once a year and kept in a garage in the Bronx—he looked not very different from the way he'd wound up in his '86 maroon Honda: dressed in the same retro, stately way: soft grey flannels, blue blazer, regimental tie.

When we arrived at this high-priced home for the exceedingly self-indulgent, she sniffed furiously at its air of rich laxity, its pool and tennis-courts; she did not admit weakness; such "homes" would not have been tolerated in the Philadelphia of her childhood—"Doesn't the girl have a family of her own?" We were supposed to think this wasn't a fruit farm but a pricey hotel—the guests just happened to be off their rockers—so Mamma, Tony and I, along with the agents, families and lovers of the other "disturbed", sat there eating sandwiches while she forcefully asked the staff if they couldn't make the coffee stronger.

When she was brought down from her room, Di wore a satin cream dressing-gown with feather-like stuff around the collar and wrists: it was like the gown in my dream and also parted above the knees. In her fingers she held the big-beaded rosary Mamma had given her. It seemed to keep her busy. What with those hysterical fingers on the beads and her painted mouth mumbling, you knew why she was there.

The accepted thing with Di, or so the doctors had been telling us earnestly, was to tell her she was looking good and all she needed was rest. Yet her eyes were so empty no one wondered why she didn't ask where or how the kids were. Di fine? Lou and I began to agree with Mamma: had Di ever been "normal"?

We couldn't tell where Tony stood on this question either, nor do I remember him ever visiting any of his kids.

Probably Mamma talked him out of it. Or thought he shouldn't be allowed anywhere near a woman in a permanent state of undress. Soon enough, however, we gave up on our one-way conversation or trying to be cheerful with the now-batty Di. Leaning forward with his elbows on his knees, his hands clasped, it fell to Tony to take up the slack. From his pocket came snapshots of the big white house and the kids. This, he was saying, was where she still belonged. The Super-Salesman was at work, admitting the errors of the Past, painting a rosy picture of the Future. The kids were fine; he'd sold his share in the greeting-card business to the Dutch partner; he'd had an interesting letter from a cousin in the guana business in Peru.

Di would have none of it. The photos, the long white house in the snow, her kids, fell listlessly from her hands and slipped to the floor, where a soft-footed Filipino picked them up before anyone could reach down. She blew her nose noisily and her lips parted—big lips like the up-and-down doors on a freight elevator. Inside you could see big pink gums. Her tongue stuck out. Anyone could see she was trying to smile. That was in my dream too.

She said, "I don't . . . I don't want to see any of you again." The line that was to become familiar. No one paid attention. She said it again.

Mamma addressed Tony a little bit louder, her latest cup of weak coffee at her lips, as though Di were hardly there: "I don't know how you can afford to heat such a big place. And where would you find a decent school?"

"None of you," Di got out slowly. She stood up.

A nurse appeared alongside and took her by the elbow. "I think we're feeling just a bit tired, aren't we?"

As I say to Harland the next time we meet, same place—same breakfast, same eggs, same everlasting explanations in my head and in the notes I share with him, "I think you can see why I wished Tony well. He was miles away from his dreams. It must have been like a desert for him, with everything sliding away to the horizon, getting lost. You know, I think what he most wanted was Mamma's car: to make a get-away."

It's the same with us. Between one place and another we do many miles in a landscape that shifts and erodes before our very eyes. The trailer park where we end up is protected by two dusty and leafless tress; it is circumscribed by a low wall of concrete and where the concrete has worn away with wind or depredation, with odd painted boulders. He handles my stories with diffidence. Mostly with a "yep" or a "nope", as though he's heard them all or knows ahead of time how they end. "The car," he says. "Queer place to die. That way, I mean. Then Rose doesn't have no car. Lost her license year ago: DWI for the third time. He might have given her a ride, your brother."

Anyway, we are going where Rose lives when she's not at Jack's Bar & Grill. We pull in. There is an office with loose boards for windows; there are, between trailers and RVs, none new, some propped in cinder block, with hooks and loose tail-lights that testify to a lost mobility trail, between washlines and discarded appliances with gaping doors, a scattering of concrete tubs, a maze of crazy paving pathways, snaking cables that trail in the sand and lead nowhere. Give me the jungles I know in Chicago any day, packed with people, huge with noise.

Rose's body sits inside like a fortune-teller waiting for a customer, at a fixed table in a dining nook. It's a loose body and half effaced in its lines by blowse. Her breasts are full and low. The mid-morning sun is behind her. Her face is the pale yellow of the desert beyond the red-and-white checked curtains of the window. Her eyes are little-girl blue; her mouth and nose a little crooked, as if they had been photographed separately and joined on the fold.

"Oh, it's you again," she says to Harland.

"Yep, I'm back. Rose, this is the late Mr Mount's brother."

"Hi." She raised an unformed hand, all dimpled. Ready for absolutely anything at all. A metal cabinet (one door is bent off its hinges) behind her right shoulder contains three frocks on wire hangers. One is little-girl blue and sways with the side-wind from the fan pointed right at her face. There is an open beer bottle before her which looks like it's been there since last night.

Harland studies the dress, which matches her eyes. "Won't fit her now," he says to me.

"You talking about me?"

"I said, that was a pretty dress. But it won't fit you now. How many months you pregnant anyway?"

"What do you mean? It's none of your business. It's got nothing to do with him or his brother."

"Didn't say it did."

"Look, he was just a *john*. I don't know why you keep asking me about *him*. I said I knew him. What more do you need?"

"You liked him. You said."

"He had manners." She turns to me. "Want something to drink?" I shake my head. "I could use something. This beer's old. You a cop too? I'm going to keep *this* baby."

"I'm no cop. I'm just trying to find out about my brother. Mr Delattre here is what you call a private detective."

"Why you want to find about your brother? He done something wrong?"

"He's dead. I need to find out how and why."

"He died, that's why. You think this is his baby? At his age?"

"You saw him often?" Harland asks.

"Often? I don't count. Three, four times. I ain't seen him in months. Think maybe he took up with Ginger. He was a good-time guy. Every Friday, nicely dressed, clean, free with the money, a crisp C-note. Laid it down on the bar: drank it, told stories, played games, balled, and round midnight got back in his coach like Cinderella. Everyone liked him. It's not his baby, anyway. You don't have to worry 'bout that. Even if it was, I wouldn't take nothing for him."

"You're not surprised he's dead."

"Uh-uh."

"You knew."

"Uh-huh. I think Ginger said."

"Who's Ginger?"

"You know, she's around."

Later, with the wind blowing hard in the Reno Airport parking lot where he's dropping me off, I say, "Harland, think about it for a minute. Doesn't it look to you like what Tony did, whatever it was, was deliberate? Maybe Eileen *helped*?"

"Nope. It was your brother did the getting around— more than you or anyone else thought. He took care of the car, he bought gas at the Texaco at the edge of town and paid cash. You ought to be asking where that cash came from, the C-notes. Not from the bank. I've asked around. Mrs Mount doesn't ring much of a bell in Sam Wells. Even in Rosedale, the only living soul recognized the picture is Rose. How do you know when something *don't* happen? But that's what my hunch is about her. She was gone some time before your brother died. Things that should have happened didn't."

"*Someone* cashed her social security checks."

"That's the funny thing. Her last two weren't cashed. Picked up but not cashed."

"So what's Eileen living on?"

"You so sure she's alive? I'm not. Not now. You could die here and nobody know, ever. Sure enough in the summer with the air on. People die off the road. Nothing out there. By the time they find you, you're just bones. If she took off, how'd she get anywhere? Hire a car? Take a bus? I've checked most things out.

"Let's see if we can find this Ginger."

What Harland doesn't say, but hits me the moment I get on the plane, is: what if Tony lost his temper once too often and took Eileen out? Then most things suddenly fit. They fit not just his dying but his nature.

X

(1949)
Mandy

Should I get married? Marriage is a complicated subject, Uncle Jim says. I tell him my boss is in love with me—he's about fifty-five and short like himself. "Look at your parents before you leap," he answers. "I have some experience. I never did see why Tony married at all. He never lacked for beautiful women. But he thought your family, the Ebers and Brunswicks, had money. They sure lived that way. I saw the whole thing unfold."

The first thing is, Dad had an official meeting with Grandpa Eber. "A tall, bald man. He told us about three times how he made his first million on Wall Street by the time he was twenty-four. He never let on he'd lost it all in the crash. Mistake Number One." Next was Grandma

Brunswick. "No one said she was completely crazy, nor that *she* had the money and got it from her lover. It wouldn't have taken much of a nudge for your dad to call the whole thing off right then."

Only then, he said, Mamma found out through friends Grandpa Eber was broke; worse, he was 100 per cent Jewish, which meant Mom was Jewish and therefore Dad couldn't possibly marry her. Of course, as Uncle Jim said, if his Mamma hadn't made such a fuss maybe he wouldn't have married her.

The wedding reception must have been awful: two batches of relatives and friends on different sides of the room not talking to each other. It was at the Saint Regis. "Your grandfather wasn't living there at all like he made out. Apparently when the wedding was announced, your crazy grandmother said she'd pay for the affair and in a smart place like the Saint Regis, for appearances' sake. But in return, her ex-husband would never bother her for money again. He should do the decent thing and drop dead. I hear she gave him a necklace to sell."

Once they were married, Grandma Mount just about wouldn't see Mom. When she got sick, she did finally go up to Connecticut. It was like her ship coming in, so she could afford to be gracious. She was getting rid of Mom and she was getting her son back. You see her now, you have no idea how potent and how devouring she was back then.

*   *   *

Jim

The year he got married, Tony was in the papers. I kept the clip for years, now I can't find it. The headline said something like PRINCETON PLAYBOY IN YACHT FIRE. He was a playboy all right, Tony. He had slicked down hair, he wore white ducks, and the yacht in question wasn't his.

He'd gone off to Florida instead of spending Christmas at home. The girl that time was called Concha, five foot four on the high, spiky heels of the day, the kind of girl we called a bombshell. A Latin bombshell. They were big in America back then. He met her hanging around the docks being handsome and suave. She said, why didn't he come along on her boat?

I don't know what as (since he didn't say), but one day I got a telegram in New York saying to come down and rescue him from an "unfortunate" situation. Which was that the yacht's owner had put him ashore in Cuba and left him to get home by his own devices: I assume because he'd been shacking up with his girl, this Concha. He'd hitched a ride back from Havana, but he was stuck: everything he owned was still on Concha's yacht.

Was that all there was to the story? Not at all. But I told Mamma I had an interview in Chicago for law school and went down to Florida to bail him out instead.

It was in a little place called Eau Gallie: trees festooned with mimosa, a small harbor, a softball lot, a few stores. I found Tony washing dishes in the place's only diner to stay alive. He quit the moment I arrived.

Concha and her boyfriend, he told me, were back now, tied up in Palm Beach. "You see, it's a delicate matter. Do you think you could . . . ?" It was a whole saga and he'd always thought of America as an adventure playground.

I took the bus down to Palm Beach, found the yacht, waited till the boyfriend was ashore playing golf, and Concha handed me Tony's bags without a problem. She said, "Hey, you cute? Next time, you tell your brother he send a grown man do his dirty work, not kid brother. I claw his eye out. *Hasta la vista.*"

Back in Eau Gallie, I handed over his clothes. I also gave him money. He said he would take the train back up and finish school.

A month later he still hadn't shown up in New York. His dean at Princeton kept calling up Mamma and she was desperately worried. "It's not like him not to tell me where he is," she said. But of course it was just like him.

"Tony's all right," I said. "He always lands on his feet. He's just having one of his little adventures."

Luckily, I was around studying one day when Tony called up from a coin-box in a jail on the Jersey shore somewhere. "Have you read the *Trib?*" he asked. "Playboy and Hired Captain Burn Yacht for Insurance. Find me a lawyer, Jim. Bloody rummy, he's not even a captain and he couldn't even get the boat to burn properly. I just went along for the ride."

"How's jail?" I asked.

He laughed—not a worry in the world: "Better than facing Mamma. Just keep things quiet."

I found the lawyer, Tony went back to Princeton on bail (drummed up by his eating club), tanned, and dined out on his exploit. When the grand jury heard the case—the yacht may have been stubby, broad and peeling, but it was undeniably *stolen*—the prosecutor hardly bothered with Tony: the phoney "captain" had a record, Tony was a war hero.

Buddy Berrigan, the lawyer, and Tony went out to lunch to celebrate, during which, Berrigan said, Tony had a fair amount to drink. It was just bad luck the "captain" turned up in the same restaurant. "There were words. Your brother started beating up on him. He's a strong guy. It took several of us to pull him off."

That told me Tony was in on the deal, but he'd got away with it again. Aggravated assault didn't work any better. Berrigan pleaded Tony's disability, the war, shell-shock, and his promising career at Princeton. The judge dismissed the case. Things were like that once and there were many ex-GIs like Tony with pent-up killing instincts; also plenty of drifters like the "captain".

I told Mandy at the funeral (she stirs up all these memories) I used to worship my brother. In part this was why. He couldn't be touched with the ordinary shit of life. In his mind he owned the yacht *and* Concha and any judge or jury he might face.

XI

(1945)
Jim

But real life had got to him at least once.

To hear him talk about the war in his regular letters home was to experience romance and adventure: his Army Post Office sent us blue V-mails full of desert oases, images from *Beau Geste*, jeep rides with British and Free French officers; promotions were always just around the corner, then came ("Kindly put 'Lieutenant' and 'Captain' in quotes," he wrote. "That's what you do with temporary ranks"). The actual war, the one we read or heard about, he made to seem secondary to a boyish sense of fun. I remember only one death: reported suitably heroically and tight-lippedly: "We set an ambush for this German troop-carrier, Dick didn't duck fast enough. A good friend."

As the war came to a close and we seemed to be

winning, a chunk of history was falling behind us, Tony would soon be back. I was the only doubter: fresh out of college, eighteen and 1-A, I longed to find out from Tony what war was *really like*: before I died in Japan, as I surely would—since Tony had always had all the luck.

At the end of that summer (I still hadn't been drafted and we hadn't heard from Tony for three months) he was repatriated and we went out to see him in a veterans' hospital a long way out on Long Island. The hospital was already a bad sign: we'd been notified of no wounds.

Yet the Labor Day weekend we went out was one of those on which one could feel hopeful. America felt fresh, even after the Bomb; the air was clean and beflagged; this good country had prevailed; it was still there; the Long Island railroad continued to rumble along its old rails and its passengers, though exhausted, were gruffly cheerful. We hadn't moved much during the war; now we saw, as something renewed from our past, clammers, rowboats, hedges still stuck with winter paper, station wagons with real wooden sides.

Cheerful, Mamma and I took a clapped-out taxi with a B-sticker and, at the other end, still hopeful, we patiently walked on miles of lino in the hospital. Overworked clerks took inquiries from anxious parents; hard-edged nurses called upstairs to okay the visit; a lot of cigarettes were smoked in the corridors before we were let in.

But then, on top of "Private" Mount (it was lettered neatly at the foot of Tony's cot and Mamma murmured, "There must be some mistake") there was Tony himself. Sweet Jesus, what had they done to him?

He sat on the edge of his army cot, one of a row, in pyjamas striped like an old-time convict only the other way, up and down, a thin blue bathrobe, toes-only slippers. He was a deep, unhealthy yellow; his eyes were spent; his head nearly bald; his skin taut on bone after visible bone. He was injured all right; he shook, he trembled. The question was, where was the wound?

All the best doctors in the world couldn't have pin-pointed a spot, for the self is invisible. Somewhere he'd lost language except for scattered fragments like baby talk. Mamma caressed him, her arms (always elegant, as if gathering up a bunch of flowers in a vase) around his head. The smart, skinny, chain-smoking kid I was then stood by watching. I was really past his ken. Anything was. Way past.

We rode back slowly into the New York dusk, click-ety-click. Mamma's face, hiding tears, was pressed to the filthy window, unconsolable. A part of her self, the deepest part, had also been destroyed. I felt a deep sorrow for him, mingled with grief for myself.

The fact is, we were in ignorance of the facts, I told Francine who was hardly pleased by my constant absences. "What about the Kid?" she asked. "Is a dead brother somehow more important than him?"

"The Kid's there, he'll be there long after me," I said. "These are unresolved matters. They affect me. You see, first, when he got out of the hospital, Tony said he'd faked the whole thing, just to get out. Then I remembered that back in the early days after the North African landings he'd got himself busted. His luck gave out. If you can believe it, because Mamma insisted on knowing where he was—he and she had this dumb code and they nailed him.

"The Army took its revenge. Probably with good reasons. Who knows what else he did. They had punishment brigades the public didn't hear much about. That's when you get sent in first. So Tony was on one of the first landing crafts to Sicily, with the Germans four deep on the beaches. The poor bastard lost his hair coming ashore, he was that shit-scared. That's in his Army records, which Harland got.

"Then he went AWOL and shacked up in a hotel in some small town just liberated—maybe Mamma'd told him of some remote cousin to look up. Again, his bad luck, the Germans bombed it and the ceiling fell on him. Thirty-six hours later he was dug out. Dazed and white with plaster, the MPs found him wandering the streets. Enough time had gone by he was now not just absent without leave, he was a deserter.

"He told the MPs some cockamamy story; they didn't buy it. He tried to attack them. Things went from bad to worse.

"So much for his illness being a fake. I think he couldn't face what had really happened to him. He'd been attainted. He couldn't believe this was happening to *him*. It was his precious self that fell apart. There were no fantasies to hide in. You couldn't lie when your identity was just a dog-tag and they were determined to get you killed. Tony couldn't face it.

"Just like his dying out there in Nevada, it always

depends on which story you believe. But it's all in his records. When he was on a troop ship to the South of France he started shivering and turned yellow with hepatitis. He grew so listless he wouldn't eat. From that he blew up full-scale shell-shock and they shipped him back Stateside because he was no one any more. He joined the head-cases. That's where I saw him again.

"What Harland says is right. He says Tony had to live with murderous thoughts all his life, some terrible *anger*. I've faced it myself."

But as far as Francine is concerned, I might be talking about people on Mars or the Honorable Morris Markey, whom I am defending against a charge of milking a mill-and-a-half on the divorce bench. She doesn't think Tony ever belonged among those who, as my friend Frank says, "know how the world works". And she doesn't understand my *useless* curiosity. For instance, what did Tony want or need with the ten or so hats and caps he left behind in his house when everything else was gone? It's one of her charms.

*   *   *

Mandy

I guess with my sort of luck, it was high time to get out of New York anyway. Last week my boss asked me to send his fiancée flowers: *as he climbed out of my bed*. I quit right there. I told him he had to give me a few months' salary or I'd bug him until he did. He actually paid up, or the company did. Then this guy—on the phone he sounds just like the Marlboro man—calls up to ask if I went out to Nevada, did I think I'd remember something, anything, useful about Dad? So here I am.

It's been two weeks now, I haven't called Uncle Jim once, and we've gotten to the point of going back nights to Harland's A-frame in the hills. He'll light a fire, scratch his beard, say a few things, charcoal a steak, we'll put away some bourbon and beer. Nice and easy. Not that I think we're going anywhere, the two of us. As he says, two bodies are a fact, so's a warm body in bed; marriage is just an idea. He makes me laugh: his legs are so thin you'd think his jeans were crushing them. In his own way he's *delicate*; he sees things differently and when I start talking too much, he shakes his head—"Some kind of whacko family you

come from, kid."

Some nights I get stuck in my motel. He says, "not tonight" and goes off. "That's what I do for a living," he says. "You stay out of it." The next day he comes back, rubbing his chin, and he tells me he's getting close. With this girl called Rose. "Know what she says to me, honey? Rose? She said, 'Look for trouble, that's what Ginger does'."

Apparently her daddy's something big in Vegas. He's into coin-games. So his little girl plays games of her own. She gets herself in trouble on purpose because she knows it'll embarrass her dad. According to Rose, her dad's tried everything: shrinks, drug programs, jail, tickets to South America. None of them's worked. Her head's fucked up.

We've been all round this place. We get in the pick-up

and just go. I can't remember much. Some of the places I stopped with Dad for a drink. Nothing useful. Everywhere I look I just see him dead in his car. How glossy the car looked in the photos, how clean Dad was.

He says, "Your Uncle Jim *envied* your dad." Not his life, but the way he started out, with everything made easy. "Seems like he thinks even dying his brother's getting away with something."

"And was he?"

"Your uncle's paying me good money to find out."

I think he first took me over to Hawthorn just for the sheer fun of it, to see what I'd say, if I was one of those stuck-up girls from back East. We went to a place called Jack's bar. It was a Friday night. He made a point of that. "Unless she's moved on, this is where she sometimes shows up. Ginger. Rose used to do tricks for your dad, but my guess is Ginger is something different."

The bar is just a long, low, flat cinder-block place on a desert lot about a mile outside Hawthorn, which is a long way outside Rosedale. Harland puts his pick-up alongside all the others parked nose in all round the building. Inside, there's practically no light at all. Just a lot of what Uncle Jim once described as "herd-muscle", the result of pushing, shoving, facing, following, browsing, stampeding. He said that if you watched muscle closely, it was expressive as any face. The customers are mostly young and there isn't a girl in a skirt there for me, nor anyone over thirty I can see.

We sit down in a booth, he orders for both of us, looking the crowd over, especially the bar. "I've just got this hunch one or t'other of the girls is going to come in tonight. Give you a chance for you to look them over, tell me what you think. Rose is some months gone. I don't think she's thinking any more. She's just got this instinct to protect. Like I'd hurt Ginger."

I ask him, "How come Uncle Jim wants to know so bad? Dad's dead. Where's the interest?"

"He loved him. He feels cheated."

"This Ginger too?"

"Least she got her own back. She killed him, I think. I mean, technically. Whatever happened was hers to make happen. Those are her hairs in the car. I'm dead sure of that. Maybe your Dad was just a new line of trouble for her. One thing I know: she's got a record running back three years. All arrests, no convictions. So you see, daddies are useful."

Nobody shows up. It's 8 a.m. and *cold.* He had to hold me tight most of the night. "You must be awful scared," he says. "The way you shiver." He has no idea it's him.

*   *   *

1930s

Jim

This is going to be my last trip out. Harland's found out where Ginger is. And what does he say about her? That "she's just a kid". I've seen enough kids in court to know they're as dangerous as adults; their weirdness is locked away in their heads, that's all—waiting to pass to the actual.

As they say in spirit messages, I see the boy Tony in clear. He is reckless; he manipulates truth; he's a human salamander, always unscathed. He climbs trees and drives a car before he knows how, falls and crashes: the moment of truth, however, is an accident forever postponed.

Meanwhile, our father has killed himself without notice or apology: not a hundred miles from Sam Wells.

Go back another year or two when we spent summers at Father's house on the Jersey shore. Girl-cousins—all on Father's side, neat, starched, bony girls swinging tennis rackets in presses—come to stay. They are seduced by Tony or they refuse and find their suitcases of neat frocks and careful underwear tossed in with the garbage. There are furious visits from Father's sisters. He won't see them. Even as the girls go home in tears and I hear the crunch of their big cars on the sand, Tony details his conquests. Back then, I told Mandy, there really were ten-year-olds to whom sex was as mysterious as God.

Whatever I did, I was like my father in this, I did it in secret; people like Tony need a public. Their lives proliferate in versions and re-makes. He would recount in shivering detail how a lame man fell, pushed, from the boardwalk into the sea. Someone else pushed him, but Tony's tears of repentance were real. He appropriated from others the lives he would like to lead.

This made him, I now realize, into countless people—the last Tony being a classic image of death out West. But even that's not so very different from sitting in a bathtub and broadcasting the sound-effects of planes over Addis

Ababa in the then-recent war, interviewing himself in what he said was Amharic. He did a number with the edge of his hand on his Adam's apple that came out *The Campbells are coming, Hurrah! Hurrah!* So he was liquid: he could be anyone he wanted.

Now I know this is the way exiles behave. Exiles always have these terrific pasts; they've all been pushed out of the Garden of Eden. Tony had bit into the apple early. Tossed out of paradise, he clung to Mamma, and for each new exile he had to invent the paradise lost.

I see the widow's peak, the way his hair rises from it, a Pompadour, smooth on both sides. When we were at school he was the first boy I knew who ordered a manicure with his haircut in Danbury. And got it.

I believe in the innocence of children but also in the terrible things they can do.

*   *   *

Mandy

Uncle Jim is due sometime after the weekend, so Harland's going to be busy, or so he says. It's little old me who sits in Jack's every night, sometimes alone, sometimes with Rose.

She wants to hear about life in the big city; I want to know what it's like *here.* The answer, according to Rose, is Nothing. "I've never even been sure that I've been here," she says, "though I could show you where I went to high school and my first date works for the electric company in town." What we have in common is we've been no good at loving the right people and we don't seem to have any future at all; what she has that I don't have is a baby, or she will have. "This will be a third," she says. "I got rid of the first two because Mom said to. Then Mom got pregnant and moved to Montana and I never heard from her again." We both feel sorry for ourselves and we drink. Each night we part somewhere after midnight knowing that we'll be looking for each other the next day.

We look up at the mirror behind the bar from time to time. What she sees I don't know. I see a mess. My hair droops down over my face, my lipstick's smeared. "How old you think I am?" Rose asks. I'm trying to fix my face. I don't know. Twenty-eight, thirty? "I voted the first time three years ago. For sheriff. He sent me off, same guy I voted for, to this reform school north of Reno. I'm going to make my own family," she says. "It's the only kind worth having."

Tonight I've brought out part of my treasure trove: Uncle Jim's letters, or the stuff he's written about Dad, his memories of who Dad was. They sit in a little pile on the bar. He types them all on yellow second sheets from back when people made carbons. I've read them dozens of times, and I can sometimes make out this or that about Dad that I recognize.

The hours pass. Rose reads alongside me, her finger tracing the unfamiliar words. She wants to know why Uncle Jim dumps all this shit about Dad on me. "So he loved his mother: is that a crime?" Buffalo wing fat collects on the letters. I'm getting drunk, so is Rose. We see two brothers measuring up against each other. They're angry and disappointed with each other.

Sunday morning, waking late, feeding hours into a vast slot machine of time, I slip out to the orange machine and buy a *Times-Gazette* and read the Help Wanted page, thinking it's time I found myself a job; I'm none of the people wanted. Sunday afternoon I'm bored in my motel room, with the view from my window (parked cars, grey sky, a thin powder of snow), the TV, the football playoffs. I shower (again) and decide my body's not right for Western clothes. A fourth time I ring Harland's number, leaving my stale little signal on his answering machine.

It's cold out. Very cold.

The night I see her, at Jack's, Ginger looks like she's been at the bar since breakfast. I just know it's her. I sit down maybe six feet away with the taco chips between us.

I expected her to be a red-head but she isn't; she had long, blond, very straight hair, none too clean, but yes with a touch of red. Some daddy's darling gone expensively wrong. About the same age as Rose, she's twitchy, her skin has a touch of lemon-peel color, and she's wearing a hand-knit from South America, big for her, New Age jewelry, a short black skirt, expensive low boots.

Whoever called four-to-six the happy hour is full of shit.

Two hours later, the only thing that's happened is a few people have started coming in. That's how I know it has really started snowing. They come in and stamp their feet in the Bud Lite mirror in front of me. Now and then the waitress passes by wiping the bar. "How you doing, Ginger? Want anything?"

"I hate this place," Ginger said to no one in particular. "I don't know why I come here." Some more time slips by and she says, not as though she's talking to me yet, but as if she might, "You know why you come here?"

I tell her, not looking at her, it seems to be the only place in town. She says it's not exactly in town and you couldn't call Hawthorn exactly a town. Then after quite a while, she says, "I hear you've been looking for me. About your dad. I saw Rose." Just then, her eyes cloud over. "You got to excuse me, hon, I got to go to the Little Girls."

She comes back refreshed. With what?

I know she's going to tell me a story. It has her head and that's why she's there at Jack's. Rose told her about me. So I wait. She wants to talk about Dad but first she has to go do her number in the Ladies. You don't live with Arpad as long as I did and not know what it's like after a fix. I just wait. Then she tells me her story: in a voice she's made up for me, or maybe for herself. She wants to tell me something. Because she has the street-smarts—that's what she seems to be telling me the rare times she looks me in the eye—I'll never have.

107

*   *   *

Ginger

Mandy, hon, I think you ought to know this stuff, 'cause otherwise you're never going to get your dad straight or yourself either. But you got to understand I'm telling you a *secret*. The two of us, we were wound up. There wasn't nobody else in the world as far as he was concerned. Just him and me. He'd got nothing else to do and Christ knows I had nothing else to do. You understand?

"Well, it was over the line. In Bishop. That's Bishop, California. Sometimes I just go driving, okay? I guess about this time a year ago. No time of day at all. I stop at a Seven-Eleven for a beer and there's this old john in the parking lot standing there by this ordinary Honda looking natty, not doing anything. I mean *nothing*. I never seen anyone doing nothing like that before. Not only he's got nothing to do, it doesn't bother him *one little bit*, see. It looks like he hasn't got any interest in life. Strictly none. Not even about being there at all.

"But there's something about him. Hard to put into words what. Like he's insulting the whole place just standing there, apart, not doing nothing at all. Like fucking monuments do. Anyway, hon, I'm sure you like to think. I don't. Used to at UNLV, half-arsed did foolosophy. Now everything I do without thinking and if I did think I wouldn't do it. Could be you just think too much.

"So I get out of my car, maybe ten feet away, and I stand there doing nothing also except looking his way. I want to see how long it's going to take before he, you know, figures why I'm standing there. I mean, I know. I know about johns in general. Like the guy in the ad, I *earn* my living. And this john I know about from Rose: same eyes, same nose, same cool. I know he's waiting to get laid, OK?

"Maybe a minute goes by, five. I got no sense of time. Then he takes out a cigarette case. Silver, like you see in the movies. He takes a cigarette out and taps it: like this. Only move he makes. Only he doesn't smoke it, see? I'm watching him. His hand shakes a bit like my dad's does sometimes. My dad's a creep like those two guys bothering Rose, your uncle, I guess, and his sidekick the cop. Guys spitting in the wind. No guts. No comparing, get that straight."

"You want anything?" his daughter says.

"I got me something, hon. I got me something in the Little Girls and I got me something here, a gun in my bag. You want to see? You scared to look? Real cheapo, see?

"Jesus, you really look like him, it's queer. Where was I? Yeah. I walk over nice and steady, a good strut. I know I look good, I can tell he's seen that. Next thing I'm standing in front of him and I say, 'Don't talk, okay? Don't say a thing.'

"I tell him, like this . . . See, I hold the gun up against my tits, so just he and I can see it. I tell him, 'Here's a gun. You want me, you go in there and show them you're *alive*.' On account he looks to me more dead than . . . more dead than alive. I mean that first time. He's scared, but also he's so cool. The part of him that's not like a rabbit has been, like waiting for something like this to happen. I tell him, 'All you do is take their money, then you walk back out here and off we go'."

"Shit. And he did it?"

"Hell yes he did. No problem. He's *wired*. You were

clerking in a Seven-Eleven, you think someone his age has got a gun? And that crazy accent of his, the way he looks? I thought he was a retired head-waiter or something. We get a couple of hundred bucks and off we go back up Route 6, me in my car, him in his. Cross the state line, pull into a Best Western. Nothing else in the world but us two. Doesn't say a damn thing. Just looks at me like a good time, the best time *ever's* about to happen. I'm telling you, hon, it wasn't no trick. It was the real thing. We real-thinged that night like there was no tomorrow.

"We done the same thing plenty times and he feels good. We pick places a hundred miles away, convenience stores, gas stations, diners, motels. The cops go crazy. *We're* crazy. I've got clippings. Here, you see? They call him the Robin Hood of the Sunset Years. Neat, huh?

"All that time he doesn't even have a name for me. I don't know where he lives, where he's from, what's going on in that head of his. I just know he's *loving* this shit. He can't wait for the next time. And each time it gets fancier and fancier."

His little girl asks, "How come they didn't recognize *him*? You know, the police or someone. They had pictures, didn't they? They got TV in those places like they have in banks."

"You wouldn't have either," I tell her. "He had a ball playing different people, different ways of talking, funny hats. Lots of different hats. He'd talk to the guys at the cash register, he's ask questions, he was lost, he was scouting for a movie company, where was the nearest doctor. He could've been an *ac*-tor, easy. Anybody would have believed him. Take any moment, he was that guy, whoever he said he was. And his idea, after the first time: he sticks tape on the plates, drives off without lights. We park someplace on a meter, we head off in his Honda or my BMW. Next day, drive back, pick up the other car. The *po*-lice, they don't figure two cars for the lousy small jobs we do for fun."

"He was a sick man."

"Sick, shit! He was *dear*, hon. More fun than I've had in years. Never met anyone like him. Crazy! Until he met me he was sick like somebody who didn't want to live. Give him something to do, he wasn't sick. The great thing was, he did it all for me. Every place we go to is a new high. 'Specially if it's touch and go. Once, prowl car stopped outside this dinky liquor store someplace. I'm at the door with my shades on. Big guy at the counter. He sees the cops, he sees the gun, he puts two and two together. Your dad, you'd never believe it, was so quick, he breaks the big guy's wrist, whacks him on the side of the head, shoves him under the counter with the gun side of his neck, takes his big cowboy hat and says to the cops, 'What can I do for you gentlemen?' Strong as hell, real *angry*.

"Neither of us gave a damn about the money. We dropped it left right and center. What we liked was *doing* it. And the afters."

"Nobody knows who he is, where you stay?"

"*I* don't know who he is. Don't ask him. No more'n he ever asks about me. We didn't need all that *information*. Don't even have a number to call—we just meet up last place we went, Thursday sundown, check things out, kinda surprised the cops do nothing.

"Then one point, he gets sick with the pills. You know, he was running out of gas. Only it was breath. That gives me a scare, and I ask him where he lives and he says Sam Wells, and finally I give him a number, Rose's number. Only Rose doesn't want to get mixed up in any of my shit, so when your uncle's cop guy comes by she doesn't let on.

"By then we were doing it most Thursdays, regular, and after we'd come here. This is *his* place. People loved him. We'd let things cool down. Have a few drinks. Anyway, he wasn't in any shape to drive so I have to take him to his house. He looks really *grey*. Not at all like I know him: like some dog you're locking up. Except you can see this dog's got a mean streak. Tight lips, his hands just in control, only shaking more, white.

"Next time I see him, it's Rose sends word he's at Jack's. Time I get there, he's had a few too many. He's in lousy shape, gets sentimental, just like any other pussy-whipped john. Shit, Ginger, I say to myself, just your luck, one guy you meet you really like and he's pooping out on you.

"We sit here, he's sitting right where you're sitting, he starts telling me the story of his life, about his Mamma, how hard it's been, about you, 'specially you, about his kids and how he's a failure, all that shit. I can't take it. That's the kind of guy I've met all my life. Sort of thing my dad does. The black boo-hoos. I tell him, forget it. Everybody's got lives. The problem's getting rid of them.

"He's going down, right? So I tell him again like the first time, let's go out and *do*, let's go someplace and make out. Otherwise you going to be *dead*.

"Damned if he doesn't get up off his stool. 'It's Tuesday night,' he says first. 'And this time,' he says, all suave, 'you're going to let me drive your car.' It turns out he *walked* into Sam Wells, then took the bus over here. I ask myself, what's so special about Tuesday night? I ask him, but he ain't letting on. But we go out, he opens the door for me, he gets in the driver's seat, spins his wheels and off we go in a clouda dust, heading towards Sam Wells."

His girl asks, is that the last night? I say, "Hell no, there ain't no *last* night. There's lots of nights. You want to hear what I got to say?" She nods. By her age, kid oughta learn to shut up.

"*OK* then. We drive through town, he stops outside the sa-*lon*, doesn't get out, just nods, drives out of town and we go to his house, some little development, nothing out there, not a peep from anyone, blue light in the neighbor's house. He gets out of the car, stands there, takes out his silver case, taps a cigarette on it, comes over and says, got a light? 'Tonight's hair-night,' he grins. 'Tuesday.' And we're going to do something he oughta have done long time ago.

"We park maybe fifty feet up the drive from his house up in the hills where I delivered him the week before and took a cab back to my car. 'What you going to do?' I ask. 'Rob your own house?'

"'You'll see,' he says. He tells me to open the boot of the car: he mean the trunk.

"I'm standing out there in the dark looking up at the stars, he vanishes into the house. It feels like a long time. When he comes out he's got his arms full of stuff: dresses, coats, aprons, shoes. He dumps them all on top of the car and wants them put in back. He goes back in. More shit. Papers, photo albums, stuffed dolls. I shove that in with the rest. He makes another trip in, as if he wants to make sure of something, and I see a car turning in from the highway, figure it might be his wife, so I go to the door and tell him, hurry up.

"Last time he comes out he's got three frames, pictures, samplers you call 'em. You know, good thoughts you embroider, A Stitch in Time, that sort of stuff. The car's snaking its way up and your dad's now stamping on them. Crazy, huh? But he's having the time of his life. Her car, I recognize the Honda, turns in on his road, it turns into the driveway into his garage, I can see him in her lights. He's wearing a light raincoat he's proud of, he likes English things, right? Cap on his head, squared away towards her, cigarette case in his hand, tapping, lighting up.

"She comes out the car. Big, red-faced woman. Cold angry. Not saying a word. She slaps the cigarette out of his mouth. Walks into the house, thank God, 'cause I'm ready to split if what I think's going to happen does happen and he kills her, right there, cold on the asphalt of a goddam driveway in retirement acres. Nothing. He takes another cigarette out of his case, taps, lights it and just walks soft-foot up to where I'm waiting.

"Hey, you can be proud of your dad. He's got a great smile on his face. A star. As if millions were watching. 'Well, what do you know?' he says to me. 'I've got my own set of keys and they're right here in my pocket!' Just as slow, he walks back, gets into the Honda, and off the two of us go."

"The last time, please. Please tell me about the last time." Stupid girl is crying instead of being proud. And I'm getting tired, the stuff is wearing off. But OK. She got a right to know.

"Last time was up North somewhere. That Thursday. We've shacked up thirty-six hours in Rose's crummy trailer, I'm sore all over and we decide we're going out because it's Thursday. We like the idea the *po*-lice is kinda expecting us on Thursdays, see? And also there's nothing left to do except that.

"We drive miles and miles, sometimes I'm in front, sometimes him, neither of us seeing anything worth doing. We stop couple of times, pull in, check a deal out. I don't know what's the matter, but it's not working out. Like we're too tired to bother. Maybe three, four hours, we're driving out there in nowhere, up in the hills where it's icy and you don't see a light for miles. Damn fool! There ain't a place open to bust, but he won't stop, no matter how often I flash my lights.

"Before I know it, I find we've taken some tiny road

joins the highway before Sam Wells. Then he pulls over on the top of this hill. Damn cold, walking over to his car. Cold and lonely. His lights switched off. I give him a kiss and a couple of pills and we sit there staring at lights way down below where you don't see another light right up to the horizon.

"He's just real calm. It doesn't matter what happens. Nothing matters. He's sitting waiting for me. He wants we should do what we always do."

"Why'd you pick *him*?" she says.

"Because he wanted. I figure all his life he wanted to do something like this. Something really *wrong*. But something real. Hey, listen, I know the type. They're people running away from some time long ago when things were going right for them. I took your dad back. I gave him a little Friday Night love. He couldn't get enough of it."

"They said the doors were locked in his car."

"He must have locked them after. I thought he was only passed out. Only last thing I saw he was fixing himself up, looking in the mirror. I knew he was happy. He liked to be neat. But I'd told him that was the last time. Then I read it was. That's too bad. But, hey, he was *happy*."

XII

Jim

When I got back my wife met me at the airport
and told me Mamma had died. She said in that queer,
rational way of hers, "I thought I'd tell you right away. I
never understood if you loved her or had a grudge against
her." Then she looked at me and said, "You don't have to
answer that now. But don't be like Tony and wait until
you're dead."

Two *big* deaths inside six months. A natural death
for both of them. Natural to each. Francine had read the
depositions Harland took from Ginger and Mandy and
Rose. We'd heard how Ginger's dad got a court order to
put her away and how she got away when the cops came
for her. "Mebbe with Mandy's help, mebbe not," Harland
says.

I don't know what will happen to Mandy, though I don't expect she'll be coming back. And in the end, I suppose it doesn't matter what happened to Eileen. Eileen took off. Before, during, after. Does it matter? In the end Tony had fooled her once too often. He was a sweet man, *dear* as Ginger said, but a liar.

Francine said, "I won't ask you how you feel. We all handle death in different ways. This was your way of coping." I asked, did she feel sorry for anyone? "For Ginger," she said. "Ginger, Rose and her baby. But Ginger, yes: who else really lost anything?"

No need to feel sorry for him. At his age! Sick and not sick, big bangs, chicks, popping pills, taking off because the money ran out, and the fun, when Ginger wasn't there any more, when she said that was the last time, doing what comes naturally, recognizing it was all over, making himself look good, sitting there at the wheel thinking all the things he'd got away with all his life! O brother!

*   *   *

1923

Jim

He was born. Lucky.

La Françoise

I have two baby brothers (Toto and Jacques are twins) eight years younger than me, and Toto's done a terrible thing, but that doesn't make him inhuman. I don't expect you to like him. I ask that you don't hate him.

When the boys were five, Maman and Papa had promised them the sea-side, but Maman turned out to be pregnant again and couldn't take them. Jacques has travelled everywhere, but Toto still hasn't been to the sea. Belfort, where we live, is as far from the sea as you can get, and the sea was a big idea to him. He talked about going for months ahead of time. The sea was like the sun, which was a ball of light so hot you couldn't touch it, like the string of bulbs I had around my dresser, around the mirror.

He and Jacques were stuck at home instead and I

looked after them. Jacques would play football in the summer street, Toto followed me around. I sat at the mirror. My face stared back at me: not great—a black widow's peak and big almond-shaped eyes. He stood behind me, his little hand on my shoulder. My shoulder felt damp. Toto was studying what I did with my eyebrows.

He mentioned that yesterday at the trial. He told me all sorts of memories popped into his mind in the courtroom: unasked. Such as the packety sound of his mother's sneakers. "Those things from way back are much less interesting than the papers make out," he said. I asked him, but no, he couldn't remember specifically when he first handled a pair of his mother's stockings. They were few, and kept in the top drawer of her dresser, wrapped in tissue. But I could tell him. It was the same summer. The shutters were closed against the heat, I watched him as he took one out, pushed his little fist inside, and carried it up over his wrist and elbow. First he held the mesh up to the light, then he laid the stocking on his lap and, through his spread-out fingers and the stocking, examined the white of his thighs.

I know all these things about him. I've always known them about him, and seen how pretty he was. You have to understand how *normal* the rest of us are. All of us except Toto, who remains vain and sweet and not like the rest of us.

Belfort is a garrison town. The citadel stands on top, with grass growing inside and cavernous, sloping, underground passages to hide in, and be caught, which he found thrilling. I often took him for walks up there. The town was always full of soldiers in training, doing their military service. There were peasant boys with impenetrable Auvergnat accents and clever ones from the streets of Paris. He and Jacques would alternate rides on their bike and hang about. The soldiers would sing songs, drink and talk about girls.

Toto would come back and say, "I don't like it when they talk about us like that." About "us"? He meant himself, certainly not Jacques. Oh my little sister! Still, he found such talk exciting and disturbing. The older soldiers talked about Algeria, and a place called l'Indochine, so he liked the younger ones better: because he couldn't think of anything worth defending. "Countries you can think about," he said. "Countries are girls. That's why you say *'La Patrie'*." When one of the judges asked him how he had avoided his military service, he said he told the Medical Officer who examined him he didn't think doing military service was important. In no circumstances? he was asked. Maman was touched when he told the court it might be worthwhile doing something spectacular, "like burning your hand on a machine gun defending Maman", but anyway, what was politics about? There was Germany right over there to the East, and there were big statues to lots and lots of dead soldiers here— but why defend himself? It was far easier to say yes. He never tried to defend himself when his father beat him—as if a puppy—with a rolled-up newspaper. Jacques says that in the yard at school he stayed off other people's turf, but also didn't cry when something was done to him.

Jacques told him, "You have to defend yourself."

"I don't want to," he replied.

Jacques kicked and bloodied his knuckles on his brother's behalf. Then he stopped, because it made no sense defending someone who didn't want to be defended.

"I was probably about eight or nine when the lady from the *Sécu*, the social worker, came the first time," he said to Maître Blanchot. "They bug you all your life, the *Sécu*." We went back over that visit, Toto and I. In his version, all six of us were there, sitting about like dummies, sulky and silent, and we were thinking, who were these people to come into our house and ask questions? Maman was very nervous, and more short-sighted and squinting than ever (therefore not seeing the powder on Toto's cheeks), Papa indignant to have been told he could "proceed" to his office (he telephoned overdue electricity accounts).

I remembered the way the social worker—depressed, even disgusted, her eye *political*—looked around the room: at the brown linoleum, the potted plants, the spotlessly-polished stained glass set into the windows that cast its dank patterns on the floor. I thought, she really does hate this room, while Maman was so proud of it. Maman who wished us to rise; the social worker who would have preferred us to be among the deserving poor.

Toto remembered bursting into tears while Maman made a camomile tea for the woman. "She hates all of us," he'd said to Jacques.

Jacques surprised him by answering in that common-sense voice of his, "Come on, Toto, she doesn't even *see* us."

That night he had crept into my bed for a sisterly cuddle, and whispered: "It's true what Jacques says, she didn't see us. We live in a submarine, in an invisible house." To me, the house looked solid enough. It was made of bricks, and the bricks were immaculately pointed. Papa was into do-it-yourself. "If she doesn't hate us, why does she look at us like that?"

After a moment's thought I said, "She's embarrassed." That was the first time I was ever conscious that to the world outside, Toto made us seem "different". A grand illusion gone in cheap pink powder! That we were just an ordinary family! By the time the papers are through with us, we'll all be in a freaks' gallery! Toto also said that when the *Sécu* lady left (I remember Maman in the front corridor saying, "Shake Madame's hand, Toto") the social worker leaned down and whispered in his ear, "You disgust me."

"I don't see where she gets off saying something like that," added Toto. "I hadn't done anything to her. I didn't even want to be like her. She smoked cigarettes like a man, out of the side of her mouth. Also, she wore no lipstick."

To the psychiatrist the court appointed, Madame Annie Stein, he said, "I thought she was right. We were disgusting."

"You weren't pleased with yourself?" she asked.

"The way I looked? With make-up on?"

His lawyer has all this stuff on tape, and he played it

125

back to Maman, Papa and me: in his big office with a view. The idea was, his family could *explain* Toto to him: for his defence. "She was a boring woman," we heard Toto's voice say. "The first one." Of the many social workers who trooped through our house and came away wondering. True, she was neither young nor pretty, and not interesting either. Plus, she wore trousers (it was winter) and he couldn't understand a woman wearing trousers who didn't have to.

"You were examined for bruises," the lawyer added, flipping the pages of his dossier.

"That's why the bitch came. The teacher said I had a black eye."

"Did you?"

We could almost hear him delicately cross his legs. "Probably. You still won't make out I'm crazy, you know."

"I'm only building a picture of your childhood."

"I told the *Sécu* lady it was my father who beat me," he answered the lawyer.

"Was it your father?" Blanchot look across at Papa without the least curiosity: as though he would have done the same himself.

"It might have been."

Perhaps that wasn't the first social worker, he told the court. It could have been any of them. They were all alike. "It wasn't any fun to be in that house, with people entitled to walk in and look us over any time they felt like it," he told the judges. "Like we were specimens. My sisters had no fun there either. But *they* never got personal interviews with the social services. One of them even got married at fifteen. That stopped them: she was married. It worked for her but not for me."

Monsieur Thècle, who taught him in *sixième,* gave him a life of Rimbaud to read. I remember him reading the book in his room, curled up in a chair and brushing his long hair out of his eyes. He was reading the beginning, where some poet—he told me, "He looks a bit like Thècle, you know, like a flabby owl"—seduces the adolescent Rimbaud. He understood what it meant to be seduced: that had already happened. The *thing,* as he called it, *la chose.*

But he didn't really read things through. Besides having weak blue eyes, he took the easy way. He read the parts that had something to do with him. He got to the last bit of the book, which took place in Abyssinia or somewhere like that, and Abyssinia made him want to get away. So he took a school trip, having begged the 125 francs it cost for the bus and one night in a hostel, from Maman. Thècle was a real man of the Sixties and took all his twelve- and thirteen-year-olds on some political demonstration, a march through Paris, arms interlocked, Toto's first *manif.* I remember Toto being really *physically* excited.

That was about as far as his flirtations with politics went. Though generally speaking, once he started dressing up, he was a communist for a few years in the Seventies, because communists had room for all kinds of people if you were willing to paint slogans on walls, distribute leaflets

127

or go out on boring *manifs*. It was just a phase, and the *Cocos* got rid of him when pictures of him and La Gazelle in frocks at some demo or other turned up in the papers. After that, the local *travelos*, the Belfort ones who hung around where the soldiers were—*travelos* are what they call guys who dress and put out as girls—turned on the Algerians and other blacks in the party and no longer went on *manifs*.

I don't know if Monsieur Thècle did to him what Toto says in court, or if it was just what Toto wished he had done. Thècle is now something big in unions and he told the *Sécu* Toto had been "a whore in politics, too". The fact is Thècle was still marching with the Party as recently as last year. The *Sécu* got back into the act because Toto had been picked up several times for prostitution. Belfort is not Paris.

"Did Monsieur Thècle make advances to you?" the lawyer asked.

"Who cares?"

We both read Simenon. We liked him a lot, because the people in his books were like us; we too were "little people". What happened to us and what's happening to Toto belongs in one of his books. Because we went through some rotten years. First a colleague got Papa in trouble at the electric company and he was retired with only half his pension. Then Felicité's (my sister who got married at fifteen) husband got fired for taking money from the till and his brother wound up in court for dropping his baby from a balcony because it wouldn't stop crying. Verdict: death by misadventure.

One of Simenon's books Toto read many times, the one with *le petit Kleine*. This Kleine was a weak and unsuccessful artist who was found hanging from the handle of the church door. "You just watch," Toto said. "Something like that will happen to me." In the story the rope turns out to have been too short for Kleine to kill himself. It's not said right out in the open in the book, but you have to think Simenon and his friends killed him for fun and then hanged him. They hated Kleine for being such a *failure*.

Toto told Papa he wanted to be an artist. But people like us don't become artists—there are different lives for the rich and the poor. Papa didn't take him seriously. "Art? That's a bit difficult, isn't it? You have to learn this and that." Just wanting something wasn't enough. I bring up those books because I think Toto feels he *deserves* to die for what he's done. Or more likely for what he is. Like Rimbaud or *le petit Kleine*. Maybe he should die in general. As if the card he'd drawn was the Hanged Man, the bad news one. But please let's get this straight. Dying isn't something he wants, it's just all round his life, any way he looks.

129

He hardly spoke at all during the trial, except when he heard things that were just plain stupid or wrong. In court, Blanchot always looked as if he'd come straight from lunch. His face was blotchy as if brawn had been dropped into a pot of boiling water. Blanchot suggested the judges might be more lenient if Toto could nail Monsieur Thècle for *détournement de mineurs*, corrupting minors. The man didn't live in a real world. His fine speeches about M. Thècle's betraying his "sacred trust" and about the responsibility of being *in loco parentis* reduced Toto to tears of frustration. Toto couldn't explain *anything* to Blanchot. The lawyer plainly thought Toto and his friends, his teacher, the whole lot of them, were perverts. "You're only making things worse for yourself," he said, adjusting the white stock on his neck. "You don't understand, those people in the courtroom hate you."

Toto understood. And why. Because he wasn't normal. "You're just one big empty hole," Blanchot said at one point, irritated by Toto's apathy. He wanted to know why his client always walked into court the way he did, as if he wore snaffles at his knees. "You get them angry on purpose, and where the devil do you get lipstick in prison?"

130

Toto said, why bother Thècle? The trip to Paris had been a big turn-off—in terms of feeling anything for Monsieur Thècle, that is. Just now, he wanted to be left alone, and not have complicated ideas about what was right or wrong, about which there wasn't a whole lot one could do. "I don't want to be explained," he said.

He was asked about his first sexual experience. They wanted to know when and how. That wasn't the heart of the matter. Blowing smoke at Madame Annie Stein, he said, "I had a tight arse before, then I didn't. Or, if you like, I found I could breathe better with my mouth full."

He told me it happened the summer before he went

to Paris: on another school trip, this one across the river to Germany. Gilles was fourteen, and his pubis was fully developed. Its coarse black hair astonished Toto. And Gilles held his hand in the last row all the way home. The rest followed—puppy love, worship, necking, fondling, stroking. Anything to please Gilles. As we three remaining sisters knew we'd have to take our pleasure from pleasing the distant, still unknown "him".

Back home, we'd have had to be blind not to see what was going on: as underclothes vanished from our drawers, and Toto walked about the house in a trance, steadfast but unsteady on high heels. As he slipped daintily into puberty (as Jacques did noticeably) he said he wanted to be an actor. That became his pretext. He spent days lighting cigarettes and posing. We girls teased and encouraged him: against the men, his brother Jacques and Papa. I don't think Maman realized; she was always distracted and more worried about Papa. Call it complicity. We all got involved, because Papa was a problem: we'd been taught to keep anything that could upset Papa away from him. So we kept guard when the lank and surly Gilles slipped up the stairs to Toto's room. When Gilles was coming, Toto experienced the same nerves we, his three sisters, had felt before dates. Would he please?

Mind you, it was Maman's house. She had inherited it from her uncle who was a priest. But Papa really *owned* it, because he filled it. Our house was a drill-field: whenever Papa's voice rang through the house, jogging Maman from whatever she was doing, she ran to find him, startled as a raw recruit. One Sunday, while Toto and Gilles were supposedly glueing together balsa aeroplanes in the room upstairs (Jacques was out on his job helping unpack newspapers) from the kitchen window I could see Papa in the back yard. He wore his old green corduroys and had a hoe in one hand, just like a peasant. I heard him shout up, "Am I supposed to do all the work around here?"

By then Maman's rheumatism was getting worse. She started climbing the stairs mechanically to protect Toto. I ran up past her. Toto was standing at the window, the elastic of a black slip up over his chest. Gilles lolled on Jacques' bed, grinning and satisfied, a cigarette dangling from his lips. I managed to stop Maman at the door on some pretext or other and made Toto get properly dressed and go down and help his father. Gilles understood I didn't want to see him there again. I realize now this was because I didn't like Gilles, not because I disapproved of what he and Toto were doing. That means I had already accepted that Toto was like another sister and could see a boyfriend, as Felicité had done with Eric before she was married.

A while later, the two of us in the garden, Toto bent over thinning lettuce while I weeded, Toto said he wished he could get back at Papa. Gilles knew a reporter: perhaps he could tell him his story, lay his whole undesirable life out like the old *Est republicain* on which the seedlings were laid out in rows, so everyone would *know*. While he worked, he told me all about the first time, the way we girls told each other. "It was like a dream," he sang softly, knowing Papa was increasingly deaf. "I was Barbara Stanwyck (the resemblance was a joke of mine) and when Gilles lifted my slip . . .''

Of course back then he would never have dared say any of that to Papa's face. Ours wasn't the kind of house you could tell the truth in. Instead, he stood around sulking when Papa was around, pretending to be a boy like Jacques by digging his hands into the pockets of his jeans. Well, who of us would have dared tell Papa what was *really* on our minds?

"Fetch the fertilizer from the shed," Papa said. "It's time you got some muscle. Look at you!" The judges might have understood Toto better if they had seen him doing the ironing with us, which he did with great concentration. But the court felt the way Papa feels: how could this happen to a decent, hard-working man? This was his own blood. It was as though something was wrong with him.

Later, after a reluctant half-hour's gardening, Toto came into the kitchen for lunch studying his hands with horror, back-garden Belfort under his fingernails. "You want to keep yourself clean," I heard Gilles tell Toto at the front door. "Just look at yourself!"

After that, Toto would skip away on Sundays, but by then—no doubt with Gilles spreading the word about what an easy piece Toto was—Toto had dropped into the *demi-monde* of the *travelos*. Or at least the fringes. When he could. When he dared. When the cops weren't around. He no longer said he was acting. This was "for real", or at least the little he knew about the real.

We all protected him. None of us thought he had *chosen* to be a girl, that's what he was.

The cinema—matinées were all he could afford—offered darkness and apprentice encounters. Marlon's back, like a stone slab, filled the screen, and his mind. He went through a phase of gun molls with crimped hair, and when, rarely, old films played, Barbara Stanwyck laid her evening gowns on him. Sitting well down in front where he would be caught in the glare of the screen, by means of his hand running through his freshly-washed hair he offered an ear; or, leaning forward, he stroked his shoulders, his arms crossed on his chest. His perfume was discreet, like that of a girl his own age. Once out of every two or three times he got picked up.

Did she remember her first kiss? he asked Annie Stein the psychiatrist he was making into another sister. "I mean outside your house. And not on a date. From someone you didn't know. And what happened after? I do."

"Who did you kiss?" she asked.

"I *was* kissed," he corrected her.

"Was he the one who seduced you?"

"I seduced him. That was Antoine."

This kiss was of a different kind than the ones he gave Gilles. Immediately he had felt the purpose behind it. It had reduced him to nothingness. It happened during an American feature. At a Saturday matinée. He was studying Sandra Dee and liked the way she fluffed and wore her hair. Antoine was sitting behind him, and while Sandra Dee walked barefoot in a garden, he felt himself being kissed on the neck and ear. Antoine then moved down a row, sat next to him and put his arm around Toto's shoulders. He toyed with the red kerchief around Antoine's neck, which smelled of after-shave.

Having learned how pretty he was, then how desirable, he now felt in control. Because Antoine wanted him. All of him. Antoine kissed him again in a room he rented in a high-rise on the edge of town. It was a twenty-minute bus ride out there, not counting the time they had to wait. He felt impatient.

Afterwards, they lay diagonally across the bed. Antoine whispered into his ear, "Did you enjoy that?"

"Yes," he said, to be nice.

"Really?"

"No, not really."

"You didn't? Why not?"

"It doesn't matter, as long as you were pleased."

He felt Antoine's head rise from below the pillow, propped up on a hand, searching for words which were unnecessary because they were so completely conventional. They occurred in countless movies. After.

"Would you like a shower?" Antoine asked. "I have a shower."

"Not really."

"Nothing happened to you?"

"I don't know. I don't want to think about it." He didn't know what should have happened, what he was supposed to have felt, what he should have liked. He was supposed to have wanted what had happened, and he hadn't really wanted anything. Once he told me he felt he'd gone from A to B. Nothing more than that.

135

"You want to go home?" Antoine asked.

"Not particularly."

"You want to stay here?"

"With you?"

"I have . . ." The boy twisted his head behind Toto to look at his watch, ". . . a half-hour left." He had an evening job waiting on tables.

"I'd like to watch a film."

"I haven't got a player."

"You asked me what I wanted. I said I'd like to watch a film. That's all. It's not the end of the world. You said you had to go back to work."

"In a half-hour."

"All right."

He told Madame Annie Stein that he lay back and became someone else, falling into a sort of half-dream that went back deep into childhood. His twin brother, Jacques, with whom he shared a bed, always pushed him away and took over most of that not very wide bed. He remembered how he used to make himself very small. Now, when someone loved him, he became very still and small, as if dead.

Somewhere in there, Felicité married Eric, two months short of her sixteenth birthday. Toto and Jacques were just turning fourteen and I could now vote, something I wouldn't think of doing. After the wedding, the house seemed a lot smaller. My middle sister, Emilie, went off to hotel school and Toto could have a room of his own, which was now where we talked. The twins were splitting. Jacques, growing up, grew silent and was passionate about football. Toto was at that stage where he chattered a lot, the way we sisters had before. He became a pale version of Feli: as blond, but less buoyant. Now that Feli and Emilie were gone, perhaps he wanted to take their places.

I felt he was beginning to understand some things about being a woman and he was jealous of Feli. She had won something permanent and desirable, a real life, and with a man Toto fancied. She was now also completely a woman. While that made me think of the sour smell of quick babies that followed, Toto said, "Imagine being dressed up all in white and then taken away in a taxi, still hanging on to your flowers!" He didn't want any rights over someone else but would have been happy for someone else like Feli's new husband Eric to do whatever he wanted with him, and more so because it was legal and normal.

137

Everything I write here is from my own memory or, in those parts before the examining magistrates or Madame Annie Stein, from the thick volumes of reports I've read— a lot thicker than the book of clippings on his brief career as model or drag-*artiste*. His book was still with him in prison. There was nothing he cared for more, and he showed it to everyone. It contained his celebrity. But as he now said, "When you think about it, I guess it's the wrong kind of fame."

Once he'd met his likes in Belfort, the *travelos* and

the queens and hard guys, and had drifted into their world
of bars and discos and clubs that weren't all that gay, he
talked to me about La Gazelle and the other girls, and their
adventures and affairs. They amazed him and he made them
into his own kind of comic book. He smiled when he
told me he was known as *la Françoise*. (His real name was
François-Xavier, but no one had ever called him anything
but Toto.) A decade later—he's now twenty-six—he's
soured on the other girls: "They're just jealous because I'm
a star."

Take the day after the big fire—my subject. There
was Toto the survivor. Front and center-page. He didn't
look his best. What he meant by being a star was having a
minister with horn-rimmed glasses bending over his hospital
bed. In the photo, the minister looked about to kiss him,
and those were real tears in the Minister's eyes: "Are you
suffering terribly?" the Minister asked him. Right there on
our own screen, still in black-and-white and therefore more
real. All sorts of people called up. Including reporters.

The next morning Papa had gone out (in his best suit,
for we'd suffered a tragedy and we all ought to be dignified)
for the newspapers. When he came back we spread them
out on the kitchen table and Maman, who was about to
take the train for the Paris hospital where her son was under
observation, sniffled. In the pictures of Toto you could also
see, behind the plastic tube of the drip, Toto's eyelids low-
ered in a gesture we all knew. That was on the TV too.
His pupils relaxed until the Minister swam out of view.
That might have been the morphine, of course, to obtain

which he exaggerated the pain from his bandaged hands.

Now, with the trial, he is a star again: in glasses which enlarge the swimming of his eyes. Looking back and adding up all the good times, like atoms, we still knew he wasn't a normal son or brother, but we had no idea it would come to this. He had always washed up after meals—Maman's apron was allowed. Now he wasn't there. He was in prison. Every night we were reminded of Papa's original outrage and how helpless he felt. No one dared break the silence.

Please, I know how you must feel, especially if you lost a son in the fire that night, but you must understand our divided feelings about Toto. To us he was likeable, tender, thoughtful. He had all sorts of gifts, including a certain charm and trustful innocence. We all loved him, especially Jacques, who would go into town with him arm in arm. They are brothers but walk like boy and girl. We think that's better than hating him for being different. I taught him to sew and helped him buy his clothes, and over the years he really had become my kid sister. But again, there were limits. I wouldn't take him out with me the way he wanted, as my sister. Except for me, there's always been silence in the house. We could only breathe away from Papa.

The examining magistrate asked him about remorse: "Don't you feel any?"

"No."

"None at all? You know what the word means? It

means your sins come back and bite you a second time."

Toto stood there humming *Cantaré, volaré* under his breath. The song had been going through his mind and it brought back good memories, until it brought back bad ones. Now he'd mastered every step of Doris Day's routine as her skirt whirled through Rome. Now that had been one of his better cabaret numbers. The bad memory was, they got rid of him. His Doris Day was too butch; *his* Doris Day was *much* too butch.

In court, the magistrates persisted. They wanted to be fair. "You obviously have talent, and even intelligence. What in God's name happened to you? We have your reports. A model student, a first in French literature when you were thirteen. Even when you went off with this Monsieur . . ." They shuffled through their papers . . . "This Monsieur Heugel, when you went off with M. Heugel to Switzerland, you still got through your school work, you weren't kept back."

"You see what I mean?" he said to me. "Once again I'm missing something. This thing called remorse. Is it something they take out of you, like in La Gazelle's op? La Gazelle's got something she doesn't want, and I haven't got something I'm supposed to have," he said. "Feeling. This remorse thing. How do they know what I feel? Why should I tell them."

Everyone knew about La Gazelle's op. Every Friday night, when Maman and Papa were out at their "circle" and I cooked for Jacques and Toto and little André, Toto brought in regular bulletins. La Gazelle had something between his legs he didn't want; his two officer lovers wanted him "perfected"; he'd saved up 50,000 francs; he was off to Tangier.

"Me it doesn't bother," Toto said innocently. "It doesn't come into the calculation." Instead, he wanted to tell me that he'd fallen in love with an Arab boy in prison.

"You really have no feelings at all about any of those people?" Madame Annie Stein asked, puzzled. "How would you like to die in a fire?"

"I didn't even know who they were. I didn't especially mean to kill them. It was their bad luck."

"There were eighteen of them. Not knowing them makes it less bad? Parents lost their children, boys their girl friends, girls their boy friends. You don't think of their loss? What does 'loss' mean to you?"

The unfairness got to him. There was Papa ripping up the dresses we made for his dolls ("Still playing with dolls, *hein?*"); Alexi, his last "great love" overdosed by a rival; the video recorder he bought during the year he resolved to "straighten out" stolen by a boy who'd faked love, pulled it out of the wall and given it to his girl friend; the only apartment he ever had that was his own, painted, decorated with his own hands, burned in one of the first fires. This was loss. "I had no idea they'd die," he answered stubbornly. "All I did was start a fire."

141

Indifference was what the press picked on. Papa sat listening in the front row of the courtroom, like a stone. The hat on his knees was his badge of respectability. He held on to it tightly. The goings-on in the courtroom baffled him. How could anyone's life be made up just of "accidents"? Toto's promiscuity was the worst thing, this long recital of lovers. All right, so my son's queer and that's distasteful enough, maybe he can't help that, with all those women spoiling him, but how can one not care who one sleeps with? Look at those friends of his! That Descombes (La Gazelle) person! One can have a screw loose, one can be sick, but what sort of person doesn't *care*? His hangdog look told the press how much he hated being there, hated his son being there, hated what the world had come to.

Once in a while Toto would sneak a look at Papa and Maman. She was in a brown rayon dress and hat. (*No one* wears a hat any more, Maman!) If by chance he caught Papa's eye, Papa's sense of guilt hit him like heat when you come out from an air-conditioned cinema. What did I do to my son? Nothing, is what Toto would have replied, this is just the way I am.

At least Papa said nothing to the reporters who crowded about him between sessions, buttonholed him while he stood at the bar for coffee and the cognac he needed to face this disaster. But his hands shook as he drained the last drop. He hoped the earth would swallow him up. Maman filled in for him. She is quoted with some pity. Yes, Toto had always wanted to be a girl: "Beyond that I don't understand a thing. He's not bad, like you say. He's a gentle boy." A woman wrote that Maman didn't even understand what Toto was. How could she? Thank God Jacques was on a contracting job in Antibes. That didn't stop the papers. Jacques was Toto's *twin.* Look how strong he is. A center-forward who tried out with F. C. Belfort.

"I'm not indifferent," Toto finally told Madame Annie Stein, "I'm *different.* That's different. I'm not like other people. I'm not like Jacques."

Monsieur Heugel, whose story came out at the trial, was Swiss. He had fussy clothes, an afterthought of a moustache, money, and one of those efficient mouths that's always working on something. One day, Toto told me he'd met this "nice man" who gave him presents. Then several times he came into the restaurant where I worked, once with Toto. I didn't get to serve them, and Toto didn't let on who I was. I understood the man was Swiss, in business, and came to Belfort about ten days a month.

Blanchot had an idea Heugel might weigh with the court, the adolescent trauma, being forced into prostitution.

"I wasn't forced," Toto insisted.

He had been out hiking. The direction made no difference, but it happened to be on the road to Montbeliard. It was the sort of day you should be happy, grow wings, fly away. But Toto was in one of his *moods*, which often began as a desire for something different, like elsewhere. Where we live, that meant he was walking out of town in his jeans and a shirt open on his hairless chest, plucking wildflowers, chewing on their stalks. "I had no idea whatsoever of running away from home or anything like that," he said to Blanchot. "I didn't have a penny in my pocket." But sunglasses, yes, which hid his eyes and made him look older.

It grew hot and clammy, the sort of hazy day when the freshness goes and your dress sticks to your skin. There was Monsieur Heugel, fresh as his Mercedes. Heat and dissatisfaction. August. People were away on holiday. *Other* people. We used to watch our friends go away. They got to see the sea. The rest of us had things to do: Feli her babies, I my job; Jacques part-timed at the swimming pool. Toto lived by people. People to watch, to gossip with or flirt. Then first X would go, then Y. How to fill the days, which were bloodless and pale? He read a lot, so his head was full of words. Words like viscera, veins, ducts. "Imagine wearing your body inside out, so everything inside you is visible," he once said.

Blanchot insisted on Heugel—the judges needed *some* explanation!—and Toto countered by regaling the lawyer with the geography of "down there", the places people like himself explored with nose, eyes and lips. Among the smells of cesspit and dry rot, and in the exhalations of the body, there were discoveries to be made. "I don't care who you are, or how experienced, it always hurts a little. At first," he told Blanchot. "Shouldn't you make an effort of some kind to understand?"

It was Toto who didn't understand. He couldn't imagine what it was like to be the lawyer, not live in an underworld, to have all that power, to be able to decide about the likes of him. What he told Blanchot about Monsieur Heugel went against the lawyer's thesis. There was not only consent, but complicity.

No, he said, the actual meeting didn't stick in his mind. Every time a new man came along, wasn't it the same thing? Weren't they all alike? You met someone, they fancied you, you opened up. Look, he remembered the summer well enough.

"How old were you?" Blanchot asked.

"Fifteen. Old enough."

Blanchot knew, but he always asked, and then repeated the word in disbelief: "Fifteen? What did you want to be?"

"*Une fille*," he replied. A prostitute.

The summer he met Monsieur Heugel, he was thinking (the *Song of Bernadette*) of entering a seminary, perhaps one of the orders.

I kept my mouth shut. He liked humility and acceptance but also, I thought, for things like that you also have to believe in God, which he didn't. He told Blanchot about his vocation. "I just love Mary, don't you?" Mary was in blue-and-white plaster. She stood up in a niche with a rosary in her hands.

I went to church with him once, because he told me he'd been chaste for three months under her influence.

The Sunday on which he went for his walk, Jacques had said, earlier in the morning, "Why don't you come and have a swim at the pool? I can get you in free."

"No, thank you," Toto replied. The swimming pools were crowded. People stared at his body. Was there a law said you had to have hair on your body?

He got into Heugel's car because it was there and

145

stopped alongside him. He hardly looked at Heugel. But the leather seat felt comfortable, the car was cool; it was pleasant that the landscape slipped effortlessly by, made of trees and rivers, shades and fields. "I'll bet you're hungry," Heugel said at Pontarlier.

"He must have been around forty," he told his lawyer. "He never made a secret of it that he wanted to share me with others." Said cold like that. Tell the man what it's actually like, which he can't imagine.

The frontier was exciting. It was the first time he crossed one. He felt a lot richer right away. Like acquiring an uncle, or being picked out in a smart shop.

"It was a business deal, then?" Blanchot asked.

"Not the way you think. Money wasn't what counted. It was being used."

The lunch Heugel stopped for was a better lunch than he would have had at home. He remembered the wine, not its name. It made him very sleepy and he curled up in the back. Who else had ever given him expensive presents? Who else understood his cravings?

"I could come and go when I wanted. I had my own room in his house. Everyone treated me with consideration. We had these fantastic Sunday lunches: anything I asked for. Champagne, delicacies. Things we'd not even heard of in my family. It was an opportunity."

Was he afraid?

No. Full of well-being, and he woke up in Lausanne. There were a lot of big, ritzy hotels along the lake, it was very clean after Belfort. Belfort doesn't have a lake. To feel

rich and clean was nice. Heugel's bathroom was gigantic.
A dream bathroom. Everything you could need. Razors,
soaps, shampoos, lotions. Great for someone in love with
mirrors. The next day Heugel took him out for clothes.
"He bought me short blue tennis skirts and sailor blouses,
white socks and sandals. He took me to the hairdresser at
the Majestic. When I looked at myself I didn't recognize
the little girl in the mirror. It was very innocent. One man,
all I had to do was sit on his knees. Then he put me to
bed in my room and read me a story about kissing me
goodnight." It was a happy period.

"You didn't call your family?"

"Didn't even think about them. But Heugel wrote
them and I wrote twice a week saying I was having a lovely
holiday. I went several times. Papa was pleased. He thought
I looked better with short hair. I have pictures."

Toto had lots of pictures of himself, dressed in all sorts
of ways and against all sorts of funny backdrops. They're in
his book of all the things and people he thought he might
really be. His special "friend" Dalila he did the rounds with
was a photographer's assistant. Maître Blanchot didn't want
to see them.

Instead he said, "Now tell me again when you set
your first fire."

Toto hated it when Blanchot addressed the court. We all
did. He made Toto out to be an orphan in his own family.
He talked about the failure of society and how Toto had

been passed from person to person in the Social Services. Even if Toto didn't have us, everyone has a family besides the one he's born into. Prison was a family, and when the moment came (he knew they'd find him guilty) when they'd say, "Prisoner, have you got anything to say?" he was going to tell them he wanted to marry Aziz, who shared his cell and was madly in love with him. "*He* thinks I'm beautiful. We're engaged."

A pity that, in all the beauty that love affair had in his eyes, it was no more than imagined. Toto was only talking about what he needed most: to belong somewhere, or with someone.

The girls, the *travelos*, were another family: Bebette, la Gazelle, Dalila. They looked after each other. But best of all, the troupe was a family. That's where he discovered his art. When he turned seventeen. They travelled around between night-clubs and little Rhine villages, in small towns that had few tourists, unsophisticated places where people found them exotic, like circus people. They had a painted bus with bars painted on its side: *La Cage aux Folles*.

He was washing up dishes in Belfort one night and his eyes jumped out of his head when he saw their act. He told Madame Annie Stein about washing up dishes, and then about Darien. Or first about Darien.

Darien was the boss, and he said he was the son of exiled Spaniards. I met him. His eyes were the colour of cooking chocolate. He knew how to snap his fingers like castanets. He was so quick it sounded like he was tap-dancing.

He told Madame Annie Stein about the kitchen, about standing by the big concrete sinks with heavy taps. "It was summer and I had to wear this long canvas apron you slip over your neck and tie in back. When it got wet from splashing, it got heavier and heavier." The plates were greasy and hard to handle. They were soaked in one sink and rinsed in the other. He wore big rubber gloves. It was mechanical work. "That was the way he treated me," Toto told the lawyer. "As though that was where I belonged. Not a real woman but a sort of *domestique*. A servant who dressed up as a woman."

But he understood why. "I humiliated myself for him on purpose," he said, watching Madame Annie Stein's brisk pen at work. He offered himself to Darien that same night.

Suddenly, it had become impossible to stay home. "Bring me your book tomorrow," Darien had said. Because Toto had told him he was a successful model, and all models have this book with pictures of themselves. Toto looked pretty good in his book: at least when he wore the kind of simple dresses he could buy off the peg. But there had been only a couple of small jobs. It wasn't worth the expense of the clothes, the make-up and the hairdresser. It was simpler to live off unemployment.

Madame Annie Stein tried to get him off the troupe for a moment. "Talk to me about fire," she said.

But he came back to the troupe all the time. "You felt you didn't exist anywhere else but with them," he said. "They were my real family and I was happier than I'd ever been. At least I was doing something." The flamenco, he

149

explained excitedly, was just one of their numbers. The music was canned. Darien was in tight pants, his "girls" wore ruffles and stamped heavy heels. There was also a number in which they impersonated great pop singers. The way Toto talked about him, Darien was this lofty, uninvolved, god-like creature, so far above you, just being around him made you a menial. Everyone was in love with Darien, and without him all the girls felt *incomplete.*

But Darien reacted to him the way most of those Toto fell in love with did. As if, if they were nice to him, they'd *acquire* him and couldn't get rid of him. It was the same with Felicité as soon as she started going out with boys. It was obvious what she wanted was to marry and have kids. The boys found that a drag, until Eric came along.

Toto wanted to be important in someone else's life. "I guess I was experimenting with this business of expressing feeling," he said. "When of course I didn't feel any. Not in my heart. It isn't feelings the body has. It has pleasure or pain, but it doesn't say things like, 'I love you'. You want to find some secret in me, don't you! You think I have some feelings bottled up inside. If you know about them, you can unlock something in me. Am I different enough to be *crazy?* That's what you want to know. Well, it's only you people worry about that. But don't think I don't know *they* feel something I don't, people who can really be in love. Something more than enjoyment. I know that. It costs nothing to give pleasure. Ask them. You ask any of them. But *they* feel something more than that. They *love* me. At least they say they do. See? So others do have this feeling. Or they say they do."

"You don't love them, ever?"

"What's 'love'?"

"So what do you think about? When you give them what they want?"

Sometimes he had an underground river down which the whole world vanished, as when you pull a plug. When they had finished, nothing had changed. He wanted to sleep for a very long time. "I hate it when they talk, after. There's nothing to talk about."

"Was that when you got into drugs?" she asked.

"With Darien, yes. That was the first time. He carried his own spoon, his own needle. It was something he needed. They were sick, the whole lot of them."

"But not you."

"I was trying to feel this love thing, that's why I tried it. I wanted to feel like Doris Day did, who went around with a satisfied smile on her face. Was it something I could learn? You don't listen to what I say."

"And fire?"

"Fires are there waiting to be lit. Sure, you get a hit from fires."

He said he never told anyone before. But the first time he appeared on stage—he was Cleopatra—painted and wearing a wig with a dark fringe and long, black hair and bracelets and collar of gold, he had his first and only orgasm.

His skit for the troupe was supposed to be funny. But I didn't think it was. My boyfriend, who drove us to Colmar for the show, called it "amateur". But it was a star turn: really his last one until the trial. The lights dazzled and cut the audience off: the world out there had become a big mirror. But afterwards there were sarcastic comments from Darien—"Just who do you take yourself for?" One of the "girls" dropped an ice cream cone on his Cleopatra dress. "She was just jealous. The act was something I created. I made up the dialogue. It was a good act. Better than Darien's flamenco."

Dressing up did it for him. "Look at me, I can't play a man," he said spitefully. Being a boy was what he played in between shows.

Madame Annie Stein kept coming back to the fires. That's what she was being paid to find out: did he know what he was doing? He put her off, or worked around to it his own way. "Suppose I worked in a factory and wore overalls, forget that those people died, who would even see me?" Drag did it. It drew people; it bewildered them; it made them uneasy. He liked that halfway world. "I don't understand people like my brother who are one thing all the time."

"But you love him."

"I wouldn't want to be him."

Maître Blanchot said, "You take that line and people will think you're just spoiled, and perfectly capable of doing something awful deliberately because you hate normal people."

"You think I thought about what I was doing? I was

drunk, I was high, I didn't think at all." When he got to that bit in court, he looked my way and said, "I told the truth. The literal truth. I was bored. The place was dead. Nothing was happening. I thought setting the hostel on fire would liven things up."

I had to drag out of him what happened. By August, the troupe was in Brittany and doing pretty well with students and tourists. After they opened, he thought he'd take the next morning off and finally get to see the sea. But when he went through the dressing room to get Darien's permission for a day off, he found his costumes trailing on the floor and some new "girls" walking all over them. His make-up kit was gone. The record he used in his number was smashed.

In tears, he went into Darien's office. Darien said, "You're not on tonight. Nor tomorrow night." He reached into his pocket and handed him a hundred francs. "For all I care, you can get yourself back to Belfort."

"What's wrong?"

"You're no good, that's what's wrong. You're no good and you never will be any good."

That was when the fires started.

I went to his prison with Papa to see him. I remember Papa's big, flat hands lying on his knees like work-gloves. "You don't see things the way other people see them," Papa said. "You really don't even see people, do you? You're sick, not wicked."

"Prison, Papa, not the loony bin. The loony bin is what Blanchot wants. Not me."

"He's doing his best for you. You really prefer twenty years in prison? Maybe in hospital they can cure you."

"Yes, Papa. But I'm not crazy."

"If you're not crazy, what are you?"

"I'm me. Why did Darien have to say I wasn't good enough? I put my whole soul into it, and there he was saying my soul wasn't enough. What more do they want?"

By the end, Toto was dialling up encounters on the Minitel. That's how they caught him after the big fire. They'd been watching this super-consumption of computer calls, and that night he made a mistake, dialing 17 and 18, Police and Fire: when in fact he was only lonely. I guess when Darien said, "Go home," all my brother saw was pictures of life as it was going to be for him. He saw la Gazelle going off every day to work at the Samaritaine, and Dalila in his darkroom from nine to seven with an hour for lunch. He'd had his fling.

At eleven o'clock he was on the station platform, shivering in a mist blowing in off the Atlantic, which was still as far away as ever. The bar was closed, the café was closed, there were no other passengers. It was high summer. Where was everyone? He made a connection somewhere around the Porte Saint Denis and was out of it for a week.

"You overdosed," Madame Annie Stein said.

"Just the once."

"You wanted to die. Had you ever thought of killing yourself before that?"

"No."

I'd like to know why he lied about that. All those experiments with plastic bags over his head? The special highs? And the one book he always had with him, with *le petit Kleine*?

"How about the drugs?" she asked.

"Just fun: when you're bored."

"Prostitution?"

"I did it for the money. To pay for the trichloride, the movies, cigarettes. My dresses cost a lot."

I know why she asked. First, the overdose. Second, the father of one of the victims—the letter (published in *France Dimanche*) lay before her—said the best thing he could do was kill himself: in his place, I'd have killed myself. Instead, he killed other people. "Send him to me," this father wrote. "I'll do the job myself."

He was reading a lot in prison, including a book on pyromania, which was the word they used in court all the time. Apparently most fires are set to attract attention. In the mood he was in, as he told her, the main thing was, fires destroyed. "You start fires to burn the junk of your life, rotten love letters, lousy poems, used hypodermics, records you've fallen out of love with, pictures of yourself you now despise, daily life."

He was in the hall outside his ward. He was lucky that a friend found him and the doctors got him breathing again after the overdose. He asked the hospital to call me

155

and I went up to Paris to see him. It was obvious he didn't know what to do with himself, but they wanted to keep him in for observation and then send him to some rehab program. After I left, he said, he lit a cigarette, and not thinking of anything in particular, he didn't blow out the match. There was a laundry room within feet, the door open, a big bin of sheets and hospital gowns just inside. He dropped the match in the bin, and went back to his ward as if nothing had happened, sleeping until the alarm rang and a nurse shook him awake.

My brother came back to Belfort. I saw him from time to time, and so did Maman, who thought he was improving with counseling, and that going to school to become a chef was also a good sign. I thought he looked desperately bored, and I heard that he and the other *travelos* still hung around in the cafés downtown. But they said in court there were thirty-seven more fires in the next year: in many different parts of town, because he drifted from one place to another.

Maman sat daily in her hard-backed pew in court. So did Papa, an extra judge: you did this, I know you did, how could you have? Maman wore a cardigan with embroidered petunias. They looked like she'd picked them from the carpet at home. We went to visit Toto together. "I've never told you this before," Maman told him, "but I was always terrified for you and Jacques. You were so small."

"What a tragedy if I had died," he said sarcastically.

"It would have been awful for me," she replied. Then she kissed him goodbye.

After the first fires, he told the court, it became a habit. "You start one, you start others." Fires were like lovers, they were all alike. The day before the last one, the big one, he'd ordered a new sofa. The *Sécu* had found him a more or less permanent room in a student hostel, the Hotel d'Europe, an oldish building. A fire inspection was due, which found it lacked extinguishers and fire escapes.

The next night, after putting in an evening on his Minitel, he went out to borrow some sugar from a neighbor. He'd seen all the ads on TV before and he hadn't got any sugar for his coffee. When he got back to the Hotel d'Europe where the *Sécu* had put him, he watched another film on TV. When it finished, around one, he went for a walk. The streets were empty. When he came back again, he collected some newspapers, carried them back to the garbage area and struck a match. Then he went upstairs, cooked and ate two fried eggs and lay down on his bed. "I thought of what I'd just done and nothing mattered," he said.

At three in the morning there was first one explosion and then a second. He ran out of his room. There was no way down: the stairs were engulfed in flames. Eighteen people died. One single man was fifty-four, the other seventeen were all between twenty and thirty. He confessed. That took less time than identifying the bodies.

In court, they asked him if he seduced little boys? One judge asked about a boy called Eric. "Eric? I know lots of Erics. No, for me, little boys are eleven." Or little

157

boys are five and get taken to the sea-side. Sentenced to twenty years, he asked to be sent to his kind of prison. Where there would be others like him.

Some weeks ago, just after I began work on a paper in Grenoble, I received a small package from my brother. It contained a little wooden effigy, carved and painted by himself of the Blessed Virgin. She wore a sky blue dress and carried a rosary. But around her neck was a noose, tied with a hangman's knot. "Pray for her," he wrote.

Along the River Plate

T he water in the Paraná, for they had not yet joined the River Plate, was lugubrious and brown. The public address system, two horns hanging from exposed wires, played the theme music from *Spellbound*, the film, on an endless loop. The music played twenty-four hours a day, but from midnight to six barely perceptibly, like the river parting before the prow.

Looking through the battered slats of his cabin door for the first two days, it was hard for him to tell: was it the far green shore that did the traveling—drifting islands, bluffs, submerged trees—or this ship? Now, on the third—a sullen siesta done, some time spent with his sketch book and a tattered paperback, smoking one cigarillo after another— there was some hope the air would start to stir. More air, anyway, than provided by the casual drift of this ancient side-paddled vessel that plied once weekly between Asunción, Paraguay, and Buenos Aires. Maybe.

Don Andrés (Andrew McAllister) found himself on the *Diaz de Solis* due to a chance encounter with a Colonel Echeverría in Rosario. The Colonel had admired his sketch book, the deftness of his hand, the treachery of a flat surface that yielded voluptuous shapes. "*Amigo*," the Colonel said, "I do not think I let you draw my sister. I think you should do a portrait of *la Señora Presidente*." It would make a fine gift for the President: a man who had everything, including the saintly Evita. "*El Presidente* is a generous man. He will appreciate my gesture."

Some months later in Asunción, he had run into the Colonel again at the Grand Hotel Iguaçu. They had embraced like old friends: as chance acquaintances become, far from home. "You haven't forgotten the portrait, eh?" He sat very erect while being sketched on loose sheets of note-paper with great steel-engraved falls behind the hotel's letterhead. Echeverría's pose suggested he saw himself as a memorial: hand in bronze frock coat. "The difficulty with me," he said, "is to make my moustache different from all others." Like the hotel's name, the note-paper lied, for the falls were several hundred miles away.

The Colonel thought him rich. Don Andrés was European, he was white. Only rich Europeans came so far up river. It would have been too complex to explain to Echeverría that his letter of credit, even kited, was long exhausted and the cheques he drew against it hypothetical. The man could be useful. In Buenos Aires he would present himself at the Casa Rosada with Echeverría's letter. Doña Evita would receive him; there would be an honorarium, perhaps an order, a star, a diamond keepsake; she would be enchanted with his skills.

When the sketch of the Colonel was done and Echeverría had written out a letter of introduction for Don Andrés, he added: "Now, if I were a painter like you, I'd go by boat. I know the Captain. He is not a drunk, though he is often in a filthy temper with his wife."

Not much of a recommendation for a five-day trip, but then this was not travel brochure country. Not in June, 1952.

There were routines to travel. Just now he would go out on deck. Between his cabin and the Captain's, 'midships, was the *Comedor* or dining room. There the oil dripped sluggishly from the nightly chicken. The deck passengers (there were only four cabins) did not eat chicken. Irregularly, they chewed at chunks of *charque*; or from plastic bags emerged round dry biscuits on which they nibbled throughout the day. The older women smoked pipes. Now that on the third day there was little curiosity left, he could stand at the rail and no longer be seen, no longer be stared at for his height and the great whiteness of his skin, whiter than his fellow passengers had ever seen. Shortly the sun would settle on the endless green and the Captain would emerge, brutish, unshaven, and tuck a soup-spotted napkin under his fat chin, and Don Andrés would put down his paperback and sketchbook and go into the *Comedor*. In a minute. It was the hour of illusions: of better trips, of elsewhere.

But tonight at the rail stood a figure he did not recall seeing before: that of a man as long as himself, as gaunt, as white. The Stranger did not turn his head. But the profile was striking, dominated by a long narrow nose that rose unusually high above his one visible eye. This eye was dark and heavy-lidded. He wore a long coat of shabby gabardine which reached nearly to his ankles, below which Andrew could see a pair of black and cracked boots with worn and uneven heels. Though it was June and winter, that high up the Paraná warmth still clung to the river. Had the ship stopped during his siesta? Tied up at one or other of the miserable docks along the river, picked up, dropped off some wretched passengers, at a hacienda, a forlorn town?

The evening drifted in over the vast expanse of water (already there the river is a mile wide), featureless, deceptively still. Such clouds as there were groaned at a very great distance to the south and some shreds of lightning were visible, belonging to another world. Darkness wasn't sudden, but as if the ship were burrowing into the flank of a large moist animal. The ship's lights came on; *Spellbound* droned.

In the door of the Captain's cabin his wife Eulalia yawned, her armpits muscular, a corn-paper cigarette dangling from her mouth, its smoke, given that the ship was supposedly moving, curiously vertical. Unmistakably her, he thought: the flat Indian bangs were the same, the purple lips like a split fig, the solid row of square teeth.

He remembered the rest of her body, dark, lustrous. This was the woman who'd come to his bedroom in Asunción and it was thanks to her his cock leaked. He scratched and pinched it through his pocket; it oozed, he squeezed, humiliated. He was fastidious, a clean traveler. How long did these things take to incubate? Stirred by the lascivious tropics the evil could flourish and destroy, like maggots in meat, within a week.

She went in. A cluster of faint lights winked on the south shore of the river. "A generator, *Señor*," said the tall Stranger, pointing. "As the stars have generators and that is why they seem to pulsate." Night having fallen, the stranger had found a hat. A tall hat. Not exactly a top hat; more felt, nearly conical. He didn't look Indian, but threadbare.

Actually it was because the stars were very far away and because the light had so far to travel.

There were four tables in the *Comedor*, two of them empty and at a third the Captain scowled with a heaping forkful of rice half way to his mouth. Don Andrés' table was covered with oilcloth. There was a cruet of oil in which a fly swam. The shot-glass with toothpicks contained two *palitos* only. There was a soup plate before him and an Indian in a once-white jacket was passing around a tureen of soup. Whole tomatoes floated in it, and drops of beef-fat.

The Stranger stood at his shoulder. "You seem an educated man, *Señor*," he said. "I may sit with you?" In his long coat buttoned up to the collar the Stranger had the grave eyes, the modest countenance of the believer. He was also as underfed as a plaza dog.

"Please."

They ate their soup and established those basics by which travelers in far-away places make themselves known to each other. Don Andrés had come from England, that was very far, *muy lejos.* The Stranger had joined the ship in the middle of the night, but in fact came from nowhere: "I take this ship, I take another ship, I travel the river," he said. And Don Andrés was an artist, he had observed him sketching. He himself might have wished to be something similar, but of course that was out of the question.

When the *mozo* took away the soup-plates, the Stranger put a heavy coin on the table. "I would be delighted if you would be my guest," Don Andrés said pushing the coin away. The Stranger nodded with old-fashioned courtesy; also no more than acknowledging his due. He said he had no parents to speak of. He had been brought up by priests (there was that clerical air) in a remote little town in the province of Santiago del Estero—Saint James of Foreign Parts; they had given him an education and sent him out into the world.

"And I am a son of the manse," Don Andrés replied. At which immediately a cold granite house appeared in his mind, and his older sister who had brought him up. And how when she took him to the cinema she would put a paper bag over his head during the kissing scenes.

The Stranger made no comment, and it was too difficult, too tiring to explain predestination. Don Andrés would have liked to ask him how the Stranger earned his living, which was obviously exiguous. Out of charity he did not. In the same way that he didn't ask why he wore a long coat, lest he be told the Stranger lacked a shirt or trousers. Instead, he tore a sheet from his sketch pad and wrote in his fine hand, *Sirs, muy Señores mios. In accordance with the regulations governing the control of venereal diseases, I wish to report that on the night of June 15, in Room 202 of the Grand Hotel Iguaçu, I was solicited by . . .*

She had knocked on his door forthrightly. "May I come in?" He had never been to bed with a *putana*. Why not? *Adelante.* Come in. England was far away. In a trice he had been entangled in sheets, coarse black hair, heavy lips, teeth that bit, patchouli, sweat, guarana and whiskey; she towered over him in a black slip, potent, squat, broad, solid. "*¡Me gustan los rubios!*" she said. She liked the fair-haired. The pads of her fingers, of both hands, lay on his eyelids and within his blue eyes swam and his blondness.

167

In the bathroom she took a tumbler, filled it with water, washed out her mouth, rubbed her teeth with one finger and came back to talk of childhood: cross-legged at the foot of his bed, above which he had lit a tiny 30-watt bulb. He sketched her—the drawing was somewhere in the back of his sketch book—while she spoke of the Chaco and her brothers, likewise while she related her meeting with *la Señora Presidente*, every girl's dream. She narrated her life (*Una vez me acuerdo que . . .* I remember once) as though it were a newsreel which he wasn't expected to believe.

His eyes felt heavy then and he found himself drifting into sleep, thinking how foolish he had been not to ask the Colonel to pay for his portrait—only the occasional remote *alcalde* or the proprietor of a bar or billiard parlor ever did; Echeverría had accepted it as a tribute. The sum he had left in his pocket was far too little to pay her. Still, she had pocketed it.

Now she walked slowly outside the window of the *comedor*, a dark blue frock stuck to her back. Only her teeth shone in the companionway light. Had she recognized him? *Me acuerdo que una vez encontré un gringo, rubio, artista . . .* Everything was a chance encounter in these parts. Memory was disorganized.

He crumpled up his letter and threw it angrily on the floor. Time passed. There was nowhere for it to go. The Stranger remained unperturbed.

By now, Don Andrés thought, many of the *Indios* would have settled down for the night, spread a blanket, be smoking a dark, curled cigar and be murmuring to each other of the incomprehensible events along the river.

When they reached the *flan*, accompanied by a shredded cocoanut confection that lived on the bar under a bell-jar, the Stranger said, "Excuse me, I have something to show you."

From within his coat he extracted a large volume, big as his father's Bible, bound in buckram boards. "It is the only one I have left on this trip," the Stranger said. "You have offered me a *coñac*, and as you have been so generous (the glasses appeared, though Don Andrés didn't remember ordering them), I will authorize a special price."

Don Andrés stared at the book. What could it be? Romances? Speeches by Don Bartolomeo Mitre? That mad tale of gauchos and honour, *Don Segundo Sombra*? The idea that the Stranger was no more than a salesman—albeit selling books—and traveling among fellow passengers only very few of whom could read, was reassuring. It demystified him. Perhaps now his own fear of being diseased and helpless, adrift on a foul river many hundreds of miles from civilization, would also evaporate.

He opened the book at random and was surprised to find it was an English book. An English book printed in two columns. True, the columns were irregular, the print was out of line like the woodblock letters in a child's printing set, but the words were in a language he knew.

He read: "AUCLAN, a citi and seapor on the east coas of Nor Islan, New zealan, in Eden counti, pop. 37,736." Hastily, almost guiltily, he turned the page: "AURA, from the Griego for breathin, a emanatión from a volatil substans by electric descargo, in epilepsi." He put the book down, astonished.

169

"I see you are surprised," the Stranger said. "I am a man of learning. This you do not expect. You see a poor man (he gave another of his inclinations of the head) and you think he is without his letters. But this is a very valuable book. It contains all the facts in the world. It is called the Britannica, after Britain, where men like yourself have acquired what all people should know." He grasped the book and opened it to its title page. "You see," he said jabbing the page with his finger. "Esteban Gomez, that is myself *Señor*, publisher. *Su servidor.*"

"But the Britannica, well, it's much longer."

"No *Señor*, I assure you. This is a very complete, informative edition. From which other humble persons like myself may learn."

"I have no reason to doubt that. But it is not the Britannica."

Gomez failed to look surprised. "You may say that *Señor*, but I assure you it is not so. It says here, Britannica."

"But some of the words are missing."

The look on Gomez's face was reproving. "Of course, if you are not interested, I will not insist."

"It's not a question of not wanting it. I have a Britannica. This . . ." He hesitated to continue. It was a question of charity. Was he not himself an imposter? This trip, undertaken to cure him of a nervous depression, had been a total failure.

"You have some imitation perhaps," Gomez answered lugubriously. "I fear there are many about."

"Tell me, Gomez: do you speak English, or read it?"

"*Ni una palabra*," he answered, not a word. "It wasn't among the things we learned. Not in the middle of nowhere. As no one taught you faith."

That was true. Don Andrés hadn't been given faith. He looked at the book and saw it clearly as a fraud. Faith was a valuable commodity, like a steady hand or a clear eye, but one couldn't apply it to this book. Faith itself and this book were incommensurable. Perhaps what Gomez said about faith was like his theory about the stars or like the book itself, simply wrong. Here Don Andrés felt on firm ground. Gomez couldn't read English, but he could. That alone was enough to make him feel sad: that in these remote parts, learning that came from afar was better, that all one required for knowing was faith.

He insisted no further. Rising from table he said he would reflect on *Señor* Gomez's kind offer and let him know.

Gomez seemed unaffected in mind by his fate. Only his body—its extenuation, its show of poverty—showed signs of the frailness fraud brings in its wake. That is if, like Don Andrés' father, you believed vice is figured on the body.

Many explanations ran through Don Andrés' mind. Somewhere in the capital city—Buenos Aires was a sink-hole of capitalist sins—someone was abusing Gomez's gullibility. He was being sold shoddy goods and knew no better. He sold on commission. The unscrupulous distributor of these frauds kept Gomez poor. That was one possibility, against which one had to acknowledge Gomez's humility, his faith, his dream of bringing learning to the unlearned.

There was also a chance that this wicked wholesaler of bogus encyclopædias was himself a dupe and knew no more English than Gomez: in short, a chain of lies extending back to the real thing, but forever less and less like the original. For there must be times on this river when not even a wise man could know for sure that Auckland was a city in New Zealand. Did New Zealand, with its green

171

mountains and its slate-grey sea, its Maori-babble and peaceful sheep, really exist? Could it be an accident that Gomez should have sought to sell his book to the one man on board who was bound to know it was false? And if one knew nothing of Auckland or Auras and knew no English, how was the information in the book wrong? The innocent reader would at least know such places, such things, existed.

Slowly, however, Don Andrés, tormented in his flesh, began to understand the true nature of Gomez's proposed transaction. Gomez had chosen him because he intended to impose his lie on him, just as Eulalia had in Asunción. In his experience, that was the nature of the continent: it told lies and insisted they be believed. Don Andrés was rich, white and a *Señor*; he would not argue; he was bound by *noblesse oblige* and could not challenge someone so obviously poor and deluded. It was the confidence trick of a higher mind. No different from Colonel Echeverría's moustache or *la Señora Presidente*.

What lay about him at whatever time of night it was could not be described as silence—the ship still moved, its engine groaned, its paddles went whump-whump-whump—but there was expectation, in the middle of which he thought he heard breathing, inspection, a rustle. He tossed on his side wet with sweat, and half-opening one eye he saw his cabin door was ajar. It seemed to be filled with a black slip that either hung or swayed in the air. Then the door shut and he felt a body press against the side of his bunk, burning.

A story materialized in the darkness, another story as

in Asunción. "Take me away from here," she said. When he said nothing, she lay alongside him, whispering. How her baby had fallen between the rotting timbers of the dock and the ship's hull.

He heard the splash and woke up. It was no nightmare. Eulalia was there, arms crossed on her breasts. "Go away!" he hissed at her. "I wrote denouncing you. What do you want of me? Why tell more lies?"

She looked more solid than ever, she had a finger to her lips and ran a rough, hot palm, smelling like the ashes of a burnt-out fire, over his brow. Like a whole continent she spread herself out over a body full of empty areas. Under her lips and through her teeth he said he was sick, he'd never been like this, he wanted to go home. She said, "Ssh."

He woke up to a smell of rotting fruit, melons among them. On the fourth day dirt had taken possession of his body and that endless music grew in his ear like mould.

Dressing in the doorway of his cabin, he saw one-story buildings, ochre, yellow, patient blue, trembling in the sun. A rusted gangplank, its stanchions linked by old rope, connected ship to land. On the jetty there was an ancient sign, written in white on blue, but not legible. This could be Zarato, where they were due to take on a cargo of tobacco, and here he knew he would have to find a doctor.

He had one foot over the high sill of the *Comedor* when he caught a glimpse of a long-coated figure walking cautiously and aslant down the gangplank and holding onto the ropes on either side. He wore his conical felt hat as

173

though it were raining in the mountains. "*Señor* Gomez," he called out. "Gomez, wait! I want the book! I'll pay what you want for it!" With what he would pay for it no longer mattered. But Gomez did not look back. "My book!" Don Andrés cried out. "It's my book. You offered it to me. I'll pay you for it." He hurried after him, unable to imagine where the book might be. It was a big book, full of information, and very heavy. He doubted such a book could be hidden under Gomez's long coat or under his hat. What would hold it up?

At the foot of the gangplank he caught up with Gomez, grasping at the shiny gabardine of his sleeve. "My book," he said again. "You must sell it to me. The Britannica. I must have it."

The sleeve escaped his hand. Gomez was hurrying away. "*No puedo*," he called back over his shoulder. "I can't. *Es un ejemplar unico!* It's the only copy."

In the world? "Wait," said Don Andrés. "I must talk to you."

Gomez suddenly stopped and turned to face him. He looked abominably sad. "Look," he said. "If you wish a copy I will send it to you."

"What have you done with it?"

"Now you ask," he said, reproach in his voice.

"At least tell me, do you sell many copies?" He felt conspiratorial. When he got back to England he would paint Esteban Gomez's portrait. He would call it "The Counterfeiter". The canvas would explain everything about his trip and where he'd been. These people—Esteban Gomez, Eulalia, Colonel Echeverría—sought reclamation. They didn't want to sink into the vast anonymity of the continent.

"In truth no," Gomez answered imperturbably. "Not many at all. It is a very hard task to educate the people. They do not all believe in education. We have a long tradition of being cheated."

"One more thing," he said urgently, feeling Gomez beginning to drift away from him. "Why do you wear this long coat? Are you not hot?"

"I must wish you a good journey, *Señor.* As I said, if you wish a copy you must leave your address. It will be sent to you. Unless, that is, you don't trust me."

"But where are you going?"

"I myself will probably be going back—should you be this way again." Again he took his leave. By fragments, it seemed. Retaining him would be like remembering the exact tune of a song heard by chance. Yet at the very moment when Don Andrés was convinced he would escape altogether, he turned around once again with the same gravity he had displayed on their first meeting. "You must remember," he said, "that up-river the trip takes longer. You see, I cannot just float down the river: not unless I am at the beginning to start with. Whereas you are going south. It is a place where you too will need a coat."

Don Andrés knew this was his last chance. "Who do I give the address to?"

"You can give it to my father."

"Your father?"

"Al Capitán." To the Captain. "He does not approve

175

of me, but as you see, being my father, he cannot very well say 'Esteban, no, you may not travel on my boat'."

"You said you had so to speak no parents."

"That is true. It was a manner of speaking. We are both *huerfanos*, orphans, I believe."

Then Gomez vanished.

Were his parents another mistake on his part, like stars having generators?

The Captain said he had until twelve noon, *más o menos*, the horn would be sounded fifteen minutes before, but *hombre*, what would Don Andrés do here, there was nothing to see.

He set off with a heavy heart. There were things he had failed to ask Gomez; he had failed to read properly the map of Gomez's past, and there was every chance he would fail to find anything he wanted in this place too.

As he walked without any particular direction, sometimes away from the broad river and sometimes along it, this place felt like all the others in this land of tiny *aldeas*. It was like having no common language, though he spoke Spanish well. One saw old men in bars, veterans of obscure wars, children playing with bottle caps, young girls sitting in windows with painted leers, and their lives went on invisibly—before one came and after one left. In almost any direction, this village or town, whatever it was called, led directly into the countryside. There were yawning doors that gave onto Levantine emporia piled with burlap sacks, empty cafés, churches with white-stoned gardens of hard grass, monuments of men on horseback; suddenly one was at the end and the street turned from cracked cobble-stones to packed dirt. Here and there were traces of recent rain, the occasional cypress, a house in the distance. Otherwise there was nothing to be seen and one turned back.

Then he saw the tell-tale sign:

MIGUEL CISNEROS
MEDICINA GENERAL
ENFERMEDADES DE LA PIEL

He walked in.

Cisneros wore an immaculate white coat. He had a highly specific moustache, was short and wore shiny spectacles. Behind him, in another room, stood a tall young woman carrying a child in her long arms. When he had explained why he had come, Cisneros said: "I have no time to waste, kindly take down your trousers." He pointed to a high enamel stool. "Sit there. Your underpants too." From the stool Don Andrés saw solid sunflowers in the front garden. Cisneros squeezed his penis between his thumb and index finger. Yellow-green pus emerged. "It's nothing at all. Just an ordinary gonorrhea. Nothing serious."

"I got this in Asunción. I want you to report the woman."

"Why would I do that?"

"She is infectious. Others might . . . Anyway, it is the law."

"We are a long way from the law. Do you think

they care in Asunción? You should be more careful of the company you keep. You do not do this sort of thing at home, why here? Anyway, today it is no miracle to cure venereal disease. You can get dressed now." He went to a cupboard and drew out a bottle of pills from which he tumbled a specific number into his hand, counting them out one by one. "You have come by the river boat?"

"She is on the boat. I am surprised that as a man of science you would not wish that she be treated."

"Very well," Cisneros answered impatiently. "Give me her name."

"I know her as Eulalia. She travels with the Captain."

Cisneros let out a short dry laugh. "I thought you'd been with a *puta*. Doña Eulalia is no *puta*. She is an unhappy woman."

"You know her?"

"*Son personajes*," the doctor replied. "All sorts of people pass through here." Characters, thought Don Andrés. They passed through, like himself, but they did not stay.

"Your name, please?"

"Andrew McAllister."

"Home address?"

"I have been traveling. Why do you need that? I won't be through here again."

"If you wish me to report her, I must report you too. You too are infectious."

He felt light-hearted. A name and an address were of little consequence. He could give any name or any address.

"I am an artist. Could I draw you, doctor? I could make a new sign for you. A bigger and better sign."

"You have no money?"

"Near as can be."

"*No hace caso.* It doesn't matter."

"I could stay. I could take another boat."

"This isn't a place for you."

"It's cool in here. Nice. You're a lucky man. You know Eulalia, you know the Captain. Do you also know a tall young man who wears a long coat and a high hat?"

"Their son? Esteban?"

"Yes. Can you explain him to me?"

"Perhaps he is simple-minded. Or he isn't. He is the unhappy child of an unhappy woman."

"You don't want to be drawn? I am a good artist. I am going to do a portrait of *la Señora Presidente.* I could do your wife and child."

"I have no wife, I have no child." Then who was the young woman in the outer room? And whose was the child?

The doctor's silence now grew implacable. Once again Andrew felt he was being cast out. Why did Cisneros feel this dislike for him? He was a stranger and strangers are hospitably received. "Tell me, Doctor, are you happy here? I mean, this is not a real place is it?"

"I was born here. This is my place. To me it is real."

It was the kind of answer one gets on the road if one asks the way to X. A finger points and one is told "straight ahead", because that is the way one is going and that is what one wants to hear. The doctor had offered him things that could be true. Eulalia's son fell into the water; someone saved him. Esteban had a family but didn't. They were the sorts of explanations given along the river, the maps they dropped on the unwary.

His arrival in Buenos Aires was damp and mute, matter-of-fact: a bump into a half-dark quay. A thin wintry rain was falling and *Spellbound* stopped. Passengers melted away, the door to the Captain's cabin, like that of the *Comedor*, was shut and locked. He shivered in his denim jacket. In its pocket he found the name Colonel Echeverría had given him: Don Raúl Apold Rexach. He was in the Ministry of Information, and the Colonel had said he was very close to *la Señora Presidente.*

As he looked about for a taxi—he had little idea where he might go, he had already pawned his watch—the Colonel stood by his side mockingly. "Seriously," he was saying. "Do you really think she will want to be painted by you? A stranger?"

He walked several blocks before he saw a blue bus. He got on, among a company of women in black. He had only his knapsack with him, and his sketch book and pencils. He had left his paperback on his bunk. While the bus advanced into the late night air, he sketched her in his head, first among Argentine women; then bit by bit he added others—Esteban Gomez, the Colonel himself, courtiers—and finally her husband, wearing (as he had been told he did) a bee-keeper's muslin about his head. There was room for all the people he had met.

The painting excited him, so he got off the bus and started trudging towards what he supposed to be the center, where the Casa Rosada lay. The lightness in his heart he could not have explained to anyone. It had to do with the completion, at least in his mind, of a canvas that would express the whole of a world he would never see again. That made it complete: unalterable, incorruptible as if embalmed. It meant he could leave. If that was what he wanted to do. His sister would look after him. He would be safe.

Soon he began to run into other pedestrians like himself, holding black umbrellas against the drizzle, the men quick-stepping with bodies bent forward, the women wearing hats, furs or shawls, their shining faces some of the time thrown back to the sky. On their skin there were either tears or rain. Everyone was going in the same direction: as though there were no other direction.

The closer he got to the center, the higher rose a murmur: the sound of vanes in a steady wind. Every once in a while he heard a single voice. They said something like, "*Se ha muerto, se ha muerto*," she's dead; and "Evita, Evita, E-viii-ta!" It took some time, as it had listening to Gomez, but as the minutes went by and he fell in step with this somber crowd, he began to understand. There would be no painting from life. At most from memory. *La Señora Presidente* was dead, the Colonel was too late, Esteban Gomez would block-print her name on a new page, to which Eulalia, unable to read, would turn when the ship turned about and went up the River Plate towards its beginnings.

If he could find a taxi he could get to the airport right then. Outgoing planes would be empty. It was the incoming ones that would be full. For people are always curious about death and go on long trips to places that can't be known.

Olga and Snow
for Nina Talbot-Rice

Introducing Countess Olga at a Memorial Service

Into thick, fresh, wet snow, still falling, she emerged from her limo. Those vast sables of hers parted and gave the reporters standing around a good look at her long, well-sheathed legs—admirable, girlish legs. The legs taupe, the furs black, the snow white. A brusque wind had just turned left onto Columbus Avenue and plucked the myriad flakes upwards, but the Countess wasn't one to sniffle. "For some pipple the snow blows up," she tossed at the *Washington Post* man. "For other pipple, look at you."

Survival, death and luck, good and bad, were her subjects. A deep Russian English—the l's deeper than at the end of "gull", the w's resonant v's, articles rare—was her language. Hear her. "What good is Nobble Price to poor Plotznik now? I have been lucky. He is not so lucky, no?"

No, the great Russian dissident poet, Adam Plotznik, was dead, shot in Wilkes-Barre PA. Whereas the lucky Countess Olga (the "Countess" bit was a commercial ploy) glowed in her seventy-fifth year. She had indeed prospered over here; Central Park West was her turf, her penthouse six blocks away. But what with the wet, Leningradish snow and Adam Plotznik, our departed laureate, her Russia continued to flourish within.

Following her out of the limo was a younger man. He wore a camel-hair coat from way back; a fedora perched on his high brow and frizzy hair. He was slightly stooped and had inexact teeth which clutched a cigarette. This was Michael Leapman, a *Times* obituarist. "This ought to make you feel right at home," he said.

"Is going to be hard, Michael. I am here and I am there. I feel such heat inside! Like I'm that continent, you know, at bottom of India, from which Australia dropped off. Adam was whole Australia, big chunk of my life."

"Er . . . It's natural. You two married."

"Barely."

"Okay. Barely."

"Or maybe not at all."

An elderly Negro with dusty, Pullman-car-porter hair stepped forward and said: "For the Plotznik service?" He pointed a white glove. "Elevator on the right."

"Shall we go in?"

The press of people by the elevator was thick and wet. The professional poets, used to midwestern readings, had

brought their umbrellas; the rich and famous, stamping
their boots, hugging each other with lips puckered, wore
that special, lupine look celebrities have, who never look
like their photographs. With their itchy skins and sewn-up
bodies, they dipped into her as into a jar of cold cream.
"Olga, darling, how *are* you?" Well, obviously fine and
dandy. "How *do* you do it? You look marvelous!"

Leapman's size-13, old-style brogues leaked. As far as
anyone knew, he was still no more than the Countess'
intermittent, unattached pal. Apparently he had met her
some years back when he had interviewed her about Armand
Hammer, a man she seriously despised. But he hadn't been
seen with her then: not until Olga became officially the
"widow" (sort of) of a dead poet. At that point he became
her "escort". He fancied that status and its ambiguity: just
as he liked to play at being "Michael the Reaper", the guy
who wrote up the dead: "Catch them whole in three hundred to two thousand words max. What do you want?
Olga's guys have all *died*, she has no one to talk to."

Michael was already of an indeterminate age. The
obits aged him, as if those ended lives had leaked into his
own; they certainly didn't help attract the younger women
he vaguely courted. With the exception of Countess Olga's
PA, Ms Zinsser, Carmen, a lush acreage of Argentine flesh
atop tiny, sharp-heeled booties.

Around the time of Plotznik's death she dined out on
stories of how Michael plied his trade. "Overall," she would
say in her hesitant way, tilting her big hair back the way
Leapman leaned back in his chair, "everybody wants an

obit: a rewrite and a lot of *de mortuis.* Nothing but the good. But how many people really *listen?*"

He had told her about a Harvard chum of his (sighing at this folly) who'd gone down from his Miami condo in long shorts and a tee-shirt to mail a letter before his daily tennis game. The baking street just felled him. "Like me, he was coming up to fifty. Right there in the street. He gets an obit? Come on."

"*¡Ay, por Diós!*"

"Yes, indeed: by God, as you say. I'll get one, of course, because I'm a company employee. 'Michael Leapman was for twenty-one years an admired obituarist for the Times group of companies. He leaves his mother, Mrs Hazel Leapman of Teaneck'."

"*¡Que chiste!*" Ms Zinsser had a delicious chortle that came from way down in her gorge.

He had cited the upcoming Memorial Service and all the famous people who turned up as an example, referring particularly to his friend and mentor, Arthur (Beau) Schoenheit. "Arthur's bound to be there," he had said. "When he talks to me, I know he's also checking out my future copy: How much space will he get? What's the judgment of history?"

"Ar*tur*? The one who writes the Countess sexy letters?"

"Sexy letters? Not the man I know. Of course, you weren't even born when Arthur was around. No, I'm talking about Arthur Schoenheit, my professor. White House habitué some time back."

"That's the *hombre*." Like Olga, Carmen had her peculiarities in English. She couldn't cope with y's. "Zhou should read his letters! Zhou do Miss Olga too?"

"One day, sure."

It was one of those days on which Carmen, who said she was twenty-seven, looked forty-one; while her employer, who was seventy-five, looked even younger, give or take a few years for the shadows of experience in her grey-green eyes. "What a woman!" Michael said.

Was he already in love with Olga? It's perfectly possible. He didn't pay much attention to the fact, but at around this time his life began to change in subtle ways. Olga was a forceful lady.

Olga and Arthur ("Beau") Schoenheit touch the mourners

Upstairs, they found themselves in a sort of lobby between the various non-denominational Memorial Chapels. There was a dripping, a melting, a thaw, on the carpeted floor. The silence was warm after the snow and the torque of New York wheels making out how they could down there on Columbus Avenue. The place was jammed. Prodigiously young men in dark suits—kids without pockets to put their hands in (rookie pall-bearers)—moved about in a subdued way. They all had enviable, very full heads of vigorous, curly, dark hair topped (this being a Jewish funeral) with yarmulkas, and moved about discreetly murmuring: "The Remembrance is about to begin."

Olga took Leapman's arm. "Oh-oh, Arthur's heading this way. I swear to you he is following me. What he wants of me?" she whispered urgently. "Here I am seventy-five. My innards are intact, I'm dermally lustrous (the phrase came straight from her hi-falutin' ad copy). My breasts have no lump or mole. You admit this smart orphan's brain is okay. I am not interested in mens. I'm rich, and the last of my guys is dead. Shot. Mugged. In Wilkes-Barre, Pennsylvania. Ha! I read it is sixth best place to live in America."

Leapman looked behind that wheaten hair and saw his old Prof indeed heading their way: thick horn-rims, little, round, shiny bald head topped with faded hair-piece, tiny elegant feet. "Lately, he writes me letters," she said. "I won't specify what kind. Arthur's *eighty*! More than eighty. Do something."

So Carmen hadn't been telling one of her Argentine tall tales. Leapman was startled by these signs of amorousness from Arthur. After Heidi (briefly Mrs Schoenheit) took off, hadn't he foresworn all women? A sign of Michael's innocence: that's not an oath you stick to.

Arthur, on tiptoes, reached up to peck Miss Olga's cheek. "Ravishing," he said.

"Maybe once," she replied tartly.

"Still are," Arthur said. "Observe this lady, Michael: she hasn't changed since we first met. At least not outwardly!"

Surprise Number Two. Arthur's name had come up often in their conversation. But not once had Olga let on that she knew him, much less shared some sort of "past" with him. Nor had Arthur even before mentioned Olga. At the Remembrance he probably didn't grasp all the consequences of this double omission. When he should have been *focused*, his mind simply drifted off. Which was better, he was wondering, Comfort (companionship) or Freedom (solitude)? Just that morning, downstairs in the entrance to the brownstone way East on 79th, he'd bumped into the lady who had the apartment below his. She was about his age and had ditched her husband ("Who needs to be married? Men are just a nuisance.") three years before, and she'd said, "Look, Mr Leapman, when I go away on vacation, I draw the blinds and curtains, right? It just hit me. I could be lying there dying and people will think I've just gone to the Island." It was like a fate: everyone talked to him about death. And he'd just nodded. But then, when he got on the cross-town bus, he thought about his neighbor and about himself. Yes, he thought, that was one of the many down sides of being alone.

Turning that encounter over in his mind, he figured Olga had to be all for freedom, for no mens. And yet Arthur's (hardly delicate) approaches clearly flustered her.

The front two pews were reserved for the "witnesses" to the late poet's life. Up in front, at a pulpit, the boyish rabbi shuffled his file-cards. Arthur was in the pew just behind Michael and Olga and Arthur's short breath fanned Olga's long neck. Then the rabbi said they were going to start with a few words from the widow. "Countess Olga, please."

Of course Olga had to go first. It was her right. Hadn't Plotznik's first poems celebrated his Muse? A high-headed, long-legged girl of the people?

Olga was no great public speaker, but she had dignity, and she was at least brief. She simply recounted Adam's fascination with America, and also his fear of it, and then described the night the dead poet had been received in Jack's White House. How moving that was, she said, after a lifetime of persecution. How complex were lives, how fatal the mistakes (What mistakes? Whose mistakes?) of youth, how unpredictable was death.

When she'd finished it took her some time to part the throng. The most famous *parfumière* in America had a public. It wanted to show its appreciation: "You're *so* fabulous." These were obligations, but they bugged her, and when she finally sat down alongside Michael again, her torso rigidly upright, her cool hand on his, she said: "Listen, while Arthur's talking, I'm going to give this place slip. Anyone who asks, you say I'm upset."

Which she had every right to be. Death was robbing her of her past. But also, as she'd explained in the limo on the way over, *this* Plotznik, the dead Plotznik—the "Nobble Price" man, the great Dissident, the guy with the lofty brow and the glazed, amused expression of a very old dog, the curly hair that started high up his skull all round—wasn't *her* Plotznik. America blurred history: "People here are born again every day. There past stick to you."

She heard out the beginning of Arthur (who followed her at the podium) impatiently. With an expression on her face as though Arthur were a restaurant kitchen to which she wasn't going to give her seal of approval.

Arthur *was* a public speaker, with years of holding

forth, and like many plump and dainty men, he had a powerful, even bullish voice. He swayed a little on his feet, top heavy from his big head; the smooth skin of his face— it fit his skull like a pink surgical glove—suffered from a subcutaneous tremor; he had trouble getting his pages in order; but once he got going, he got all the cadences right. "As with the dreams of long ago," he began reading, "a murdered poet is now joined with a murdered president." With the best of motives, he emoted on the waywardness of the dark-skinned Leroy Lennox (Plotznik's putative killer), whose failures were somehow Theirs. His voice rose. "Why are we so violent?" (Yes, yes, *why?*) "Why this dark side of America?" He turned in melodramatic stage despair to the embalmed Plotznik center-stage: "Where has the hope gone?"

It was an old-time tent revival meeting, and where Leapman admired it, Olga found it over the top. "You can say one thing, Michael," she hissed. "Arthur never misses an occasion." More confidentially, she added: "I had a peek in the coffin while I was up there. Adam looks like he's made of wox. He who always slept curled up on his side like a baby. What a waste, no? All the hours they spent making him up? A fine job. But to burn such good coffin?" And Arthur up front all but stamped his little feet. She wasn't paying *attention.*

In Sleepy Hollow, Arthur makes certain confidences

Arthur called the Catskills house to which he had retired "Sleepy Hollow". Actually, it was a two-up and two-down frame house largely surrounded with skunk cabbage, and the hollow was a sort of muddy gulch with a pond. Leapman went up there more or less every other week to work on Arthur's papers. He would get off the Short Line bus by the gateway to Irena Fyvel's hotel, the Mount Zion (Mrs Fyvel, a one-time "star of the Yiddish Stage and Screen" was a great friend of Olga's) and walk the rest of the way down to Arthur's cottage. The routine was unchanging. The Professor, his body always impeccably turned out (though his mind wandered), his odd little belly held out before him like some insignificant tumor he had failed to check in at the counter, would greet him at the door, Michael would work an hour or two, sorting and checking facts, and at around four, they would sit in front of the fire and Arthur would serve tea and hot biscuits.

These visits were not unlike visiting Mr Leapman Sr in his last days. He had been Arthur's Teaching Assistant as he'd been his father's son. These were both subordinate positions. "Of course my father did his best to make it easy," Michael would say, "but it was always a queer mix of the cantankerous and the coy. You know, I was never sure if you really ought to like or hob-nob with your family. More than that, whether Olders and Youngers can ever really get along. They have the high ground, being around longer, but it's queer being fifty and having your father still call you 'Mike'. In his eye I'm always going to have a first-base mitt on. Same with Arthur: I'm still the bright Sidekick of twenty-five years back."

Arthur and Michael's father also shared a tendency to back into what they really wanted to bring up. On this visit, towards the end of November, Arthur started by announcing—his breath was sour, his hand trembled, and why was he so angry?—that in his opinion all too much fuss had been made about Plotznik, a "greatly overrated poet, I told the President he was a phony dissident. Maybe he was OK back in Russia, but the man couldn't handle English. As a matter of fact, none of Olga's guys amounted to much. A bunch of deadbeats if you ask me."

Next Arthur started chaffing Michael about his "hundred years of solitude" and what a bozo he was. What was Michael waiting for to fix himself up? So he'd missed out on the glamorous, flower-struck birds of the sixties, so he'd had a brief, unhappy fling (i.e. marriage), what was the matter with the supply of older women in these big cities? That sort of "frank talk" was his way of getting along with the young, whom he wanted as pals. Unfortunately, Arthur often got the tone wrong, sometimes *offensively* wrong. "*Intrusive*," said Michael. "That's what Arthur could be."

Reverting to the subject of older women, Arthur said, "When you think about it, behind their nail-lacquer and night creams, many of these older women must have hot innards. Walk into Lord & Taylor, go to the theater or Lincoln Center, what do you see? Countless ladies wanting for full-time company. Half the bounty of the world circulates by someone's pleasuring ladies of a certain age. How else has the New York Public Library got rich? That Armenian fellow whose father stabled camels."

"I know, I know," Michael admitted (What was the man getting to?). "I haven't even been divorced once." Which was half-true, and the excuse he usually gave the aspirants Mrs Hazel Leapman (Ma) sent up from New Jersey.

"Except for what's-her-name," Arthur reminded him.

"Quite. Bunny." Whose name and fate Arthur knew perfectly well.

The lovely part of this was that where Michael thought old Prof was offering this fleshly solace to him, in fact Arthur had this particular turf sussed out for himself. He looked down at his tiny shoes, which shone like ballroom dancers' hair, and said: "I like to think I have what it takes to please."

"Ah. You have somebody in mind?"

"See if you can guess. You're smart."

"The widow Fyvel?" (She of the Mount Zion, up the hollow.)

"A charming lady, but no consort. She runs a hotel! But how about Countess Olga! The crazy Russian *parfumière*? I'm wild about her, and I can see you're pretty chummy. You think she'd do? How do you find her these days, by the way?"

"Terrific."

Leapman had a city brain. There were too many leaves and too much wet grass for it to work up to speed in the country. Well, Arthur obviously wasn't kidding. Michael's first thought was that an Arthur took a lot of looking after, and that so far as he knew a condition of Olga's lease on life in America included her own version of the Monroe Doctrine: no entanglements, no pets, amorous or otherwise. His second reaction, he admitted, was purely jealous. "Of course, she's getting on," he blurted out treacherously. "Around the eyes. I mean it must take longer and longer to moisturize, things like that."

"Bah! The body's packaging! It's the contents that count. You could indicate my willingness, you know. Unless you have designs of your own, ha-ha."

Arthur's "willingness"? Come on! Olga was a catch-and-a-half. When she blew him away in the divorce court, the spectacularly tall and anorexic Heidi had stripped Arthur of every asset except his father's house in Cambridge. His only real capital was his reputation as a friend of a long-gone president, while Olga's millions just accumulated. They were one part of America she'd never really grasped. She took money for granted. "First thing you think, you come to America," she was quoted somewhere as saying, "is this is rich country. It isn't money make you rich. But here you want to be warm, you turn up heat. That's being rich. Back in Russia even Big People can't have what they want."

Nor did Michael think about money. That wasn't why he stuck around Olga, about whom he was always deeply respectful. Or inhibited.

"You see," Arthur went on, "a *rapprochement* is greatly overdue, for in the past we have missed each other's boat. Her life has not always been a happy one and mine could use some improvement. Never underestimate the grabbing power of an old flame."

Doubting that, Leapman said, "Are you asking me if she'd say yes? Er, who knows with a woman of such a strong and determined character?"

Arthur looked surprised and even alarmed. "Olga and I have a past, we could have a future. Surely she's mentioned me. (Actually, not the way he wanted to hear.) She stayed with me a weekend once in Cambridge. She illuminated the house. The servants noticed it."

"That was when the boat was missed?"

Arthur huffed: "She was fresh off it. She didn't have a bean." Yes, and now it was the other way round. "A Golden Opportunity has presented itself, Michael my boy. I am on the Plotznik Memorial Committee and so is the bereaved Countess."

"Already? So quickly we have a committee?"

Arthur was pained. "The Family asked me. Teddy called me from Florida."

Which Leapman thought bad news. That family wasn't good for Arthur; it was his hobby horse, his Subject, and too often his *raison d'être*. Michael stayed around until his bus was due, but by then Arthur was disconnected again. Lately, he didn't make all that much sense.

Olga wishes her past revisited

"Tonight, we go out and get drunk," Olga said some days later. "I don't want to be *alone.*"

And at midnight they had already been sitting for some hours—with Olga between Michael and her chauffeur, Vladimir—at the bar in a Polish drink-shop high up Second Avenue. The vodka was smooth and heavy, lubricating. By then, Olga and Vladimir were trading snatches of Plotznik poems. A sort of coarse and agreeable murmur—he knew no Russian—the poems allowed him to sit there studying the world outside: the way snow froze with a stiff, metallic glitter; traffic slithering by; the limo attracting some attention from a handful of local multiculturals in beaded stocking caps.

"Nothing serious," Leapman assured Vladimir. "A

little antenna-fingering, a little testing of their pump-up sneakers on its tires. That sort of thing. Just trying to keep warm."

"Wilkes-Barre," Olga said. "Adam give reading in coffee bar. Wire service say he went off with girl, after."

"I saw her picture. A big California hoyden with life-guard shoulders." The girl, Cornelia Watson, he remembered, had looked something like his wife Bunny. Who was on his mind.

"The man, the Negro . . . Leroy . . ."

"Leroy Lennox."

"He look like Pushkin. He has widow-peak and he is *very* short. Bullet go straight up."

The vodka Olga had chosen, oily and a special green, grew more oily as time went by, more green. So did Olga's eyes. Two dozen John Paul II's, mostly in blue-and-gold, were tucked into the mirror behind the bar. Olga's agreeable voice, steadily deepening, rolled on, and a quartet of Poles at a back booth played cards: for money, and with excitement. But Outside?

"You, Czeslaw," she said to the barman, who was reading a dog-eared Polish paper. "People don't know what life was like back then, am I right?"

"*Pana* is right," he said, without looking up.

"Last week, two girl call in 'sick'. I tell them, when I was their age I could have been dying, I still worked. I say, 'Did you start here stirring oily messes with a wooden paddle or have you got spotless factory, white smock and good wages?'"

It took her some time to really *see* Michael. Memory was working her and causing her pain. ("You have to hand your past to someone," Michael would say. "Otherwise it's lost forever.") How she slept on a trunk in the corridor; how the toilet woke her up "like a Niagara in my ear"; how she was groped in her sleep by Mexican heavy-breathers and pinched as she toiled at their filthy underwear in the kitchen tub.

"When's this? Where's this?" he asked.

"In Peter. In Leningrad. You know what *Dietski Dom* is, Michael?" she said, resting her head on his shoulder. "Is where the Revolution put the mother-and-fatherless. Irena Fyvel and me, we are unhappy orphans together there. We are both sixteen. Comrade Director of orphanage send Irena and me to Labor Exchange. We are grown-up, smart Soviet girls now. Exchange give us jobs, real life. In 1936 maybe."

Olga got a family of Mexicans; Irena got to sew theater costumes for a traveling company and a husband, the long dead Lev Davidovich. These weren't ordinary Mexicans, however. The Señora had an important job. "She had *valuta*, special money for important communists, and a big dusty apartment near the Yekaterinsky Sad in Saint Petersburg." Where the windows were sealed tight, summer and winter: "Five, smelly Mexican bodies in that apartment to fetch and carry for, plus Captain whose apartment it once was. Now Captain live in tiny maid's room by the kitchen, and I have to sleep on trunk in corridor. Captain live in open air with window wide open because of perfume.

Old, heavy curtains, mantillas on sofas, parrot in cage, portrait of Vladimir Ilych, all get daily *psscht-psscht* of perfume from me. But it does no good. It smells like everywhere tropical plants are rotting."

Mexicans in Russia? Yes, she explained. "She train the man who kills Trotsky with an ice-pick."

Vladimir interrupted. "Is a good thing, Countess."

"What is good thing?"

"Is a good thing they do, Trotsky, *tschak!*" He showed how.

"Vladi, go home." The chauffeur brushed an imaginary spot off his boot with his handkerchief but did not budge. "Is there I meet Arthur first time."

She related how she was in a pale blue, much-shrunken dress when the doorbell rang. *Drring-drring.* At the door was a soft, golden-curled angel with light feet and soft little boots, who said, "Olga, is it? I'm Arthur. Ar-*tur* Germanovich Schoenheit. *K vashim uslugam.*"

"At *my* service?" she translated. "Help! He's going to kiss my hand! He speak fruity Russian. Must be American, I think. Look how rich he is! I don't know what to do."

"Arthur? Wait a minute. What's Arthur doing there?" Arthur had gone from Berlin to Oxford, from Oxford to Russia. He was writing a series on the fifteenth anniversary of the Revolution for a Berlin newspaper, and he had a letter from high up. Arthur had connections, Michael said.

There he was in the Mexican salon, shedding his coat. "This is raglan, *etot Raglan,*" he said. "No shoulders, see?" Olga had to pass the coat round. The Mexicans wanted to feel the wool. "It is called that," he explained, "because Lord Raglan had only one arm."

Said Olga, "The Mexicans stare at him like he is mad. *¡Rag-lan? ¿Quien es?*'Raglan? What's that?' A man with such a coat," Olga said, "is too polite to notice the smell. They sit around for hours talking about old politics and Trotsky. *No one* talk about Trotsky in Russia, but Arthur does. Señora Mercedes was very suspicious. Even with letter. I stand behind door, listening. I fall in love. But he never even notice me. I am not in his world. Wallpaper is what I am."

And to think sixty years later Arthur wanted her back! Leapman was indignant. He looked down into her face, which still lay on his shoulder. She had un-aged. It was uncanny how he could see her as she had been.

"I weep for days," she said. "I am in kitchen sobbing like stupid teenage girl. But good Captain comes in. He puts finger to his lips and takes me to his room. 'Olechka,' he says to cheer me up, 'there has been an Earthquake and there is no more Mexico.' He has schoolboy globe in his room and he show me where Mexico used to be, in bright yellow. He has scratched it away with a pocket-knife. In some things—let's not talk about important ones—Murad Ilych, Captain Vakhtangov, was a foresighted man. Sure thing, Mexico, our Mexico, was about to disappear. But at the time he was just being kind. He sit me down on the icy cot next to him; he put arm round my shoulders like this, the only thing warm."

The Captain told her Kings of Fashion would break her heart.

To Leapman's surprise, Olga was sobbing: as she said, in a stupid, wet, but now seventy-five-year-old way. "Is enough for tonight, Michael," she said unsteadily. "Vladimir takes us home, I think."

Hidden in grey plush behind tinted glass, miles behind the imperturbable Vladimir—except for the icon and vigil light where the TV would be, the pair of them must have looked like the Man making his big-time, night-time deliveries—she said: "You have to admire Arthur's courage at this late date."

¡*Hasta la vista*, baby!

Some time went by, unimportantly. Olga made an out-of-town trip or two, during which Michael and Carmen managed to have the odd lunch together. To both Michael and Carmen, these trips of Olga's were mysterious. Who knew where she went? Olga wouldn't talk about them and she made her own arrangements.

By then Olga and Michael were seeing each other more regularly. Their usual meeting-place was Goldfarb's Deli on Broadway, a block or two west of Olga's apartment building. She had her own mid-afternoon Klatsch there. These ladies, the regulars, Michael had got to know. He identified them by their eccentricities of age. There was Mrs Brown-Spot, Ms Frizzy-Hair, and the Regular Bagel. They were women with solid pasts, with children and grand-

children and regular checks from Social Security, but likewise with a solid interest in the life around them. They
listened, they were *Times* readers, they made him feel at
home ("He's ever so cute," he'd overheard Mrs Brown-Spot
say. "Does he live round here?") Unlike Olga, who might
never be completely assimilated to America, they were
natives like himself. Their stories were straight.

It must have been an exploratory time for Michael:
by giving him her life, wasn't Olga intimating that there
was more on offer? She had a way of picking up where
she'd left off, Michael said: as if she were turning a page.
In her mind, her life was clearly a story—perhaps she'd
been rehearsing it for years, waiting for someone to tell it
to. But he had to be attentive. She tended to skip connections. For instance, that one day Mercedes and the rest of
her family, all men she said were brothers or cousins, were
picked up by the police.

Was Mercedes surprised? Uh-uh. Soviet society had
dispensed with farewells. Olga had sat up on her trunk in
the hall and the whole family had tramped glumly past her
with their cardboard suitcases—sooner or later, *everyone*
suffers for the cause!

"*¡Hasta la vista,* baby!" as Ms Zinsser said when
Michael told her.

These ancient cataclysms, so Michael said, seemed
inapplicable to life in America. If anything like that happened here, would his Ma drop her bridge game? Would
Mr Leapman Sr have harangued the State Troopers about
being dictators when they stopped him, in his later years,

for "irregular driving"? No. One of the great things here was that rooted hatred of the arbitrary. To Olga, whose whole life seemed to have been arbitrary—Would an American have been assigned to be a maid for a bunch of Mexicans?—this was not only acceptable, it was a way of life.

"They leave behind parrot," Olga said. "We eat him for Christmas, Captain and me. We get to sleep in Señora's bed. He says, 'Sometimes it is best to be exceedingly modest.'"

Michael liked Captain Vakhtangov. He was nuts, but he was honest and he looked after Olga. "The old boy was right," he told Carmen. "Enthusiasm is what gets people in trouble. I don't believe in revolutions." (Carmen, always pliable, merely said they were an Argentine habit. *Muy aburrido.* Very boring.)

But every morning, Olga said, her stomach would not sit still. "Captain explain to me I am pregnant." Here the problem lay with the District Housing Committee. "One day they show up: with new tenants who have many cases and scientific instruments. They are Soviet-type optimists who plan to turn Siberia into tropical garden, very blond and happy with future they are building. And they have German vacuum-cleaner, they grow vegetable indoor. They have no need of pregnant maid."

The Committee said Carmen and the Captain could only stay if they got married: and even then only because Olga was of irreproachable proletarian origin—"Hey, you can't be more proletarian than orphan. So I become *gospoda*, a married woman, at seventeen."

The ancient ears of the West Side ladies at the neighboring table perked up at that. Ms Frizzy-Hair had the floor: "What I'd like to know," she said, "is why we BOther." "Oh, Fran-CINE," said Regular Bagel, and Ms Frizzy-Hair bit her lip. Only to return to her point: "I still want to know. We look at insects, at ants, nothing stops them carrying a crumb from here to there. Don't you ever wonder why?" Mrs Brown-Spot said it was because they were ants, and that's what ants did. "Right," Francine shot back. "And why do *we* go on?"

Leapman, getting up to go back to the office to polish up the day's dead (it had been a slow day—only a minor captain of industry and a Nipponese trade official had departed), wanted to tell them not to worry. About adversity they should learn from Olga.

"You are writing this down?" Olga asked, getting up herself to say hello to her friends.

"Yes," he said in parting, as Regular Bagel fluttered her hands this way. Yes, but. Yes, biography was beginning to cause him problems. It was just a mild complaint on his part, but Carmen said: "Not everybody wants to take on a lot of old history."

And Michael said, "I should not *listen?*"

Well, he couldn't help himself. At the Deli or twenty-two floors up in her penthouse with its acres of sea-green carpet, he was getting sucked in. Several times a week he had to shift between two worlds: between Olga's Russia and a New York which in his childhood had been a visit-to-the-dentist's town, stable and even matronly, and was now full of gyms and women going to them with bulging, span-dex-clad thighs, of crude and murderous-looking youths with beaded bonnets, and large oriental families with slabs of black hair. It was no easy job. But then he had a refuge, didn't he?

For twenty-one years the *Times* had been that refuge. For as long as he remembered, when it was cold outside—which it was, crepuscularly cold—the paper had overheated its offices; as when it was hot, it overcooled. He was a creature of rituals. The first of which, on any given day, was to drape his coat (the same he wore as an undergraduate) on the stacks of brown filing cabinets that filled most of his office. Then he sat down at his desk and turned on his computer, on which he played a great many games of patience. Now, instead of solace, there was a message for him from his departmental boss, Web-Master of the *Times'* Underworld, (Doctor) Gino Fante: could Michael spare a word?

No. Michael wasn't ready. He got up and walked around, thinking of Olga and (more peripherally) Carmen, only to realize it wasn't coffee (another of his rituals) he needed, but a reformed life—Less history, kiddo, he said to himself. What is it about you that compels people to dump their lives on you? It had been slowly dawning on him that what he needed was a few laughs. All this death was bad for him. Returning to his desk, he also realized he had a subconscious desire to open up this subject, himself, with Carmen. Preferably resting his head in her large, black-clad lap. That mature—maybe even ripe—*señorita* had taken off her glasses, and her moist, large and dark eyes were swimming aimlessly. He could count on her for understanding, after which comes who knows what.

Only then Fante (compact body, violent face) leaned over his shoulder. "You got so much time on your hands you can write a *book* on Countess Olga?"

Michael said no. "Come on, Gino. What the hell would I know about *success* stories? Now go away, will you? I have to think."

"So long as your copy's on time and real short. We all have to remember our Employers, Michael."

Yeah, yeah. He was writing up Olga on company time. He was *way* over two thousand words max on her. So what? For a quarter of an hour, then, Michael drained his mind of sex and tapped out a short version of Olga: "Married for the first time to retired Captain Murad Ilyich Vakhtangov . . ." No. "*Née* Olga Frunze, a foundling raised in an orphanage, at fifteen the Countess found herself in a nest of old Bolsheviks . . ." He deleted every version. He really didn't know who Olga was. Just that she touched him in a way no one else ever had. Her emanations wouldn't go away: worse, they competed with Carmen's, like ice and fire. He brought up on his screen Olga's data base grey-green eyes in their myriad pixels. They stared back at him enterprisingly. He too was feeling pregnant and his stomach wouldn't stay still: inside him, Olga was growing restlessly— so matter-of-fact but powerful were her memories. Like kicks.

On the nature of light (and darkness) in America

Now when Olga came back, around Christmas,

she took to calling him early. Very early. For instance when, having intimated the afternoon before that Arthur had invited her out on something like a "date", she caught Michael at what he thought of as the crack of dawn. He tried to make it like any other day—As on other mornings, he rose, shaved, and dressed, he turned on the TV to check the weather but got sports instead, and managed an espresso—but it wasn't an ordinary day. Olga's wasn't a friendly call, it was a summons.

Still only semi-conscious, he donned coat, perched hat on top, and wrapped scarf (at Mrs Hazel Leapman's insistence) round thin, susceptible throat and prominent Adam's apple, and set out. You could say he walked his

two flights of stairs down to 79th Street and lit up his first
Camel with no particular expectations beyond a certain
uneasiness. Not that Arthur was queering his pitch—he
didn't have one, and he wished his old friend well—but
that he couldn't see the Olga he knew connecting to Arthur.
Old flames or not.

Yet down at Manhattan street-level and past the heavy
street door he saw right away something had happened to
the light. The top of the world over New York was solid
black and the sun, rising, was trapped in a few yellow inches
over the East River. It gave off a lurid, horizontal American
light which made everything stand out like a billboard. It
was light from under a lid, light queer enough to slow him
down, to make him *look*, as one might on the plain at
Armageddon, before the earthquakes and clashes.

He felt uneasy and maybe reluctant about crossing
town. He said: as though Olga were laying on this sky for
him.

Picking up his papers from the one-handed Mr
Schwartz, blue of beard and disabled veteran of some other
war long ago, he heard himself say, "I'm a city boy, Mr S.,
I don't like Nature rearranging things like this." To which
Mr S. answered, "What's that you're saying?"

Heading West towards Lex, the weirdness continued.
As in some drive-in movie on the moon, the laundromat
Leapman passed daily seemed excessively lit. A few of its
many machines tumbled and sighed. On the wide screen,
a clean, young kid stood in there in fatigues and tee-shirt,
doing a week's wash, and two nurses who wouldn't be able

to smoke in their hospital snuck quick ones on plastic chairs. Passing through the park on the crosstown bus, full of squat, dusky Olgas going to work, he spotted glinting supermarket trolleys hung with black garbage-bags and frozen snow on the well-spaced knolls. By Central Park West, the yellow light behind him was being banked, like last coals. The city looked like an Emergency Room. Fresh snow must be forming above it. *Sauve qui peut.* You're on your own, buddy. Where did light go when it went?

He said (sometimes these fragments of his past just emerged: usually when he was in trouble) he would have liked to hear his father on this highly-politicized, dictatorial, red-and-black sky. Long ago, when Michael was still a kid, Mr Leapman Sr had described the carpet in front of Mussolini's desk, the desk itself, the mappamundi nearby, a divan by the window and the *light* of the Roman afternoon, sleek, golden, and it had stuck in his head. In that setting, Michael's father asserted, Mussolini leapt upon women, any women. His father had gone on to explain that the dictator had been much too *praecox,* and that power and/ or fame were better than rhinoceros-horn. The young Michael's reaction had been that it must be great to be a dictator. He had told the story to Arthur once, who said the Kennedys didn't need any special light. Still, it was an unsettling story.

Lights blazed all the way up Olga's building: to the very top, where she met him at the terminus of her private elevator, wearing an extravagant silk kaftan, the general effect of which was purple. She looked like millions of dollars. When he made some remark about the weather, she agreed that it was *extreme* all right. But it didn't make *her* nervous. "You're shy about women," she said. "That's what Ar-*tur* say."

"Yeah? What's that supposed to mean?"

She half-smiled. "Come on. Why mens are like little boys? He's your friend, you have investment in each other. Don't be jealous. He thinks no one has made you entirely happy."

He was resentful. If Olga wanted to make him happy, this wasn't the way to go about it. Women were forever swimming into one's soul, he thought, one didn't really see women until they were lodged—and asking questions. How dared Arthur discuss his soul? Somehow Arthur was always around when something awful happened. He loved a good shipwreck. While Olga smiled teasingly at him, he remembered that it was into this very kind of morning and this inhospitable hour that his wife Bunny had crept out of their apartment in her nightie and slippers. Cambridge had been this dark and ugly, and anyone seeing Bunny must have thought she was coming back from a tryst, for she had flowers in her arms.

From the garlands Bunny strewed on the Charles to the knife she used, where and how she wound up, Arthur knew it all. And that gave Arthur, he thought plaintively, access to his soul. He had no right to talk about that with Olga.

Luckily, Carmen walked in just then, shoeless. "*¡Ola, hombre!*" she said with cheerful complicity, a girl who could talk a man out of the apocalypse. This morning, she was again all black-and-white: black the hair in untidy heaps, the velvet choker, her tights and a scarab on her fourth finger left; white her vigorous, tiny teeth, and her skin, chalky as rice-powder. By electric light, the result was complex.

He had grown up seeing plump and voluptuous girls like her not being invited out on the dance floor—basically, because most guys were scared of appetites in general. On the other hand weighed the power and availability of her flesh. Olga took Carmen off to do whatever it was they did and Michael was spared having to answer Olga.

He walked over to the window. A ribbon of joggers jogged down there in Mr Olmsted's park, never once looking up at that Doomsday sky overhead.

When Olga came back, they sat down on one of her vast sofas. She said, "Look. I didn't want to give you impression from what I said the other night that I didn't love my guys." No one was she fonder of than the Captain, she explained, gold teeth and all: wasn't he kindness itself, and hadn't he made a mother of her, however briefly?

Funny thing. Whenever Olga talked about her "guys" it was early morning for her. This was her time of day. Early some kindly soul had taken her to the *Dietski Dom*, early every morning she rose among sleeping Mexicans, and early now the Captain rose. The first sound she heard, she said, was of icy water from the basin cupped in his hands, of vigorous splutters, snorts and then slappings to bring color to his cheeks. There followed: like a cat at work on an armchair, the bold five-minute frottage of his scalp with alcoholic substances which made his scalp drunk and the room reek; further minutes naked by the open window to do his teeth with a finger and salt, his ears with a corner of hand-towel twisted sharp as a pencil, and his moustache with patent tweezers.

During this time she lay half asleep and half awake with the luxury of a full cot to herself: watchful as any nineteen-year-old with her first regular, night-and-day man to look after: and observant: of details previously unfamiliar.

When he'd finished that and chewed on onion for breakfast, she went on, he went down to work. At the Moscow Station, hours before the booking office opened, he stood at the window. By the time the staff strolled in, the line stretched back into the distance. With careful timing, knowing the clerks and their routines, he then marked his place with his wooden box and traveled back up the line, asking where people were going. In essence, he bought their tickets for them ("Little Mother, rest your weary bones with a cup of tea, Murad Ilyich will help you out") and sold them at a small mark-up. This he shared with the railway staff. Michael felt Olga's pride at this rudimentary capitalism. She said, "He treated me with real respect. Murad Ilych was romantic. He made love so delicate you'd think he was afraid I'd break in his arms."

The result—between night-shifts in a factory packing shell-cases—was two baby girls. "They have no luck," she said, returning to her theme. "No warm, no food during German siege. God did not intend I should be a mother.

Same as Captain." He was in a business without a future in war-time. "There are no ticket to anywhere except the cemeteries. Much of the time he drinks so much because of the death of his babies that he can't tell one season from another. They find him frozen to a lamp-post—out where the Zoological Gardens had been, where the elephant had been bombed. That was the terrible winter of 1942. There were the craters and stumps of a jungle there and one big, black, burned-out palm tree. It used to be an exhibition, Africa under glass. Captain think he was in Africa. It makes him feel hot, so he undresses. Is not a nice story."

Just then Michael saw a look on her face he'd never seen before. It was like a spasm. He took it to be apprehension; or it could have been pain. She was looking out the window—past the door where Carmen stood with something for her to sign—the way mothers look if they think they hear a child cry. Those babies of hers weren't really dead, were they?

No. They still tottered about in one of the many untenanted Guest Rooms of this de luxe place, forever aged two and three months. Not nice.

Michael said without explanation: "That was Bunny's word. 'Nice'."

Fished out of the early-morning and freezing Charles by an Indonesian jogger, and interned by her parents in a Sacramento psychiatric hospital, that's exactly what Bunny had put on the last postcard he had got from her: "I am not nice," she wrote.

Timor mortis

Heading home one evening, Leapman lingered, hot dog in hand, lots of mustard, among the Hispanics along the West Side, vaguely thinking he ought to get something for his mother and perhaps something for Carmen. (What could you give Olga? At most you lent her your ear.) In midwinter they still sat on upturned apple crates, music to their ear. "¡*Oye, hombre!* You got dollar?" In their mouths the word had a sweet sound, "Doh-La." Their hands looked like they were peeling potatoes in their pockets. A rubble of lottery tickets lay at their feet. Their moustaches did a down-turn at his passing, as though he didn't deserve their attention. "Peace to you too, brother," he said, it being just before Christmas. Finally he bought Carmen mangos and his mother, when he reached the vicinity of Olga's apartment, the latest book on bidding at bridge. He actually passed Olga's building, wished a good evening and a Happy Christmas to a doorman he thought he recognized, but decided what he really wanted was a quiet evening to himself.

At home, he had settled down to watch the Knicks with a microwave dinner on his lap when Arthur called: "Not a word to our mutual friend," he said. "You must come here. I need you. Don't worry, I'll explain. I'm in 809 at the Lenox Hill Hospital. It's just round the corner from you." Which in a manner of speaking, it was. Just thirteen blocks in the cold. But ever the pal and the obedient assistant—Arthur in hospital?—an alarmed Michael buttoned up his coat, stuck his hat back on his head, re-wrapped his scarf about his neck, and hurried over.

The hospital seemed deserted. A sort of non-denominational tree languished in the reception area downstairs, the clientele was aged and patient, and "Schoenheit, here we are" was at least not in Intensive Care. Though it didn't seem all that *un*intensive when he found Arthur's room and the door ajar. Arthur had obviously come down in the world, for he shared a room, and nearest to the door was what looked like a stiff, a body that lay flat out and hairy-legged under half a sheet.

"Arthur?" He moved round the body, skirting the wall, and was relieved to see his friend at least breathing. "Phew!" he said. "You're not out, I see. I mean, it's not very reassuring, seeing that guy . . ."

"Ah, Mr Next Door," said Arthur. Certainly not,

Arthur answered. He wasn't out. The crisis was past and he was just kept there for observation, though he admitted he'd been through a tough time. "You don't need to write me up just yet," he said. "You realize I've been here all week?"

Michael sat down. "I hate these places," he said.

"You think I like them?" A big black woman came in and cranked him up to the Sitting Position before extracting some blood, giving Michael a few moments in which to absorb the apparent facts of the situation. A mass of clear plastic tubes—which wound up in pink, extra-large, nipples on either side of the stray white hair on Arthur's chest—connected him to a monitor. Other tubes attached him to bottles. So obviously he was still plugged in to the real world. But inside Arthur, hardly a young man, what was going on?

When the blood had been taken, Michael asked, pointing to the other bed, "Is he, er, all right?"

Arthur's speech was slurred, and Michael now noticed that Arthur wasn't entirely in charge of his movements either. His hand, released, drooped; he lacked his toupee; his mouth was aslant, though still full of pleasantly regular teeth; his tongue, between them, lolled. "Next Door stopped altogether this morning just as the shifts were changing," Arthur said. "I rang and rang and they brought him back from the dead."

"How'd you know?" Leapman ventured.

"He stopped breathing. You hear him now? I checked this monitor." Having got those sentences out seemed to make things a bit easier for Arthur. More like himself. "Just how Euclid describes a line, something with extension but nothing else," he said. "He's asleep now. It makes you think, doesn't it?" There were little early tears in the corners of his eyes. "I saw things, Michael. I looked over the edge. How's Olga?"

"She's OK."

"The Plotznik Committee's meeting today, and I'm not even there."

"At least you're *here*, you know. It looks like you could not have been."

"Not even in a joke, Michael, please." But where was the usual easy banter? Arthur struck Michael as just going through the motions. He was glad to see somebody he knew, but essentially what was going on around him was no longer of any great interest. He sensed that Arthur was clinging to himself like breath to a mirror. "Just before you came in I thought I was having another one."

"Another what? Another attack? Were you?"

"They don't know. Things just stopped. These little round doohickeys," he said, scratching his chest, "are what's supposed to tell them. Everything's on a screen now. Mind you, I guess I'll know before they do. There's no pain, you know. Just an in . . . infinite lassitude. Your brain does your breathing for you. You can feel it wheeze. It comes up not with words but sensations such as you might have under water."

"So what happened?"

"If I knew I'd, I'd tell you. If they knew, they'd tell

me. I'd like to tell someone about it. The people here don't *listen*. I expect they've heard it all before."

As far as Michael could make out was that at three in the morning in the two rooms he kept at the Chelsea Hotel Arthur's heart, which should have been resting, had started to play games. It had wanted to wake him up. It had a message for him. "Your heart's so goddam intimate at that hour," Arthur said. "You remember I had a little . . . a little . . . an attack a few years ago? After that, you become aware of the slightest murmur. You are expectant. You realize you're tied to a machine, an appliance, a mere pump. And what do we know about plumbing?" His voice was cavernous. "You're *alone*. You understand?"

"OK, OK," Michael said soothingly. "It's OK now." The old *timor mortis* had poor Arthur by the shorts, Michael understood. It was taking him time and effort to get his story out, but he didn't want to let Michael go. Arthur didn't want books or flowers, or cable-TV installed: he wanted his heart's ease.

"What I was seeing while waiting for the EMTs. Those weren't flashbacks, Michael," Arthur says. "I was really there. In the cold, like Olga's dead guys. You notice how they all die *out of doors*? None of her guys have *homes*? It's the last thing I remembered thinking. You know, con . . . consciously. Then the molecules stopped moving around and it got bitter cold."

His teeth were beginning to chatter. "You want another blanket on you?" Leapman asked.

"I kissed my mother. Her hair was braided up on top

of her head. I kissed her on the lips, p-p-passionately. Her lips were icy. I never expected anything like that. The cold, I mean. She didn't *seem* dead."

Michael nodded. Parents had poor timing. They popped in on you when you were confused: in dreams, coming out from under anaesthetic. Generally, they had a reproof to make: "How could you have done this to a nice girl like Bunny," said Hazel on that occasion. He took Arthur's inert hand in his own. "Maybe this isn't the moment to discuss this, Arthur. Your body's under a strain. The psyche feels it."

"There's more," he answered. "Many more things I saw. I could tell you about the next world, where I went. It's a place of extreme sensations—from all of which you want out."

"You've had a bad scare, that's all."

"A bad scare? You know what they call it in this laza . . . lazaretto? An 'incident'. My whole life. My mother. An incident! Isn't there something pitiable in wanting love from someone you don't really *like?*"

"You're OK *now*," Michael said.

The effort of understanding—Would he, could he kiss his own mother on the lips?—was making Michael's hair crinkle.

Meanwhile the night staff had come in—routine is routine—and was banging about, auscultating Arthur, altering his drip ("There now, that should make you sleep like a baby!"), bringing Next Door briefly back to life to take some blood. In Michael's eyes the place was just like his laundromat that peculiar morning: the same bright, mean-ingless light, cubicles full of prostrate people submitting to their cycles, being tumbled and spun. He thought about how while they were living and in pain, people thought intensely about dying, because they had to. But there was no thinking at all after.

What was awful, Michael thought, was his cowardice. He had absolutely nothing to say; and he was relieved when the morphine shut Arthur down and the nurses shooed him out. It was like when he'd been summoned, in sneakers and sweat-pants, to Bunny's bedside at Mount Auburn Hospital. His mouth had hung open, he craved his morning cigarette, and for nothing in the world would he have hugged her life-givingly as her nurses seemed to expect.

Leapman and the amorous Carmen

Of course life went on. Michael saw Arthur daily until he was discharged and went back to the Catskills just before the New Year. Arthur wasn't dying or anything, or so he assured Michael, but he was both enfeebled and snappish, as though the doctors were trying to cheat him. On the Friday Arthur went home Michael had a date with Carmen. He nearly forgot it wondering how Arthur would make out alone in his cottage, whether Mrs Fyvel would help out, what it would be like if something of the sort happened to him. (No, solitude wasn't that hot a proposition.)

He was very late. Racing down to the Village by cab, on the surface his assignation with Carmen seemed to him simplicity itself: two aroused and consenting adults were about to embark on an Adventure. Right? Maybe? By the time the cab reached 14th Street, he was less sure. Despite the fact that he clearly foresaw the way Carmen's high heels would be slipped off under the table and what would follow that, he knew that nothing was that simple for him. And when he finally arrived and spotted her at the bar, surrounded by men, the fact that she shot him a hot, hopeful smile, that she wore a red silk scarf round her neck, did not entirely convince him. The shock of Arthur's attack hadn't worn off: he was still scared.

"What's the matter?" she asked right away.

"It's Arthur," he said as they sat down. "He had a heart attack or something and he's being kind of peculiar. What'll you have?"

"¿*Verdad?* You're kidding me. Three tequila sours please."

There were other problems. This place, to start with. He had chosen "Daphne's" because it was a journo hangout; he thought of it as *his* place, in the sense the waiters— though not tonight—usually recognized him. So little did he know about Carmen's other life, her non-Olga life, he hadn't foreseen that Carmen, too, was known here. No— more than known, better known than he was.

While he tried to give her a meticulous account of Arthur's "incident", his refusal even to consider surgery, the ups and downs between bullishness and despair, people kept coming over to their table. This one was a painter who'd filled vast canvases with Zinsser flesh ("Whad'ya mean you haven't seem 'em?"); the next was a poet who hopped around like a sparrow. OK, New York wasn't Cambridge, Massachussets, much less Teaneck. It was a bawdy, crude, trying place. But each time one lot of riff-raff went off, another came up and grabbed some part of her that was handy. And with each one she grew more incandescent. He said, "Couldn't we have dinner in private? What am I, just another of your conquests?"

She said, "Now you know how we girls feel." This was between tequilas two and three, and she went on to explain: "I like to please men. Ideally, I would like to have one of these smart, sexy people for myself. I'm still waiting for lightning to strike. You know how it is." Carmen had her fruitcake side: she wasn't very *consecutive.* A tall, sulky youth who made films brought his chair over to their tiny table, and she spent a good ten minutes rabitting on to him about the sheer beauty of banks and statues in BA. "Of course it's a flat country," she said. "They stick out. They stick up. Banks, generals on horseback."

They ate vast steaks, while all this was going on, and in between Carmen's admirers and mouthfuls of meat, Michael made his sort of pitch. He wasn't any great bargain, he said, he was reasonably smart "but I've always had problems with sex". This got her attention and she intimated, leaning across the table breathily and clasping his free hand, that this would not be the case with her. "That would be great," he said. "You see, my second thoughts often come before my first. And my third and fourth."

There were no second thoughts with Carmen. She wanted another steak and she wanted him. But *his* second (third, etc.) thoughts were about Olga and Arthur and his own fears. Great chunks of his talk was about these other figures in his life. Did Carmen think Olga was leading him on, and if so why? "There are times," he said, "when she really *leans* on me."

"That's just her way. She's the Ice Lady, beautiful and unattainable. It must be all that money. Hey, I'm not jealous," she said, catching his look. "Little Orphan Olga still has a big teenage come-on and it works: men's guards go down, their pricks come up. Take my word for it, you and Arthur aren't the only ones. It's not the way *they* look at her that tells me what's going on, they all have their tongues hanging out; it's the way *she* looks at them."

"And how's that?"

"Like all that money and that penthouse and the business, they're not really *her*. The real Olga is someone else. Any Russian is her friend. Especially crazy ones. She gives them money, they drink together, they tell each other sad stories. She's a professional waif with not a hair out of place."

"Jesus, I'm glad you don't work for me."

"Hey! I'm not writing her down. You are."

"What would you say about me?"

"You're cute. I think maybe you're a little backward. You know, old-fashioned."

"So you think Arthur doesn't stand a chance. I mean, not even taking into account his condition."

"I don't bet. I don't think she *likes* respectable people, but some part of her gravitates towards them. Look at you. You're respectable. She likes to have you around."

"I'm also disreputable."

"You are? Every day Mrs Fyvel calls up to say, 'Olechka, you need a Man. Arthur is so Dignified.' Maybe so. I've got plain old lust; she doesn't. Having a man around for her would be protection. At her age this could be important. For sure, I don't think you're disreputable. You're just the sort of man girls *marry*."

Surfeited with meat and fermented cactus, she was turning sullen on him, her head and hair sinking on to her scarf. But what could he answer? What she wanted was her dessert, then bed, then for lightning to strike; while what he wanted was less clear. "You want to know what I think?" she said. "I think since she's in this country she does like Romans: she owns things and people and makes them learn her history."

"Does she know what you think?"

"She thinks I'm some sort of droll peon, half-civilized. Mexico, Argentine are all the same; we speak Spanish. I guess she had bad experiences and I think I have been drinking too much. When I drink I am not so nice."

Nice?

That was when she mentioned the invitations and put them down on the table among the steaks. He spotted Arthur's meticulous handwriting. "Your Arthur's invitations," she said. "You're on the list. You could have told me you had a wife. But why not, everybody I meet's got a wife." Simultaneously her dainty, nyloned toes caressed his ankle.

"What invitations? When did these come?"

"Today."

He looked down at the sheets of paper in his hand: "M. L'Ambassadeur André Malraux et Mme Clara Malraux, Nikita Sergeyevich Kruschev and Mme Nina K., Mr Norman Mailer [and current wife, CK], Mrs Margaret Thatcher, Mr Michael Leapman and Bunny Leapman . . ."

"But this is outrageous," he protested, genuinely distressed, working his way down the list. "Half of these people are dead. Arthur must be high as a kite. It happens sometimes when you survive, you know, some big-time disaster, when you think you're going to die and you haven't."

"That's what I told the Countess when Mrs Fyvel brought the invitations."

"How about Arthur? Mrs Fyvel thinks he's all right? He's going to make it?"

"I guess so. You know what the Countess said about some of the guests being dead? She said, 'You shouldn't worry, they may come'."

"Yeah? Well, those two Russians crazies may live with ghosts, but Bunny won't show up. She's underground in Pasadena."

"Mrs Fyvel says their being dead is just a detail; it shows 'how considerate the Professor is'. She thinks they're all in his mind. Like All Souls' Day when all the dead come back."

"A detail? But Bunny really *is* dead!"

"Dead like Kruschev? You're a widower? *¡Hombre!*"

"Anyway, what are these invitations to?"

"His last fling, that's what he calls the party. The

Countess didn't even know he'd been ill. She's puts me in charge of finding musicians for the party. In the Catskills. For the dancing."

"I'm a bad dancer, too."

His appetites had fled. Carmen saw that. With great delicacy, she looked up first. "Please, can I have dessert?" He understood her to mean that if nothing was going to *happen*, dessert would be a consolation.

Later, when he found a taxi to take her home and they rode uptown together, he saw there was hardly any snow left. Just dirty grey patches. Where had it all gone? he wondered. Hadn't he been looking? "Some other time," he said to her door on 54th. "I don't think I'm myself tonight."

"Sure," she replied. "Let me know when you are."

Down on a Saturday afternoon

The TV was on at Olga's—the weather channel on mute—and the Countess was in some other part of her penthouse, so Michael sat there waiting. For Olga's past to move in, like some Siberian high. His here-and-now offering him a bunch of intangibles, the past was safer ground—at least it was *over*. The past, once you got it sorted out, was *really* real. While he was waiting for Olga, for instance, the not-nice Bunny became much more real than Olga or Carmen.

He found himself back in the Mount Auburn Hospital and her hair was still wet. She looked at him as though she would now rather kill him than herself. "Goddam you!" she said. "Why can't you just leave me alone?" As if he'd fished her out of the water and not that jogger-by. Of course he was responsible, even if he was fast asleep. Thanks to the young English instructor she'd been having it off with, or so she said (she'd paid him back by stabbing him several times with their own silver carving-knife, a present from Arthur), she had a brain full of Henry Adams. "You've made me into a mere, mad rabbit!" she said furiously quoting the author of his own "Education". "You'll see, Michael!"

Then at the opposite end of the illusion-scale there was his mother, Mrs Hazel Leapman. A quarter-century ago she'd said, after Bunny, "How could you do such a thing to a nice girl?" Now Mrs Leapman and her body both divagated. She was convinced that a cancer had lodged itself in her belly, and if in her, was striking ruthlessly everywhere. On the rare occasions Michael visited her, she sat in her black moiré dress, smoothing down the pleats of its skirt and consulting, the way pregnant women do, the kicks and murmurs within her stomach. It wasn't quite a monomania, since she still spent hours, when not playing bridge with her club, playing bridge by herself. Still, the tumor was imaginary. Every so often, Michael verified this fact with her doctor, who'd seen him through the various diseases of childhood. But this didn't keep her from imagining that replicas of her tumor wandered quite independently over the face of America. Bill Clinton was a lymphoma ("He and that *creature*, a chancre"); the inner cities metastasized; the cells of sin multiplied. If he differed from her she said harshly, "Have you got a *growth* in your brain?"

Bunny was right. Michael had regularly dreamt about her wet hair ever since. A mad rabbit she became. Mrs Leapman was right. A lot of people were sick.

Some time later Olga lay on a divan with her long legs lifted up and curled under her and he sat at her feet, receptive to the next chapter in her life. He felt he was drifting away from New York into one of those damp, discontented Chekovian country houses. It was raining outside, and if the actors just gave it a chance, their silence would last until the spring. By which time the gun seen in the first act would go off. At the end of Act One, the Captain had died. Olga must be twenty-something. The curtain was rising on Act Two.

But then he was brought sharply back. With a shrug of her shoulders, Olga went over to a cupboard and brought out her special vodka, green as her carpet, and two glasses. They were going to settle down.

While she poured, he leaned back. Then when she'd knocked the first one back, she said: "I am so tired explaining, Michael. At least you don't ask me dumb question. Ar-*tur* Germanovich, his favorite question is, 'Yes, but what was it really *like*?' How do I know what 'it' was like? My life is not separate from me and I can look at it.

"Hasn't it never happened to you? Someone comes along and you think they want you? But really they want to appropriate past and everything belong to you? Director our school, Irene and me. Happily married, nice man. Not too Soviet. Pretty young wife, good children. Comes new mathematic teacher. Is bachelor. Director invites him into home, is kind. New teacher fall in love with whole shebang: home, children, pictures on wall, atmosphere, good cooking. Young wife divorce him, and Director shoot himself in linen cupboard.

"Arthur is like teacher, no? Am I not happy as I am?"

No Ice Lady, Olga was sobbing: in big drops that stood out on her cheeks.

"Germans were all around St Pete. People starved. It was *xolodno*. Cold. Very cold." She shivered in her tears. "Snow is high as heads. Men holler up from street, 'Bring out your dead! Let us have your dead!' I yell down, 'Can't you see roof is gone? Glass is gone from windows? Captain is gone, my daughters are gone. You want more dead? You must be crazy!' Like wind, people can see right through the building. I'm all that's left on the fourth floor right. They come every day. Some job, huh? I meet Adam at end of siege, 1944."

Hearts were bursting to get a grip on life again, she explained. Everyone wanted to breed, as though coupling could make up for all losses. Olga too. "Some guys," she said, "have survived; others drift back a few at a time. Offers I have, but the men I meet are overcome by sorrow. Their skin is like ash, their eyes look back into their heads; they've seen too much. I am young, twenty-four, twenty-five. I try. I am hungry. All Olga want is baby. One who stay alive."

Michael had to get up and move around. He felt he was being eaten up by Olga's life. When she was like this, age slipped off her like a woman stepping out of her clothes. The distances between himself and Olga—of time, of age, of place—foreshortened. What if they came down to no distance at all? He went to the window. Here, the curtains were never drawn, and the night sky of the big city looked black and swollen; low, floodlit skies scudded past, like a threat. Why had she chosen *him* to tell her story to?

"Why you move around, Michael?" he heard her say. "Come, sit down. I tell you how I meet Adam."

She poured them each another glass. "You see," she said. "I know nothing. I'm twenty-five and I'm ignorant. All my life I do stupid manual work. I read about Revolutionary University. Is open to anyone. What a joy-shop! Anyone can teach, you can study anything. Everything is gift of God: food, light, learning. We pay our teachers in bread, cigarettes, a light bulb or two. We are surprised and scared: to be alive.

"There I find Adam. Adam is shivering nineteen-year-old waif wrapped up in a coat. He teach me street-smart. 'Where you come from?' I ask. He show me his old German *Ausweis*. It is his photo all right—his Jewish face—but name on pass is 'Gumbel Aprahamian, merchant'. He says, for last two years of war he has been running risky black market over ice from Novaya Lagoda to Petersburg: through German blockade. 'Keep it for me, hide it,' he says. 'Who knows when it may be useful?' Probably if he got through blockade in war he works with Germans. The Party kill him if it finds out: lot of people like him get disappeared. I say, 'Come home with me', and he does.

"He teach me English. Not just English. He teach me baseball, *tri straikh* and you're out, guys and dolls. We talk English together far into the night, to practice. He recites poems: Valt Vitman—*I wandered off myself, In mythical moist night-air.*" Her voice was resonant, deep. "You are surprised I remember, Michael. Ask me what I did in last thirty-five years here in America. Make money. Nothing."

But back then . . . ? That hung in the air.

"Adam needs place to stay. I get him onto Housing Committee books as my brother, Adam Frunze, records lost in war. 'Now you have three names,' I say. 'Plotznik, Frunze, Aprahamian. Which one is you?'

"I wish I can say we make passionate love or baby. Trust me. There isn't enough of him to keep me warm in bed. He doesn't even make draught when he gets in. I told you: we are married, and not at all married. He says he loves me, but has no need for sex, so no children. Instead he sits up reading or writing poems half the night: wrapped in Mexican curtains—they still stink of their cigars and perfume. He says I am his muse."

Her eyes were luminescent, like emeralds embedded in snow. This was a tale of unhappy, unequal love. "Really, he doesn't want me," she said. "It is because of my daughters he move out. One day I remember my camera, wedding present from the Captain. Film still in it which nobody could develop during war. I take film to shop. I have all but forgotten them, Michael. Now ghost-kids get in the way; they cry at the wrong moments. I cry and he doesn't even ask why.

"It goes on for long time like that, but then I fall in love with last guy."

"Plain as the nose on your face," said the mother who always spoke to Michael at the wrong moment. "You may be smart, Michael, but no one could accuse you of being *aware* of what's going on in others. You get involved. You don't see."

On uncertainties

No great discovery in this. Michael was torn between desire and fear. His guilts, his fears, were like a *corps de ballet* twisted into a knot. For a week he worked out; twice he lunched with Carmen (Olga was away again). Neither led to anything. One afternoon he took the bus out to see Arthur.

The path down to Sleepy Hollow had turned soupy. There was a bizarre thaw. But also in Arthur's brain—his heart was still pulling his chain. Never had Michael been received in bathrobe, nor in disorder. "I know," Arthur said, looking round the room. "I just don't see too well, and I forget things." He sat down in his favorite wing-chair. "I'm just t-ticking over, Michael. Ticking over. But I don't want those guys slicing me up."

"Never mind. You're feeling better? Up and about?"

"Better than what? What's the name of that girl at Olga's? Has she sent the invitations out?"

"Carmen. Olga's away just now. You sure you want to have a party?"

Arthur bit his lip. "I'm not sure of *anything*, Michael. The other day I was trying to remember when I saw Olga again, after Petersburg. It took me the better part of a day to get through to the switchboard. I wrote it down somewhere. I knew I'd forget if I didn't. And I have. Look on my desk. Maybe it's there."

The desk too was a mess: full of names and dates scribbled on bits of paper. "Here it is," said Michael. "1947."

"That's right. She came to Berlin with the Cobbler. Sa-something. It ought to be down there."

"Sapozhnikov."

"Thank God. Sapozhnikov, Yevgeny Borisovich. It means 'c-cobbler' in Russian. Sapozhnikov does. Tolstoi means 'fat'. You get flashes of lucidity. The rest of the time it's fog. It's demanding, I tell you. You want to watch out for Sapozhnikov. He bushwacked Olga. She was crazy about him. Stayed with him for years. Through thick and thin. Good-looking man with curly, Soviet-style hair and nasty violet eyes."

"Her last guy. She says."

"Maybe. I'm not up to it."

"Tell me," Michael said. "I'll make tea."

"He was an official poet, Deputy Minister for Culture.

They were at some congress I went to in Berlin. In '47 you say."

There was a long silence while Michael was out in the kitchen. Was Arthur asleep? No, he was shuffling around in slippers searching for his glasses.

"Here." Michael handed him his glasses.

"I knew they were somewhere. You wouldn't have recognized the old Olga in Berlin . . . Gawky stick from the boondocks, that's what she was. First time. Now she was a smart cookie. Sh-sh-she talked literature and wore smooth stockings and imported perfume, *Je reviens*, which her boss—Sapozhnikov—brought back from gay Paree." Arthur looked pleased. "See? Clear as a bell. Her perfume. *Je reviens*. Everybody was crazy about her: her pencil-thin, long skirt and her big shoulders. I wasn't unaffected myself."

"You weren't unaffected, but nothing happened."

Arthur answered crisply: "The conditions were not propitious. In my position, I couldn't very well woo a Soviet bureaucrat, however good-looking. We danced: once or twice. She seemed delighted to see me, but she had her own agenda."

There he lost the thread again. Night fell. "Yes," Arthur finally said. "No one understands. I wasn't looking for romance with Olga. I . . . I . . . It was a *rational* arrangement. My heart can't cope with more than that." Michael turned on all the lights. He saw Arthur hadn't drunk his tea. "Is it time for your bus already?"

"I'd stay if I could," Michael lied. "I'll stop by and see if Mrs Fyvel can't get you some help."

"Think about what I said. Think about the bad choices she made in life. The Countess can worship beyond the grave. It doesn't matter to her people are dead, which what's-his-name is of course. She tells stories. Think what she's trying to tell you."

"I do."

"They're all about death," Arthur said. "I thought I was going to join her collection. Watch out. That's what you're writing."

The violet-eyed Sapozhnikov

Often we don't know when the ground shifts under us. Michael Leapman saw *some* things very sharply, but were they what mattered? When Olga shunted him to very early and irregular mornings—we're talking now about any time between four-thirty and six—he saw these unsocial hours as something like adventures. But was that what they were? No, they were something Olga imposed on him. The hour at which the police, and executioners call. Yet he who'd so far ignored all wake-up calls and burrowed beneath bed-clothes like a teenager found himself waking up before Olga called or Vladimir buzzed downstairs.

There was no pattern to these a.m.'s—neither in the getting there nor in what they had to say to each other when they met—but a lot of eye-opening stuff that was changing his life. He learned, for instance, that at night Vladimir's limo became his home, and when he glided East to pick Michael up, that the dim bulbs in the back had clip-on taffeta shades and an oriental rug had replaced the sleek, grey Cadillac flooring. The effect was spooky—he might have been traveling many versts in a Russian imperial wagon-lit. One morning he might head West in a cab with a broken window ("Hey, you suffering, man? What 'bout me?" the driver said) and get fresh insights into all-night preachers and end-of-night hookers. On another he might see squat trucks dump his obits, wrapped in a pound's worth of news and Bloomingdale ads, on icy corners. He kept his eyes open, he learned; as Olga's people croaked, he felt more alive. Breakfast at the Deli ("We are open twenty-three hours a day") became a habit. He found himself full of thoughts; the talk of others filled his ears.

Odd people were on Broadway at that hour: musicians leaving their gigs, cab drivers who hailed from every corner of Russia, Iran, Haiti, or Darkest Africa. The Deli reeked of White Owls. By the cashier, held like a fortress by a blonde grand-daughter of the original Goldfarb, a gypsy woman with an upstairs fortune-telling-and-séance salon next door explained how come some of the dead wouldn't talk to her. "Yeah? Who?" Ms Goldfarb asked. The gypsy answered: "Like, you know, babies, suicides, the dead-for-love, and people who didn't get buried."

By February, when Olga came back, his friends hadn't seen him in weeks. And when they did, he was breathless. He was reading Plotznik's *Collected Poems*, just rushed through the presses. His copy was heavily buttered on top where he'd marked his place. "This is the first time poetry's meant anything personal to me," he said. "Listen to this."

> *They tell us the turnips we plant are taking a wrong turn.*
> *They grow upside-down into the soil, so many carriage-tops*
> *Whose fringes reach deeper than oil, down to where Saturn*
> *Brews his schemes. On winter nights a charred curtain drops*
> *As from the sky: on the thought of your sweet frocks, lollipops*
> *And summer. The cold-hearted, the many, those whose snows burn*
> *Your kisses, gather in their smiles; the stiff-legged coach-man's cloak*
> *Drops on the Antipodes with a sour, leguminous croak . . .*

"Olga says 'those are my frocks. The coachman, I think he is Stalin'." Michael was struck by a new purity in her look, pale and severe: she wore a nineteenth-century white blouse that reached high up her neck. She'd been "putting things in order", Michael said. That accounted for her travels.

She had fallen in love back then. One day the Deputy Minister for Culture had given a speech in her factory. It was about "New Trends in Soviet Art", the idea being that factory workers like her would itch to take up a paint-brush or write epics. This child of the Revolution, "born nearly in Year Zero of the new world" as she liked to say, had been in the front row: "I stare at his eyes: they are deep violet. I am struck by health of his skin, his aura, medals on his jacket, *two* Stalin Price!"

She was one of the factory's Exemplary Workers, a fact of which she was proud, and as such she had been introduced to Comrade Sapozhnikov. It had been a great moment for her. She shook his hand. "I smell romantic hair, I feel *solidarity* in his eyes. He gives me embrace. I am magnetized. I am bunch of metal filings from shop floor flying towards Yevgeny Borisovich."

She was given the day off, because the Deputy Minister said workers like her should be in the party. "I was not fooled. After he examine my knowledge of Marxism-Leninism—exemplary—we go to his apartment. Now in the morning when I get up to go to work, I sit on edge of bed and watch hog bristles grow on his cheeks; I watch him rub them with his upper arm, smooth them in right direction; I watch him bury his face in pillow. I know this is man for me. Is not politics. Is fulfillment. My luck. And first time in my life I have hot bath."

Early morning again. Her men woke up and she studied them; they were awake but she feigned sleep. She was with them but apart from them. And her own stories had now begun to emerge in the same way: in things seen briefly, and then it was as if the story, having dressed and shaved, went off to work. She would get them out, but then she had to back away, to break off her story. Often suddenly. "We ought to finish," Olga said, but she didn't. Michael didn't dare ask her why. He didn't *see* the pain. If that was what it was.

By then Michael had succumbed to those stories. They were exclusive to him; nobody else heard them. At those hours they couldn't even be overheard. He thought of her life as recovered memory, of the sort the papers spoke of, disasters buried for years. "She produced them," he said, "like some movie she'd seen when she was a kid."

A new theme came out, though, She was often resentful about Adam. "Basically, two men needed her." When Yevgeny Borisovich was away on business or at his office, Plotznik would come by, stretch himself out on the Deputy Minister's thick carpets and read the latest books from the West, American writing, poets, the sort of stuff ordinary people never got to see. ("He pass Statue of Liberty many times in a night, reading. It was his Trip," Olga told Michael.) On summer weekends he'd turn up at Sapozhnikov's dacha in a car driven by one of his war-time pals. He'd eat with them and then walk through the woods with her while Yevgeny Borisovich slept off a drunk. And on one such visit he said, "Olechka, I am going to become a dissident." He explained that if he became a dissident, we dumb Americans would invite him to read; the Soviet government would deny him a visa; the rest would follow. It was all calculated. He had a plan to become world famous: "Olechka, why would a girl like you stay with a poet who has an official dacha?"

Olga hid nothing from Yevgeny Borisovich. "Sapozhnikov was decent man," he said. "He never inquired—so long as I stayed with him. Of course, the authorities held that against him. For me, Yevgeny Borisovich protect Adam."

For a long time Michael thought there was no way Olga was going to stick with Sapozhnikov. Adam Plotznik was surely her true love. Sapozhnikov sounded gross, carnal; as Arthur had said, he was an apparatchik, a commissar. Where Adam's first poems came out in tiny editions or even cyclostyled, Yevgeny Borisovich was a public man with his collected works coming out in many horse-glue-bound volumes. Adam recited in Petersburg cafés or in private homes, Yevgeny Borisovich was a star, a man who read to thousands. People knew his poems by heart; they were taught in school. But today Adam had his Nobel and Yevgeny Borisovich was a nobody.

Michael was wrong.

Not so long after the meeting in Berlin Arthur had talked about, Sapozhnikov had fallen from grace, and from grace into drinking. Who ever knew why people fell into the black hole and disappeared? But Olga still allowed his soul to flow into her. In violent, sporadic bursts. Willing a baby. "He could not write any more. Every line was political mistake. Complicated thoughts clog his brain. He says it is true, he betrayed Soviet people. From mild attacks in Writers' Union to expulsion; from big Zis to small Zis to no Zis at all. They close his dacha 'for repairs'. How long before they arrest him? He beg me to denounce him. All accusations is true. He wanted to repent. 'What can I do?'

I ask him. He says, 'Save yourself. Inform on me. I don't mind, it's all over. But they'll get your Adam,' he say. 'They know all about him.' This is true. They put Adam in crazy place."

At some point like that she'd stop and Michael would go away: only to be called back the next morning, or the day after.

Once he brought up Arthur. She said peremptorily, "If Arthur want dead guests he should have them. They still live in his mind."

Olga, Michael thought, felt that life should be carefully punctuated. Like with a comma between each death. At the very least. That's why she'd suddenly stop. But always at the end she'd come back to Sapozhnikov. "One day," Michael said, "Olga threw away stockings and perfume and walked out of Sapozhnikov's apartment with nothing to her name. Why? Because she was in all of Plotznik's poems and Kremlin insiders knew that? To save Yevgeny Borisovich? Or to save herself, who'd always been as she said 'a good Soviet woman'? Adam was always waiting for her, and it was to Adam she went and to Adam she returned later in America. After Sapozhnikov died. The stories I heard were Adam stories; she told them to him and kept them alive that way. Until he was killed, of course: just when she needed him, needed *someone*, more than ever."

Always that bit of self-reproach. But he added: "All her 'mens' were faithful to her, to the end. Me included."

A certain intimacy arises

N o, Michael wasn't attached to his mother but
to his father. He had Leapman Sr's mannerisms, his body,
his awkwardness, his humdrum habits. (Leapman Sr had
been an insurance adjustor: no great distance between that
and the *Times*.) Hazel had been a flighty McMahon girl in
a large family of withdrawn sisters and hunky, football-
playing brothers, his aunts and uncles.

It was like a Sign, he said, when he found his old
Teaneck house-keys in his stud-box one morning. "I'd
simply *forgotten* her, what with Olga and Carmen," he said.
"You don't get forgiven for that."

It was some four months since the Plotznik service
when Michael decided to make up for his neglect. He took
the train down and—no taxi, no travelers expected in the

middle of the day—he strode from the station through the seasonally brown and leafless lawns and two-car garages of good old Teaneck. His galosh-covered shoes squelched from the rain; his portable snap-open umbrella was blown out by rude March winds; his thin hair, usually enthusiastic and curly, lay lank and flat against his cheeks. As for his mind, that part of him dwelled on his failures. A rotten son, he'd not even produced—even in the modest way that men do their duty—a blessed thing. Nothing, no heir, no grandchild, no continuity. He would be *nice*. As nice as it was possible to be with Hazel.

His first impressions were OK. When he let himself into what had been home ("Well! Look at what the cat's dragged in!" his mother said, laying her cards down) he found the aroma of spray-on wax and canned soup (chicken noodle) deeply alleviating. It told him there were and always had been excuses for his laches. He'd have to go through a tongue-lashing, but in the end he would always be forgiven. Like every only son.

Hazel wasn't a large woman by most standards—she was short and diffuse, like a spread thrown on an old sofa—but she had what all mothers have, a special, uterine claim on their sons' lives. Michael described it as "a debt I incurred at birth and could never pay off. The interest was greater than the capital, and I was always in arrears".

Her health was part of the debt. This one-time slip of a McMahon girl (which was how Michael remembered her from his youth) had a body which had steadily expanded over the last decade. Wrist and ankle, thigh and upper arm were all involved, but the middle of her body was outstripping the rest, and in Hazel's mind this was something her only son had done to her. Cancer was the result of stress, of disappointment, of sacrifice: all on his behalf. She'd risked her eternal soul and backslid from the church of her fathers into Episcopalianism for him, so he could go to Yale and Harvard and be a success. How had he repaid her?

He got a brief kiss on his high brow, then she put out another bowl and he sat down. "So, how are we feeling today? OK?"

"I don't complain," she said. "Dr Morgenstern says I have an erratic pulse. He wants me to lose weight. He thinks 'this' (laying a hand on her belly to indicate her imagined tumor) is just weight. Not that other thing. I should exercise: if I had a dog I could walk him." Hazel did not take long to get to familiar ground. Each of the women in Michael's life had her own obsession: Olga's past, Carmen's future (waiting for lightning to strike), Hazel's tumor. "They start inside you like nothing at all, you know," she said. "A rough spot like you might get on your skin. Then they take on a life of their own. You can kill them if you spot them early. Morgenstern's a young man, he's got a lot to learn."

"He checked it out?"

"I don't even ask him about that. What can *he* do? It's a punishment from God. Even you don't think of your mother any more. I suppose some woman's got her claws into you."

"I wish I could get down more often," he said. What with the *Times* and Arthur's papers, he was pushed. Also, he'd been working with a fascinating Russian woman. "Just because I can't get away more often doesn't mean I don't love you."

"What Russian woman's this?" she asked.

He countered: "How's the bridge?"

"Bridge. Thanks for your book. But don't try to distract me. Your mind's set on her, isn't it? That's what you came down to tell me. A mother can tell. You're finally getting married to someone you know I won't approve of. You haven't taken your galoshes off."

The soup was going to his head like wine. The house was overheated. It was like living in a winter coat. He looked down at his feet. At the puddle that had formed around them. "It's not like that at all." It was true that lately his dreams had been invaded by Olga, but they weren't always pleasant dreams. Recently Olga had made an appearance in the form of a Siren. One of those women who sang beautiful songs and all their sailors died. "It isn't what you think. It's not her, it's her *life*. She wants me to write it."

"So now you write up the living? I'm still here, you know. I take it she's young and good-looking?"

"No, Ma, she's an older woman."

"I knew it. A mother-figure!" She put down her spoon. Moments of ferocious energy like the one that followed would hit her sometimes: for instance when she faced the dummy and decided to finesse the enemy king. At cards she could be possessed.

He'd mentioned bridge, she began. Well her club—
Mondays, Wednesdays and Fridays (Sunday night
optional)—had ladies aplenty: ladies eager, divorced, spin-
dly, rich, earnest, many without fellas, the natural products
of neighbors, of school committees sat on and doctors'
offices sat in, clean, frank *American* women, not Commies,
not trash. What kind did he want? They were all just waiting
for him. Why just last week . . . "You've turned them all
down in the past, you'll turn them all down again, I know
you. You hate yourself, Michael Leapman," she said. "You
want to damage your constitution, which I handed you full
of health! You're *prejudiced.*"

"Against who?"

She had the cards automatically reshuffled and dealt
them out. "Against *everyone!*" she answered. It calmed her
down. "You're catching the 2.35? You never stay long.
Come again," she said, giving him a distracted kiss. "Does
she play bridge?"

He left her with four hands laid out.

All the way back in the train he carried on the argument with her: "You think I wouldn't like a normal life?
Who made me this way?" Just before his train bumped
under the Hudson to Penn Station, he had made up his
mind. His problem was the woman thing. Despite, or perhaps because of his marriage to Bunny, he had to admit
that women were *terra incognita* and he was no explorer.
Why not let things just happen? They happened to others,
didn't they? So when he left Penn station he walked towards
54th Street and Carmen's apartment. He still walked up and

down in front of her brownstone (there was a restaurant downstairs) for at least an hour: if she comes in the next ten minutes, the next five . . . She didn't come. He caught a documentary about Eskimos in MOMA. He rang her bell. Still no answer. He went into a bar and thought. Yes, this was a plea for asylum. The way he saw it, Ms Zinsser, young as she was, was consoling. And not *that* unlike a mother. A fine, patient young woman. Who knew? Michael thought. She might even play bridge.

He nearly missed her. He caught her coming out. "*¡Hombre, por fin!*" she said and took him in.

Her pad was tucked right behind the Museum of Modern Art. It was just the place for the seduction of Michael Leapman. Was it cold outside? Her lair was heated to the subtropical. Was his life cluttered? Her decor was what Leapman understood to be Zen. The walls were black, the floors of polished aluminum, and utilitarian objects of any kind, apart from a bed and cushions, were few. Was he hungry? Carmen was there: oversized and naked on the walls (courtesy of that painter fellow he'd met at Daphne's) but also in the flesh, cooking up a storm. And he was able to say to her all sorts of things he'd said to nobody else.

Halfway into the night—he had been talking about Olga luring men to their death—she said: "You want to make love to Olga?"

"No. No!"

"She doesn't even sleep in her apartment," Carmen said. "She goes to 22B next door. Nobody goes there but Mr Aprahamian."

"Plotznik? Well, *he* died, didn't he?"

But Michael stayed. Pretty much OK. It was always Sunday morning there. Carmen's bed was always warm, day and night. In a Japanese black silk peignoir, Carmen sang to herself. That was cool. And Carmen liked being a big girl, big as the sculptures in the MOMA back garden he could see from the back windows. She it was who said, rising from the bed like milk sloshing in a saucer, "*¡Ay, Hija!* These heavy genes! Ah well, Michael, you seem to like them."

Her story, too, was cool. She was the youngest of three sisters and *her* mother, Doña Lulu, still glowered at Leapman from Carmen's night-table, thick, dark and solid as a solitary tree. "I'm just like her," Carmen had said.

Made of the same stuff, was she? She too had a dresser with an assortment of silver and tortoise-shell combs, pins and all the other things you can stick in your hair? Her father was a chemist, a Social Democrat from Berlin. He emigrated before the war, married, lived in a pink house in the suburbs of Buenos Aires and built a business in cosmetics: until the Countess descended on workshops and bought him out. Or rather Mr Aprahamian did, Carmen said, who between poems and for old times' sake, did that sort of thing for Olga. "He could be very persuasive," Carmen reported. "I became, you know, a part of the deal."

If he was happy there, why did he tear himself away? She listened to idiot music: well, no girl is perfect.

But it wasn't that. It was going out for a walk the second Sunday of his stay on 54th Street. And winding up at Goldfarb's Deli. There a certain ache afflicted him: at the penetrating smell of hanging salami, the sight of potato salad yellowing in metal trays, the heady mix of steam rising, tea stewing, and cream soda sparkling behind green glass. After the sharp, red-nosed air, the Deli was just right. There he could observe, there he could think. He felt himself again.

The elderly ladies at their familiar table looked up hopefully as he walked in. They too were minus one of their own, the Countess. Without her, there was that much more space between the gherkins on their table, which gave Michael's nostalgia (was that truly what it was?) room to settle.

Perhaps he called his Ma and she said Carmen was far too young for him. Or Olga called him from wherever she was. In fact he couldn't bear to be without her. And by miracle, minutes later, there she was. As if she'd known he was waiting for her.

Elsewhere

The Countess had come back by train (she'd summoned Michael from the station) from somewhere cold. From where, she didn't say. By contrast the air inside Goldfarb's was thick and buttery. At first glance she looked in the pink: power-suited, smooth, athletic, and smart enough to tease—"You seem younger, Michael. You've been to Argentina?" But her heart just didn't seem to be in it. Deep shadows, like grief—they made her look younger yet, as though she'd just woken up from a lousy date—surrounded those emerald eyes: her life *elsewhere*, of which he was deeply jealous.

"Younger? I'm a wreck," he replied. Something disturbing had happened to him in the short walk from the BMT (73rd Street) to Goldfarb's. He was walking along and suddenly it was time to get up in Cambridge, Massachusetts and instead of being himself he was Bunny. There was the on-the-floor mattress and there was himself rubbing his eyes and rising groggily from it. In disorder. Next thing he knew he was (being Bunny) padding desultorily about the tiny egg-yolk yellow kitchen. His (her) fading, thin hair was rubber-banded into a bun and he or she was turning eggs in a pan. The toast burned in the toaster. Then Michael walked in: with this look on his face that said (meaning Bunny), "Oh, you're still here?" A few minutes later, as Michael watched him through the kitchen window the Bunny he'd become mounted her bike and pedalled bravely off to the Peabody: to deal with fossils or insect-remains.

All true. Most mornings he watched Bunny go off like that. He'd simply disregarded her. But where was Bunny *really* going? To her English instructor? He would find cantankerous notes, allegedly from this demon lover of hers: absent-mindedly (or *deliberately*) slipped into the phone book or scribbled on a shopping list as if saying, "You see? Someone loves me!" Being jealous was like biting into an unripe apple: everyone had an Elsewhere. At least, all the women he knew did. Olga did. Elsewhere was exactly where she'd just come from. Real or invented (for of course he'd started many a novel), the Elsewherians (like Carmen's vile painter or the instructor in the English department) quivered in his memory, waiting to be turned into something. Much more potent lovers than Michael, they stared him down from their quires of paper and said, "What, is this the best you can do with us?"

He couldn't say any of this to Olga, he realized. Olga

wasn't there. Olga didn't listen. Olga didn't want to hear anyone else. His soul was in turmoil. Couldn't she at least have asked why he felt a wreck? No. She was talking in her usual voice. He might as well not have been there. "Nineteen-Fifty-Something," she said. "Vladivostok-Nakhoda. Nakhoda-Vancouver. From Vancouver across Canada. Arthur fix it so I have Refugee status. Imagine how I feel landing in America."

Imagine how she felt? How about her imagining how *he* felt? And what was this hurry? Her life was turning into shorthand: "I had suitcase and one hundred bucks collected from consul in Shanghai. I sent money back with first check from business. It was crazy trip. I had seen movies in Khabarovsk. Outside train window I expect Indians and arrows. Over Rockies, then thousands of miles of snow." Khabarovsk? Shanghai?

When Bunny was taken away with her mother, Michael felt his mind had been stripped down and cleaned. He had felt sharp, equal to anything. Then he began to hear from her once or twice a year. A postcard. Messages as brief as Olga's: "I hate you." "I am not nice."

"Where have you been?" he asked Olga. "Why won't you tell me?"

"Because it make no difference."

She was willing to hand him her life, but she denied him any part in it. This was just about the last time he saw her before Arthur's party, and still she *had* to deliver herself of her story. It was something he had to undergo. Like an ordeal. And then he might be worthy.

At the same time he noticed that by some peculiar trick, her life was becoming more and more remote from her. In their time, people like Adam disappeared from her story and became distant moons. You could see a whole sky, but no close-ups. Every tale had its end.

He now learned that after walking away from her French perfume and Yevgeni Borisovich's violet eyes, she went back to Adam. He was flush. This was the heyday of Gumbel Aprahamian, the entrepreneur in wholesale pilchards. And a lot else. He had his whole war-time black-market gang with him. "Underground," she said. "Making big pay-offs." They were: "Social parasites, *kapitalisti*. Money by day, poetry reading at night: it couldn't last."

In fact, he and she were walking across the Litteiny Most one afternoon when the police drove up alongside and picked Adam up. She screamed, but "good Soviet people" had become oblivious to alarm. Anything that happened was, by definition, normal. "In Pennsylvania, they leave Adam on the sidewalk in his blood. Is same thing. They took Adam off to crazy house after trial."

"They didn't arrest you?"

She sipped her tea. "Why they take me, Michael? They already *have* me."

Michael couldn't avoid the contrast between those lives and his own. How could Russia and America ever mix? Even people who did suffer—and he hadn't—people like Bunny, couldn't measure up. Bunny had spent twenty years in a loony bin. That meant she wore a faded smock and mooned about on tranquillizers. Whereas for two years

Adam's bunk was one bunk away from an ex-Minister of Health who sat on the foot of his bed and ate his own excrement: with knife, fork, napkin and finicky manners. And what did they put in Adam's veins? Such people could beat you over the head with their sufferings. You couldn't ever suffer enough for them. Did that mean you should go out looking for ways to be hurt?

Eventually Olga and the "boys" (in raspberry waist-coats and azure shoes) rescued Adam: with pilfered release forms, official stamps and money. Said Olga: "This is what is left out about Adam. One side is hoodlum, con-man; the other is poet. He was *fun*. We have fun. For a while."

Michael wasn't fun. The good thing about that, he thought, was that he was still alive.

"They catch the boys for stealing truck," she said. "Adam is gone. I get postcard from Tiblisi. Story going round is he snitch on them and run with the money, I hear. I don't see him again until America."

"Did Arthur bring *him* out?"

"I tell you. Ar-*tur* is jealous of Adam. My guys believe in God. You don't believe in God, there is no Upstairs. Everything is Downstairs, here. Sure Ar-*tur* fascinate me. You find butterfly in your glass, you're fascinated. Forty years go by now since Yevgeny Borisovich. My babies are dead, now my guys are all dead. I'm like an envelope some-one seal up. I tell you truth, Michael. I don't want to live forever. What's left to tell you or anyone?"

The hog-bristle merman

For several mornings on his cross-town bus Michael caught glimpses of the Countess's high windows, sometimes glinting with sunlight, gunmetal and then painfully sharp orange: like a ray-gun. March had blown in; a freak thaw followed. He waited for his summons. Up there was the remainder of Olga's story: before Olga came, and Adam came, to America—the place they'd dreamed about when young. Before they both made their good fortune and reputation. When Adam had slipped away to Tiflis under a cloud, Yevgeny Borisovich was sent to manage an electricity plant in Siberia, and Olga must have been all alone in Saint Petersburg. Sending letters to Arthur: help me.

A "sealed envelope", she called herself. Do not open me up. Like all obits, Michael's concentrated on the life; far more interesting was the ending. Michael hated unfinished stories. People would tell him great stories, and always he asked: "And what happened then?"

At just about the time when he first met Olga, the mail had brought him a "We thought you might want to know" letter from Sacramento. Her mother wrote that Alison (Bunny) had passed on. No how, no why. Did he dare write back and ask if Bunny had a hand in it? Leapt out a window perhaps? Did he want to know? It had been a shock: like the death of his friend Bart in Florida as he set out to play tennis. He couldn't understand either. For Michael, life was rewarding. It was full of ideas, of fresh air, of the mysteries of women—he couldn't have made an inventory, but they were all preferable to such a stupid end as death.

He wrote Bunny's mother back a conventional letter: the loss of an only child, she should think of it as a deliverance for Bunny. To think some people—parachute-jumpers, drunk-drivers, and people like Bunny who hated themselves—go looking for death! Michael didn't even like skiing, sledding or roller-blading or anything similar. After spending so much time managing to stay upright, why risk falling over? Think of the time human beings spent learning to *live*. There were stoics like Mr Leapman Sr who could take it (life) or leave it—but what did indifference offer that was so much sexier than living?

Repeating the same journey after work, light lasting now until nearly five, most times he wound up sitting in Goldfarb's Deli waiting for Olga to show up. He didn't want to go home; it was no longer *safe*. It was safe with Isidora, the one-time Met constumière (Frizzy-Top); Mrs Loeb (The Daily Bagel), who lived on a patent used for guided missile direction-finding; and Francine (Mrs Brown-Spot), who had greedy eyes and a body that had never filled out. They were survivors and relished the fact. But how to explain his state of mind to them.

This they pre-empted. "You should be old like us," Isidora Frizzy-Top said. "The Countess is so young!"

"But everyone dies round her," Leapman said as tactfully as he could.

"So?" put in Francine. "That's normal. You get to be like one of those stones on the beach. Your age, the stone's buried in sand, right? You're comfortable, you can hide. Bit by bit the sand's washed away . . ."

"Your friends go, your enemies go," said Mrs Loeb.

"When they're all gone you're the only stone around."

"And that's not scary?" he asked.

Isidora said, "The only thing a stone's got to worry about is loneliness."

"That's why we get together."

Then, right there in the Deli, like an act of God, who controlled the *life*-rays, came the call from Olga. To come up, please. Right now, if he could. "I have Adam's wallet," she said. "Police send it. Michael, I have no time. Olga is too old to keep souvenirs. I think I finish story." Again she sounded in a hurry, wild. But what about?

He arrived out of breath, and right away, the elevator door shutting behind him—her long hair undone in her

haste as he'd never seen her before—she handed him a scrap
of paper that had been among Plotznik's credit cards:

> *. . . the hog-bristle merman,*
> *he swam and he swam and he swam . . .*

The lines must have been a fragment of his last poem-to-be,
she said. The hog-bristles were Yevgeny Borisovich's and
one day he did swim and swim and that was that.
"Michael," she said. "You don't understand despair. Is not
American characteristic. Here, holes get filled in: witness
streets. People here fix."

"You're not OK," Michael said. "Why won't you let
me help?" Bunny had talked the way Olga now talked: in a
hurry to be done with it. Life, her sentences, him. Whatever.
"Why do you tell me these stories? What do you want out
of life?"

"Nothing. I told you. I've had my life. Please, sit
down. Just listen. I want to talk about love. And being
loyal. From long ago. Is about Yevgeny Borisovich.

"He was a man with powerful needs. This is 1951 or
1952. He write me many letter asking me to come to
Khabarovsk. Everything go bust all around. I have no job,
I have no man, I have no money. I want normal life like
other people, not crazy guys, not heroism. I don't want to
be somebody's muse; I want to be me. I want love like no
girl today still dream of: frilly-aproned love, domesticity,
curtain with splashy, yellow flowers, seeing child off to
school. No one ever offer me that."

Yevgeny Borisovich had offered the most far-away curtains in the world.

"I am past thirty," she said. "Is time to think of new
life. Forget Adam. Make baby. I go to Khabarovsk because
I love him. Ten days on train. Khabarovsk is up on hill.
Below is river Amur, downstream is other countries, China,
the Koreas."

She married Sapozhnikov, a ruined man. On a day
with sullen, yellow, mosquito-rich sunshine. "Spring is sudden," she said. There was still snow on the ground: only it
was melting like ice cream, the soil couldn't take all the
water. At the House of Soviet Weddings Olga was in a new
pale blue frock; the ex-Deputy Minister sweated in a thick,
dark blue suit. A week later they hired a car and went to a
village some way away where there was still a priest.

Marrying Yevgeny Borisovich properly was the Chris-
tian thing to do. "We find God together," she said. "I have
faith God will help me. Captain must have been happy.
He never go to bed without prayer. Yevgeny Borisovich still
have lovely hair. Maybe violet of his eyes is darker: who
knows at night during power cuts? But God can also be
cruel. A year go by, a winter worse than in siege; it rain
one month, it blow and freeze for five. Still I am not
pregnant. I tell Yevgeny Borisovich he should beat me for
failing him. Instead he cry. He cry and cry. His current
fail: when it counted. I did what I could for him. I've done
that for every man in my life. But I see I am not going to
get curtains. Was God's will.

"Don't ask me what he was afraid of. Maybe when

he's young he gets shiny train set; maybe he break it first day. I hope Yevgeny Borisovich forgive me, because while he was at power plant, I make deal with Chinese business man who takes people across border to Port Arthur and off I go on back his motorcycle."

They stopped five nights on the way. She lay on a straw mattress on the floor, he hanged up a yellow leer, she said, somewhere in the vicinity of the naked bulb in the ceiling. Then one day in Port Arthur she saw an old *Pravda.* "There it was," she said. "How he go swim. Several dozen people see him on beach in Nakhoda on Japan Sea. No one swim there. They see him swim straight out to sea. That is why Adam write:

> ... *the hog-bristle merman,*
> *he swam and he swam and he swam ...*

I don't know why Adam was thinking about that.

"We have one last thing to do," she now said. "I marry Arthur. We make him happy. At last I give somebody life again. A little. No?"

What Michael failed to see was the *cost.* He said, "It could have been an old piece of paper. It could have been in his wallet for years." As if he had the box-score of a game he'd caught at Yale: Leapman, M., c.; ab, 4; h, 2. Neither very good nor a complete failure. Stuck in his wallet: a bit of his youth he couldn't bear to throw out.

Arthur's last fling

The weather-man said the rain they were driving through would "turn to snow some time after midnight". He didn't say how much. Vladimir up front told Olga she was *crazy* to be going up there into the wilds—"Look what happened to Mr Aprahamian." There were plenty of portents. Who was in the mood for a party?

Olga's sables, spreading out on the back seat next to Michael, gave off an animal heat, but she herself was remote: she swallowed pills, twice. What did she have, a headache? Once she asked about the musicians who were supposed to be somewhere behind them in their taxi; she catnapped. Only Carmen, slowly knocking back champagne, talked at all: she said she couldn't recall ever having been on an unlit road before. And "this *rural* weather," she said. *"¡Jesus*

Maria!" Maybe the Trio, used to Manhattan, would get lost "with all this green and trees".

Crossing the Tappan Zee Bridge Michael got a glimpse of the Hudson below: pretty terrifying: light on its banks, dark in the middle, and in between wet as inter-crural space. He had visions of his mother chugging up from Teaneck in her old green Dodge. "I lied to her," he told Carmen. "I told her I'd fix her up with a bridge game. 'Bring a friend,' I said. I mean, you can't have a party without *people.* Maybe she can pass herself off as Clara Malraux or someone. I thought it would cheer her up."

Somewhere around Poughkeepsie, Carmen was still talking. Pretty much talking to herself. "She was trying to make *conversation* in a vacuum," Michael explained later. He could still sniff her on his clothes, but his mind was on other things. He felt like a phoney. Though he didn't believe for a second Olga intended to become Mrs Schoenheit, he didn't feel like taking part in a *lie.* How could he play along with giving Arthur an illusion of happiness?

Irena Fyvel greeted them at the front door of the Mount Zion Hotel and Resort. (She was a motherly woman, but not soft. Embracing her, you bumped into costume jewelry, whalebone and her anxious Capital Letters.) No, Arthur hadn't Arrived, nor Michael's Mother: "You know how long he takes Dressing. Enough people here, he won't know the difference. Like a crowd-scene on stage, soldiers marching into the wings and back the other side."

She showed them round the Imperial Ballroom, a dark place with a few disconsolate out-of-season waiters waiting, and plate-glass Panoramic Windows that gave out on the howling night. In the middle of the dance floor was Arthur's inscribed ("To Arthur from Averill") wing-chair which Irena explained had been brought over that morning: "So Arthur feels At Home."

Then the Trio arrived: Sasha the mournful cellist, Jules (Jooley) on the fiddle, and serious Miriam the pianist. They poured out of their taxi into a wall of rain (already speckled with snow) that blew their umbrellas inside out. No longer young virtuosi in Saint Petersburg, they ran into the lobby, shedding soaked, belted overcoats and wet, soft black hats, clutching their ribs and instrument cases.

Soon after, the dependable Green Dodge (it had been Michael Leapman Sr's car for years) drove up and Michael went out to extract his mother, to push her before him up the slope under his umbrella. Then at the front door, before she could say the weather had cancer, he said, "Ma, I'd like you to meet Olga. Olga Frunze. Olga, my mother. Oh, and Mrs Fyvel. This is her place."

"Pleased to meetcha. Where's the bridge, Michael? We got four? Assuming you still remember how I taught you to play." She turned to Olga and said, "I don't travel much. You know, pain," she said to Olga. "I've got a cancer."

Already pale, Olga went whiter. She hated physical imperfection. Michael took his mother aside. "I hope you haven't eaten on the road."

"In my condition?" She looked around her furtively. "Pardon my manners," she said. "That's your Russian you're so crazy about?"

"There's a very good dinner, Ma. Anything you want, it's on the house. Then we'll play."

"*Is* she?"

Mothers required patience, and prudence. They loved their children more than they were loved in return, which is the stuff of heartbreak.

"It's a party," he told her. "To make Arthur—You remember him, my old professor, Professor Schoenfeld—happy."

"It's his birthday or something?"

"Er, no. A . . . well, a kind of tribute to his Life. Look, don't worry if he calls you Madame Malraux or talks to you in French. You just nod, OK?"

"You mean you're not telling me the whole truth, that's what it is. You never did. A tribute to his life, huh? I'd like one of those. In case you think you're it, forget it." She cast a look over her heavily-padded shoulder at Olga. "She looks healthy anyway. Sometimes the cancer doesn't show. You know she can't be your mother, don't you Michael? You've got one of those."

Teetering on high heels, her black wool dress soaking up the rain, Ms Zinsser held a bright red golfing umbrella over Arthur as he trudged up the drive. The illusion was perfect. He was trussed up for the occasion in *frac*, crisp white tie and opera cape. His shiny glasses looked circumspectly down, but the beau of the ball—high brow and a thin surface of curly, discolored hair, breast sparkling with the Elephant of Siam, a Bolivar, a Southern Cross—looked spiffy. When he laughed at something Carmen said in the lobby he went jingle-jangle-jingle. But was this apparition Arthur?

Carmen took a moment to shake out her umbrella. "Hey," she said urgently to Michael. "I don't think he knows where he is. He called me 'Maggie' and squeezed my arm. 'The same perfume as always?' Then he says, 'This trouble seeing is just temporary.' *Hombre*, this shouldn't be happening."

But it was. The Trio played *Hail to the Chief* twice because Arthur was taking his time, bowing left and right to waiters and busboys (including a few locals Irena had invited, Mrs Schwarz of the Dry Cleaners and two uniformed State Policeman who'd been pressed into service in return for a free meal) as if they were foreign ministers or valued ambassadors. The state cops might have been *presidentes*. Arthur introduced Carmen to all sorts of people who weren't there. Was that Susan Sontag? One of the Bouvier girls? This was supposed to make Arthur happy? What would happen when he woke up from this daze? What if he didn't?

"You can't do this," Michael said to Olga. He got that blank Elsewhere look in return. Was she drunk? Loaded up on pills? "Who is that with Irena?" she asked.

It was his mother, waiting for her turn with Arthur, concentrating on lobster.

"Little short back legs, Malraux," he heard Arthur say to Miriam the pianist. "The way he got up on t-tippy-toe around people taller than he was. Very *aviator*, the ingratiating, ingratiating . . . arrogant look, those little dark, beady eyes. Yap, yap, Indochina, who he knew in Shanghai, flying in the S-Spanish Civil War. W-would you trust a man who'd been *only* to places where no one could check up on his story?"

"Arthur's not nuts," Michael said to Carmen. "He's just stuck in the past. Is Olga really going to marry him?"

"First I heard of it. She doesn't tell me things like that," said Carmen, who was not quite upright. "The Countess is drinking."

"She is also feeding on pills. Steadying her nerves?"

"No. *Duele.* She's in pain."

"What from?"

"If I ever get married, I am going to pick a man who has all the things inside you expect. Pumps, bellows and diaphragms, muscles and cartilage, brain tissue. Working all the time. What do you think of Sasha the cellist?"

Irena, between managing people for Arthur to talk to, said to Olga: "You never had Love-Life like I had with my Emmanuel Davidovich."

They were all drunk, Michael thought. They were all in pain. Every one of them Elsewhere.

Just then, the Trio struck up a fanfare. This was followed by a Slavic version of "Happy Birthday to You". Arthur stirred on his throne.

Irena delved into her handbag. "Silence Everyone!" she called out with a sheaf of perforated telegrams in her hand. She then read messages: from Teddy and from Ethel; from ex-Presidents George and Gerald; from Jimmy and Roslyn with Wishes for World Peace; from Babs ("Nothing much to be done for *her* complexion," Olga muttered) and members of Havana-in-Hollywood, Robert Redford and the rest; and of course Hillary as well as Bill, as if her secretary and her husband's didn't talk.

Michael sat with Carmen while the messages were read out, each to applause. It took him a moment to work out why she was grinning. Pride of authorship was why. Those greetings were her work. Invented. The whole place. All of them. "*Muy* smart," he said.

"I think Sasha's cute. Cute and soulful."

Olga had made her way carefully over to Arthur and Michael followed. Arthur recognized her, only he asked her to sit down next to him where there was no chair. "How kind everyone is," Arthur said. "I'm having a little trouble with my eyes. Hello Michael. Where's Bunny?"

Irena came up fussily. "Can't you see he has an urgent Need of Nature?"

In the Men's Room—pine-paneled, basin-brightened—under the framed self-projecting smiles and shiny hair of Milton Berle, Lenny Bruce, Zero Mostel, Ida Kaminska, Maurice Schwartz (all save the last in their prime), Arthur stared blankly down into the porcelain, fiddling with the elaborate buttons of his trousers. Olga came back to life. "You want me to go away?" she said. "I didn't know your eyes were so bad."

"No, no, stay. Am I in the right place?"

She told him his shirt was in the way. Arthur's lower lip quivered. He was reassembling himself with difficulty. It moved her. "Here, I help you," she said.

"So many people just disappear, my dear," he mumbled. "Where have you been?"

It was a shock to Michael how quickly brains went and how far. Mr Leapman Sr had declined by fits and starts, this was headlong. How *did* one hold on to one's marbles? Or was it all OK because one didn't know they'd gone? Tears welled up in Arthur's eyes. He must have known. There might have been lucid moments, but at present there was a whole Viet Nam in the mechanisms of fastening together the critical aperture in his pants.

Arthur said, "Can you explain any of this to me, Michael?"

It wasn't that Michael couldn't, he just wouldn't have.

"There, you look fine," Olga said, straightening Arthur's waistcoat and grinning unsteadily. "Come on Michael, we better go back. You know how people talk."

They delivered him back to the ballroom where Michael's mother, with too much of the champagne Irena was pouring into her, sat angrily shuffling four brand-new packs of cards, and where Arthur, suddenly shedding Olga's arm (a gesture of pride?), now held court with the musicians, talking a mile a minute, first running his fingers over music-stands and sheet-music and then, when a ray of sunlight slanted down into his mind, sitting down at Miriam's piano and knocking off some show tunes.

A little later Arthur seemed think he was at the White House playing tennis. He had arranged the musicians as if they were playing doubles, and now he demonstrated different services, holding an imaginary ball in one hand and racquet in the other: those of Dick and Pierre and an unidentified State Department man who cheated. It was all obviously real to him, because the exertion caused him to break out into a sweat.

The Greeks had it right: heart-break, head-break.

Irena had the presence of mind to sail up the middle of the ballroom with a towel in her hand. "Dry yourself off, Arthur," she said. "That's enough tennis for now. It's time to dance." But in Arthur's mind, Doctor Max was somewhere upstairs feeding the President amphetamines and animal glands. First he wanted to go up there: he had some urgent message for the President. Then he half-collapsed back on the piano-bench and started saying "Olga, Olga. Who are all these awful people, Olga? Where are we?"

"Olechka," Irena said, "Come and see. It's Snowing."

They all went over to one of the big windows. The flakes were thick, heavy, and brutal: like bits of bad dreams you remember in the morning. "What if we have to stay the night?" Jooley asked.

Miriam was slumped over the piano playing something melancholy to which Carmen and Sasha were dancing, locked in embrace.

Olga felt Arthur's head. It was hot and wet. She said, "You want to get out of monkey-suit." She tried to open the window: without success. So she made Arthur lean against the plate-glass cold. Below, as the snow drifted, the four of them, now joined by a drowsy Hazel Leapman, cards in hand, could see a field that sloped down and away, the recreation area which was whitened out, and bits of blue canvas on the half-Olympic size pool.

Arthur shook his head at the view with the uncertainty of age, aware something was wrong. "No one came," he said to Olga. "No one at all. Just you."

"Nonsense," Olga said. She led him out on to the dance-floor. His face shining, his left arm high over his head to clasp Olga's, his movements elegant and natural, he seemed to think this was what should have happened long ago. And Olga? Olga looked blissful.

That was the image he carried in his head as he passed out. And when he came to, maybe an hour later, the first thing he saw was Carmen. She looked dazed, she carried her high-heeled shoes in her hands, her black hair was hastily pinned back in lumps, like plastic bags tossed on a dump, her black dress was askew, her face de-painted. With her, trailing behind, looking guilty, was Sasha. "We take Señorita home," he said.

"What, in this snow?"

They went anyway.

Michael saw his mother stretched out on a sofa in Irena's office. There was not a waiter in sight. A few minutes went by and he heard door-clunks, winsome laughter. Irena and Olga, the last ones there, were sitting at a table, talking to each other in Russian. Olga's head rested on her arms: Irena's rigid corsetry kept her upright. Michael went over and stood by their table. Irena looked up at him and switched to English. "What do we do Now?" she asked.

"*Chto delyaem?*" said Olga without lifting her head.

"*Ne znayu.* Michael? Is hard to leave this life which is so beautiful. My little darlings."

"Lev Davidovich was a fine man, too," said Irena. "I was a long time Happy."

All three of them thought Carmen and the musicians had taken Arthur back down to Sleepy Hollow.

The Abominable Snowman

Just about at dawn, a slate-grey, lightless affair, with the snow now falling in more brittle and precipitous flakes, Michael and Olga were both woken up in their rooms by the same ice-laden gutter abruptly breaking off the eaves just above their windows. It was end-of-the-world icy: no heat, no light, desolate, silent. They met—she wrapped in a blanket (why not her sables?) and shivering, he in his overcoat—in the corridor that ran past their rooms. What she wore under her blanket, some sort of garment, was nondescript, and against the pale window at the end of the corridor, she looked tall, scrubbed, young and frail, not alarming at all. Michael hadn't before noticed she had tiny, neat feet.

She didn't say a thing. She just looked at him. Or

invited him to look at her. To see she was defenseless. Everybody was asleep, he thought. He said, "My mother will panic, she won't know where she is."

"No, is just snow. Snow is good. Come see. Is Spring. April Fool." She took his hand and led him to the window at the end of the hall. The snow had obliterated every detail: the possibility of deck-chairs, the lawns they knew were there, underneath, the pool and its blue tarp, all the couples who'd been and gone. Michael said he understood for the first time how Olga felt. Like the weighted-down trees, the occasional fence-posts, the bright red top of a playground swing, she felt the very last of her kind. She was in an exile from her whole life deeper than anything an ordinary emigré might feel, he thought. Everything familiar around her and everything she had known or learned had receded—been lost, misplaced by accident or misadventure, taken away through malice—and no one she knew had sufficient energy to care. This was the way the old felt. And that was why they shed, they let go.

She said: "*Dietski Dom* is in Ekaterinograd. I wake up like this many mornings." She shivered. "Don't be afraid," she said, kissing him little-girl lightly on the cheek. "There is nothing extraordinary about Olga. Your mother is OK, Olga is OK, Mr Leapman is very much OK. Mr Leapman, he *listen*."

Michael thought what she was saying was that you went out of the world as innocent as you came in. You died when you had too many memories and you had to let them go. And when you let them go, it was like letting a bird fly out of your hand. That was when you were ready.

They stood there some minutes and then both of them went back to bed.

Michael read the book he'd brought with him – *The end of Beau Brummel* – in the cold. *He greeted them, these relicts of his thought. He kissed the ladies' hands. And when his world was full of those spooks, who came next? Reason. Suddenly. The poor man saw through the illusions; and into his madness. Then he would fall into one of the many unoccupied chairs, and one found him weeping there.*

When they gathered for breakfast (they still had gas) something had changed in Olga. Again.

Only Irena had fresh clothes. The rest of them— the stranded staff, the guests, those "relicts" of Arthur's thought—stood about or sat at table in what they'd worn the night before. Whenever someone finished a plate Olga mechanically cleared up, taking dishes back out to the kitchen.

"What are you Doing?" asked Irena sharply in Russian, and Olga sat down again with her hands folded in her lap. "You think you are still working for Mexicans?" She started pulling back the ballroom curtains. "Look everybody," she said. "Snow is still Falling. Lines are still Down. Who knows if you Get Out!"

Michael said he wondered if the musicians had made it.

"Ms Zinsser tell me to give them chains I keep in back," Vladimir said to Olga in slow, dignified Russian. (Where had he been the night before? Michael didn't remember seeing him.) Irena translated for Leapman. "I thought was your order, Countess. I take shovel and dig now."

Olga looked right through him. Vladimir shrugged.

"So you saw them off. And the Professor was with them?" Irena asked, this time in English.

"How else I have shovel back?" said Vladimir. "They cannot take car down to Professor house. They borrow shovel too."

"And Professor, he made it Home?" she persisted.

Vladimir replied that the Professor's stove had been out and they had even re-lit it.

It must have been around two or three in the afternoon when he went out to see Arthur. Those who remember the April Fool blizzard will know what it was like—as the snow diminished and the cold deepened—for Michael to make his way out the foot-wide path Vladimir had opened up to the limo, then through the drifts; to trudge down an invisible driveway to the unploughed main road on which only an occasional vehicle had made its way; and then in faltering light to find his way down through the thick shrubs to Arthur's cottage, whose chimney, he said, he could just make out, and from which no smoke rose.

Arthur was dressed in the kinds of duds kids drag out of the attic to dress the Snowman in: over his tails and boiled shirt, a long woolly scarf, a discarded jacket, a wool cap. The musicians had taken Arthur home; they'd dressed him warmly; they'd lit his fire. Then for some reason he'd decided to go out, or he'd gone out of the house by mistake and started up his path toward the main road. But he'd toppled. There had been no one around to call.

Michael found him on his back with two stiff arms stuck out of a snowbank some ten yards from the house. His glasses were adrift nearby, all powdery.

Arthur had named Michael executor. The formalities, the inquest and Arthur's funeral took a week. It was Michael who decided the funeral would be private and local. Then he went back to New York.

Olga called him immediately. "I have been calling for days," she said.

Not a word about Arthur. She said she was tired. She wanted to be alone that night. She wanted to sleep and sleep. "I think I have no more stories. God will look after me," she said. But Michael was to come the next morning, early. She said, "I think I leave early as airplanes. You come when you want. The best time in New York is just before light. I can see first planes out of La Guardia. They climb up and blink and it's all black all around. You see things so clearly."

Through the Looking-Glass

Just as Michael's fallen asleep, or so it seems, the alarm goes off at Carmen's where he's been cuddled needily for much of the night. He untangles himself from sheets and Argentina's gentle hillocks and plains, and goes to the window—by full moonlight the sculptures in MOMA's back garden have an eerie post-mortem gleam. He ransacks her disheveled drawers for a sweater he knows he left in her apartment a month ago, finally finds it and pulls it over his wiry hair and glasses, and says, "*¿Un cafecito?*"

It has given him heartache for much of the night to think of her in the Mount Zion lobby with Sasha the sheepish, soulful cellist. Now, though he pauses to admire how Carmen, rising from her sheets, copes with every desire, his mind is hardly made up. "Thank you," he says.

Soon the pump of her coffee machine groans. She knows how many sugars he needs (two); she stirs for him with a tiny spoon. What more can she do? They have talked Olga out until the small hours. For Carmen has her stated views: Michael has a hang-up about proletarian women. *¡Ay que sí!* His wife was from Sacramento! He had shown Carmen his only photo of Bunny. Bunny was patting a dog. She looked sad and the dog looked very sad. "Michael likes orphans. He doesn't understand people until they're *dead*! You think (Zhou think?) a girl like me can make him live?"

He says, "I have to go up first thing. Olga's off somewhere again. I owe her that."

Carmen says, "If you want, you go. I'm not going anywhere."

He travels uptown through warm tunnels in the city's bowels on one of the earliest BMT trains. It is mid-April. Only patches of snow remain, heaped up against brick walls, on roofs, on the sunless northern extremities of vacant lots. Only newspaper trucks are about. Shivery cats arch their backs against a wind that is still chill.

In the warm lobby of Olga's block with its 24-hour security, a guard leads him back to the elevator that is Olga's only, and opens up a brass panel with two separate keys, revealing alarms and controls that he disarms. "The Countess said she was expecting you and the door would be open. If it isn't, I'm afraid I cannot help you. There is no bell and I don't have a key."

Now the elevator rises swiftly and delivers him twenty-two flights up. It opens up both its doors and reveals two more behind. One Michael knows—He's been there often: coaxed, lured by Olga's siren-song. Back there Arthur's no-longer-needed invitations lie stockpiled on a table.

This door he pushes, but it doesn't budge. He pushes the other and it silently gives way. The cold that comes rushing towards him—there must be an open window somewhere—is well-traveled. On its way here it has visited Saint Petersburg and Siberia.

He is in an ante-chamber, a sort of vestibule, empty but for a single suitcase. Because Olga is going somewhere; because she thinks she will leave, as early as airplanes. This room is high but small. The cold rises through his feet; so does doubt. It's the early morning: Olga's time.

There is no light in here. In fact the darkness is from before electricity. In New York that's odd. In the city things hum and whir. Always there's a dependable rush from refrigerators; bells jangle, hair-dryers are to be heard at all hours and faxes unwind. "Olga?"

All there is, is a sort of distant glimmer. He can just make out a couple of rooms to his right. They seem to be crowded with very black shapes, which might be furniture. As his eyes adjust and he walks cautiously on carpets that once were brightly-colored but are now thick with dust, he touches beds, commodes, high-backed chairs on which gents' trousers are draped, he makes out a further room. Perhaps the rooms are endless. The late Adam Plotznik may be here writing poems in the dark. Unmistakably, however, these rooms were once, long ago, inhabited. He walks among the dead.

He steps into this further room. His impression is that it is hung with cloths, or perhaps curtains. He peers uncertainly at what seem to be oval frames on the walls. There is also something gilt like a cage, and a smell, mingled with perfume, that might once have been cigar smoke. Every wall he touches to feel his way is cold. The paper is damp, and in places peeling.

There is a faint glimmer, but where is it coming from? It is a grey and unhappy memory of light.

At Harvard he is rising early in the morning, has cigarettes on his breath, and winter is going to be endless. Twenty years later he feels the same anxiety he felt almost every day in Cambridge while Bunny was going to pieces. Somewhere in this morning dusk Bunny lurks. She is about to open up her bathrobe to expose herself; she who almost never wears make-up appears with lips painted a bright and glistening red; or she frowns in the kitchen and explains bleakly how she is pregnant, but not by him, and what should they do about it? Standing there in the semi-dark he feels Bunny's cold, grey eyes contemplating him and wishing him dead. Or perhaps this is later, when she'd gone, and there's the blight of her few dresses hanging in the closet without anyone in them. In the silence, Michael addresses Bunny: "Do you understand? *I should not be here.*"

Nonetheless, he has a duty and he pushes Bunny into the back of his mind. He's given his word. Arthur's had his spread—six column-inches on Page One (Tributes inside). The office can wait; the dead can wait. Michael thinks: no more writing about the dead. He has yet to absorb the death of Arthur. The trio is still playing, the medals remain pinned to Arthur's breast, Arthur's arms still breast-stroke through the high drift.

But soon, he thinks, perhaps in an hour or so, it will be light. Already he can hear the city far below: the awful busses, the roar of their leaving their stops, the whir of a garbage truck.

Somewhere, here, Olga is waiting for him. He knows that for a fact.

A queer lassitude overtakes him. It is something like an afternoon ennui, in which the wind wanders without direction or purpose, a vague sadness which he has read somewhere particularly afflicts the solitary. Yet the longer he remains silent, the more he is an intruder.

"Olga?" he calls out. No answer. A little louder: "Olga?" Her silence reassures him. It has to mean she is still asleep.

Or it means she is already gone. "Olga!"

He is disoriented. This apartment should be the mirror of the one he knows, but it is nothing like it. Somewhere (but which way?) there has to be the equivalent of Olga's bedroom and her study, into which Carmen would disappear. Here at least there are, he finds out by fumbling, a pair of old-fashioned light switches, little copper switches such as he's seen in European hotels. None of them work.

Suddenly, as he stands in the door, about to call Olga again, a light goes on behind a transom of frosted glass to his right. Just long enough for him to see a bundle of bedding halfway up. A toilet flushes, very loudly. Then the light goes off.

His hand shaking, he lights a cigarette. "Olga?" Olga must be rising, dressing somewhere back there.

Sometime later, back in the room, waiting—What else can he do? In movies and dreams time is imprecise—he finds himself at a window and tugging at cloth. A handful comes off in his hand, and then another as he fights with the drapes, a great swath of which falls over his head and shoulders. He tears at the linings, which came off their rings, only to leave tar-paper that has been glued to the window since the beginning of time. With his keys he scratches at the paper, succeeding only in opening up a tiny hole that gives onto darkness.

Finally, exhausted, he sits down and lights three matches in succession. In their flickering light he catches a glimpse of Vladimir Ilych Lenin in an oval frame. When he next looks up, the room is resolving itself by degrees, like photographic paper in a bath. What he's seen as a flash of gilt becomes a bird-cage draped with a mantilla. By his side, on a little round table, are two bottles, one big and one small. Both are empty. The big one turns out to be Olga's favorite green vodka, the herbs in it still moist.

He hears a plane fly by. Then another. He knows where he is now. New York may be out there beyond the tar-papered window, but here he is hard by the Yekaterinsky Sad in Peter, and this is the Captain's apartment, more properly his mother's, taken over by Doña Mercedes, the assassination instructor. He thinks, "I have but to go out the door, turn right, and I'll find Olga sleeping on her trunk."

He lights a cigarette with a match he finds in the kitchen. The smoke curls into a limitless grey that's worked its way over here from the Neva, and he walks confidently by her, for he's pretty sure she won't wake up. He knows the geography of the place. There's the kitchen where the Mexicans' laundry was pounded; and further on, the second maid's room, with its window always open. That is where the cold has been coming from. It will contain the Captain's globe and his narrow cot.

There is also a letter which has fallen out of her hand onto the floor. Her hand has been shielding her eyes. Her mouth is slightly open, her teeth bright and even: with her tongue between them, she seems to be in fierce concentration. He would like to touch her long legs or her face, but he doesn't want to spoil her dreams.

Epilogue and letter

The letter contains instructions. Where the keys are, how to get out. She asks to respect her privacy. It says she is tired. When he gets back to Carmen, he is to use some pretext to call the police: tell them he's worried; that she's missed an appointment, she's old, whatever he wants to say. When the police have finished, her lawyers have been instructed to let him back in. It says both apartments and whatever he finds in the trunk are his. She says Adam has always claimed there are bars of gold in there. She has never looked. Maybe there are. Michael's head is light.

He does as he's told, except that he calls the police from the lobby. Then he walks West towards Goldfarb's. It is just a habit, and he feels nothing less than thick, strong Russian tea will do. He has matters to think about. Were it an hour at which the ladies would be there, he would walk in, his coat buttoned up to his throat, and he would say, "Ladies, the Countess is no longer with us". He would bend down to their hands, the way Arthur would, and kiss them. He wouldn't talk about the pain she describes in her letter, for it might be as she says, something terrible that eats at her inside, or it might just be the pain of her life.

Of course they are not there and he can't give them Olga's last words—how no longer for her, but for some people the snow blows upwards. Too bad. That would get a laugh out of them, for they're big kidders, these ladies.

About the author

Keith Botsford
Photo by Ulrich Mack

After a notable early career as a novelist and editor, Keith Botsford describes himself as having been 'sidetracked' into journalism (*The Sunday Times, Independent, La Stampa*), variously in sports, as a columnist on food, and a US correspondent. Born in Brussels, educated in England, half Italian and half American, he went back to fiction in 1989 and lives in Boston where he is a professor of journalism, history and international relations and edits, with Saul Bellow, *The Republic of Letters*.

The fonts used in this book are from the Garamond and Bell Gothic families.